CW01494662

WRAP

Martin Charles

AuthorHouse™ UK Ltd.
500 Avebury Boulevard
Central Milton Keynes, MK9 2BE
www.authorhouse.co.uk
Phone: 08001974150

The whole WRAP is a work of complete and utter fiction and the product of my vivid imagination - as are all the situations created and characters portrayed. No allegations are suggested or made - nor should any situation be misconstrued or interpreted as fact. Any resemblance to anyone alive or dead or any situation past or present is purely coincidental and should not be read as suggesting anything else.

First published by AuthorHouse 04/28/2011

ISBN: 978-1-4567-7714-2

Martin Charles was born in Essex, into a traditional military family who had, for generations, served in the same regiment. When he was only a few months old the family moved to Hampshire and he regards Portsmouth as his home town.

Despite being academically bright, his family insisted he became a tradesman and suggested he become a broom maker's apprentice. To escape this fate he enlisted in the army at fifteen years of age and undoubtedly Boy Service shaped his life. However, he disappointed his parents by refusing to join the 'family' regiment and instead served in the Airborne Forces.

On leaving the army he pursued an adventurous overseas career, within an organization that assigned him to work and live in various conflict zones. To date - and he has no intention of improving on the statistic - he has survived unscathed a helicopter crash and by pure fluke missed being in a truck that was blown up. On another assignment he should have been on an aircraft that was shot down by a missile, killing five friends and colleagues. During his career which took him to Sudan, Ethiopia, Syria, Lebanon, Pakistan, Afghanistan and many other countries, he survived mine fields, ambushes and aircraft catching fire.

When his wife died he resigned from his career and sold the family home and he now lives in a cottage where he writes and is working towards self sufficiency.

Foreword

Unfortunately, many but not all Politicians are somewhat fat faced and overweight, which indicates a chronic lack of physical exercise. As a result many Politicians lack personalities, charisma and are about as inspirational as squashed slugs and appear incapable of leading a horse to water. The country's Leaders should be physically fit, charismatic, mentally alert and natural leaders, in fact be idols the public can look up to for inspiration and guidance. Strangely, some Politicians appear to be physically flawed, with extremely long sticky fingers for extracting money from various sources. In this day and age Politicians should tell the absolute truth and deal in indisputable facts, but some appear significantly more slippery than greased snakes. Honesty and leadership is required by the public from every elected Politician, but unfortunately they the Politicians seem to be incapable of fulfilling such requirements. Therefore, fundamental change is required, with particular emphasis on the methods used for selecting potential Politicians by the political parties they hope to represent. Primarily this is because the public has become very disillusioned with what they have had to endure in the name of modern government.

Therefore, Oliver Cromwell's Speech on the Dissolution of the Long Parliament, given to the House of Commons on 20th April 1653, would have significantly more meaning if it were delivered to today's money-grabbing, far from charismatic Members of Parliament.

'It is high time for me to put an end to your sitting in this place, which you have dishonoured by your contempt of all virtue, and defiled by your practice of every vice; ye are a factious crew, and enemies to all good government; ye are a pack of mercenary wretches, and would, like Esau, sell your country for a mess of pottage, and like Judas betray your God for a few pieces of money. Is there a single virtue now remaining amongst you? Is there one vice you do not possess? Ye have no more religion than my horse; gold is your God; which of you has not bartered your conscience for bribes? Is there a man amongst you that has the least care for the good of the Commonwealth? Ye sordid prostitutes, have you not defiled this sacred place, and turned the Lord's temple into a den of thieves, by your immoral principles and wicked practices? Ye are grown intolerably odious to the whole nation; you who were deputed here by the people to get grievances redressed, are yourselves gone! So! Take away that shining bauble there, and lock up the doors. In the name of God, go!'

But of course the self-protecting hides behind parliamentary privilege, Members of today's Parliament, will do everything and almost anything to stay within the hallowed historic walls of the Palace of Westminster. But while they look through rose tinted glasses MP's get upset on being told they are the ones clutching at straws, as they caused the country to become a sinking ship and of course the public is wondering what type of vessel MP's will grab at next to - save their souls.

However, unbeknown to the authorities across the country a number of disillusioned individuals, were coming together to change the political establishment of the United Kingdom. Lack of finance was a major constraint, but one of those involved was told about a supposed hoard of diamonds in West Africa from some forty years ago. Plans were formulated to recover the diamonds and the money raised, when sold, would be extremely useful in helping the movement to achieve its ambition of bringing about political change.

ONE

At midnight on 27th April 1961, in Freetown, Sierra Leone, the green, white and blue tricolour flag was unfurled into the night. Sierra Leone had been under British rule for over 150 years and during that period there had been stability of a sort. But now it suited Sierra Leone's intelligentsia to take control and Britain's leadership to divest itself of the responsibility. So, on the stroke of midnight, as the new flag took its first breath, Sierra Leone grasped its independence and Sir Milton Margi became its first Prime Minister. There was great hope for a peaceful and prosperous future. Milton Margai was a man of honour and high principles and his rule is still regarded as a period of prosperity and social harmony. Thereafter, though the expectations of the nation were to be dashed again and again by political intrigues fuelled by corruption, and increasing violence which would lead to a civil war. At which point the old colonial rulers took it upon themselves to help put right that which should never have gone wrong.

A group of young men, and they were all young and male, were also in the crowd that night. These men were British Intelligence Officers who had been in country in a number of guises but would now stay and become scribes, recording the deeds of the new government. For most of them the next few years would be seminal to their careers, this was their apprenticeship. Here they would learn to observe, recognise what was politically important, and analyse it from all imaginable angles.

Before independence started to spread through Africa, the Intelligence Services could work comfortably at a regional level since they, or their close friends, controlled most of the borders. Now people had to be deployed at a country level, and better cover was needed. To this end, a Shipping Agency was established in Freetown, business expanded rapidly and it easily justified the number of British men in its employ. The Agency was even rumoured to make money.

Sierra Leone, herself, stood a fair chance as amongst her natural resources there is an abundance of alluvial diamonds. First discovered in Kono district in the 1930s, diamonds have been mined ever since, legally and illegally. Tragically, to maintain their illegal mining, the Kabudu gangs who controlled certain areas used some of their significant profits to buy political favours. Was this a cause or effect? Whatever, it was another step on the road that would lead to the civil war.

In 1961, the diamonds were officially exploited by the Sierra Leone Selection Trust, known internationally as the SLST. From its base in Yengema, managers coordinated vast resources and facilities, not least a security force that bordered on a private army. The force was officered by former colonial policemen from all over the British Empire, who were happy to work alongside the local forces, many of whom were former military personnel. Sierra Leone soldiers had built up a solid reputation for themselves over many generations of fighting for the Empire. Men from Sierra Leone had fought with Wellington at Waterloo, those who returned established the town of Waterloo near Freetown. Soldiers had gone to fight in the First and Second World Wars – where many saw action in Burma.

The licensed mining area was split into three security areas - Yengema, Koidu and Moinde, each with its own headquarters and accommodation. The security areas were sub-divided and controlled by security posts, manned by ten security men, often with their families. These security posts, protected by barb-wired entanglements, were the frontline defence against the Illicit Diamond Miners. Also known as Kabudu gangs, these IDMs, had huge incentives to protect their own stakes and would stop at little to do so. These men were only identified officially when they were caught alive, and, upon their appearance in court, it was realised that they were from all parts of the African continent and elsewhere and that they were illegal miners.

Lebanese merchants dominated trade in Kono District and they fell into two categories. Firstly Maronite Christians had come from the Lebanon in the late nineteenth century as economic migrants, who had been displaced by the collapse of the silk industry at home, then part of the Ottoman Empire. Later an influx of Shiaa Muslims arrived. It surprised no-one that they soon controlled much of the illegal mining and the smuggling of diamonds; becoming extremely wealthy in the process.

In 1965, George Turhan-Cooper, a junior Intelligence Officer, was posted to Koidu, a town also known as Sefadu and the capital of Kono district. Located within the Diamond Protection Area, the DPA, Koidu was unquestionably the headquarters of the illegal diamond industry and probably the most ethnically diverse town in Africa. George's first operational assignment was under the cover of manager of the local Shipping Agency office. In later years, he wondered whether he should have persevered in business, as almost effortlessly he created a profitable business importing household goods and vehicles. George had no illusions about his appearance. He was short, slightly built and frankly quite ugly. This did not hamper his ability to gain people's confidence. He would regularly call in on the Lebanese traders to drink tea and chat about business. It was surprising how freely they talked about fellow diamond dealers. George was always surprised how gossip so easily turned to the subject. So he heard about Farid Nicey bribing government officials, Bashir Rezek smuggling an extra blue diamond into Liberia and other specific incidents. A name that cropped up frequently was that of a black African, Amadu Jalloh, who according to the Lebanese was ruthlessly efficient and extremely successful, but wholly untrustworthy.

Originating from Mali, Amadu Jalloh was an ex-French Foreign Legion Paratrooper. His first language was French, but he also spoke fluent Arabic and excellent English. Operating within the boiling cauldron of political manoeuvring, intrigue, corruption and violence that was Sierra Leone was difficult even for him.

Early one evening during the rainy season of 1966, Amadu was returning on foot through a thickly forested area, having checked one of his profitable illegal mines. These mines, or Maraka pits, were dug by hand to reach the diamond bearing gravel to an average of around eight feet deep. Tunnels connected them, and here the danger lay, as the tunnels were rarely properly propped up and often collapsed. Several times a year men were buried alive. Nevertheless, there was always a queue of men prepared to dig, in the hope that they would discover a diamond that would change their lives forever.

To a city dweller, visibility in the forest would have seemed to be zero, but Amadu's night vision was keen.

He was making reasonable progress, when he reached a distinctive incline, he knew his exact location. Stopping, Amadu remained motionless for several minutes, checking for lights and unusual sounds, before continuing his journey. Moving cautiously, he eased down the incline, but slipped and, cursing himself, lost his footing. It was second nature to Amadu to go into forward roll, to protect himself as he fell. Coming to a halt, he stayed still for a few second to regain his breath and then, he put his right hand down to push himself up. An excruciating pain seared through his wrist. His Foreign Legion training clicked in, subconsciously he realised that such pain was death if he lost control. Fumbling in his jacket with his left hand he reached for and switched on a small torch, which illuminated a slight difficulty. The Gabon Viper, Bitis Gabonica, is a short, fat and sluggish snake, which can kill an adult with a single bite. Not that it seeks out humans to attack, indeed quite the reverse, it would rather hide, but if disturbed, it can hardly be blamed for biting its attacker. Just as it must hang on to prey to ensure that it can eat them once dead, it also hangs on to a human who happens upon one. Now, an eight pound specimen was hanging from Amadu's wrist by fangs that might have been up to two inches in length, but since they were buried in his flesh it was hard to tell. Squeezing the snake's jaw, he managed to persuade it to let go, but the pain as it removed its fangs was excruciating. As he staggered away, he was aware the snake must have injected a large amount of venom, and he threw caution to the wind. By the light of his torch, he fastened his belt around his upper arm as a tourniquet and set off back to his vehicle. Getting there took a huge effort of mind over matter, but as he struggled to open the driver's door, he collapsed.

Early the next morning, George Turhan-Cooper was a passenger in a helicopter carrying out an aerial survey of the illegal mining areas along the Sewa River. It was the pilot who saw a vehicle with a body slumped beside it and he landed the helicopter nearby. Both the pilot and George got out and walked cautiously to the Jeep. It is interesting how the mind works in such situations. They did not question who he was, they did not comment on the tourniquet or the badly swollen right arm and wrist, although both guessed what had happened and, they did not express the surprise they both felt that he was still breathing. 'I can't take him,' said the pilot ruefully. George knew there was no safe way for him to be transported in the small helicopter. 'Let's get him into the back seat of the jeep; I'll then drive him to the Selection Trust Hospital in Yengema.' The keys were in the jeep door, but it would have delayed them little had they been called upon to hot wire it.

The medical staff had seen fang marks like this before and administered the appropriate snake bite serum. George had got him to the hospital just in time, they said. Amadu was in hospital for seventeen days, but made a full recovery. George soon found out whom he had saved and visited regularly to see how Amadu was faring. From this developed an interesting and informative relationship. Amadu owed George a huge debt of gratitude. Eventually, realising that George might be a little more than he seemed, he became an exceptionally reliable source of information, providing superb insights into the political corruption that affected every aspect of the countries daily life.

Meanwhile life went on in Koidu. There was always something to concern people, and George was an affable fellow in whom you could confide. So it was one day in September that he set off with three Mende tribesmen, at their behest, to drive to Lungi Airport near Freetown. They had seen many aeroplanes over the years, and generally they held little magic for them any more. However, now it was rumoured that there was one without propellers. Was this possible they wanted to know. How could it fly? George had suggested the outing to Lungi, and timed it so that they could see the BOAC VC10 land. The spectacle bemused them, and provided them with a story to impress their fellow tribesmen with for months.

Some weeks later at one of his clandestine meetings with George, Amadu expressed concern about his own safety. They continued to meet regularly and Amadu did not reiterate his fears. Then several months later in 1967, Amadu asked George to meet him in Moindema. It was late afternoon when they set off in Amadu's Jeep for Tumbadu junction, and from there along a rough track towards the villages of Nemesdu and Gbondu. Stopping the vehicle Amadu guided George on foot along a bush track accompanied by the noise of grey parrots, until they reached a narrow river spanned by a jerry-built suspension bridge, constructed from cable, which looked extremely rickety. Ten paces from the bridge, Amadu sat down at the base of a huge cotton tree and beckoned George to do the same. They sat in companionable silence for a long time, listening to the sounds of the forest. Eventually, Amadu declaimed, 'We are in the middle of a triangle between Yardu Seneor, Yumbaikamadu and Gbondu. Within a few paces is buried a clay pot, filled with diamonds,' he said.

It was clear to George that he had not been invited out for a picnic, but this is not what he had expected. Rather banally, as he thought later, he said, 'How many?' 'The pot contains a selection of best quality uncut extra clear diamonds, many of which weigh over one hundred carats, with some gold.' 'Gold?' George asked, somewhat taken aback. 'Yes. You wash the diamond-bearing gravel in sieves immersed in water to recover the diamonds, but you also find flakes of gold. I have kept the best stones for when I go home. They are worth millions of pounds. If anything happens to me the contents are yours for saving my life. The location is an approximation. I am not going to show you the pot. You have heard and seen enough to find this place again, search and dig, the pot will not be difficult to find.' George did not try to locate the supposed horde and wondered whether this could have been some sort of test. However, the quality of information obtained from Amadu continued to be accurate. He often divulged facts days before events actually occurred. A sort of friendship developed between the two men. Amadu adopted George's custom of buying the caged birds at markets and freeing them. Without any sense of irony, George joined Amadu for meals at which local bush meat was served, including occasionally, monkey and cane rat.

Young Intelligence Officers had lots of opportunities to witness the vagaries of African politics at first hand. Sir Milton Margai had won the first general election in 1962 with a landslide. The fairness of the elections was never doubted. Tragically for the country he died in office in 1964 and was succeeded by his brother Albert Margai, who had been Finance Minister in his government. Albert was as desperately bad a Prime Minister as Milton had been a good one. Not for nothing was his Mende nickname "aptaka", which roughly translates as wild, fat man. As Milton had been honest, Albert was corrupt; as Milton had been a committed democrat, Albert favoured a one-party state, his party of course; as Milton had done everything possible to unite the traditionally antagonistic tribes, Albert implemented a policy of affirmative action for their own Mende tribe.

Milton had headed an exemplary democracy, which, in early 1967, Albert stood ready to deal a blow from which it has never recovered. In the run up to the general election which was due that year, Sir Albert Margai PM, made it clear that he would not take kindly to anyone standing against candidates from his party, the Sierra Leone People's Party. If he could not change the constitution to affect his one party state, then he would try to intimidate the political class into giving him what he wanted, which was, of course, an effective life time premiership. Despite his corruption and mismanagement of the economy, there was a still a spark left of the spirit that had inspired the people on Independence Day. In response to Albert Margai's plans, there was rioting in the streets. He was perhaps too far gone to consider retreat, and he imposed a state of emergency.

Somehow the elections went ahead, the opposition leader, Siaka Stevens of the All People's Congress, won with a small majority and was sworn in as Prime Minister on 17th May 1967 by the Governor-General, Sir Henry Boston. If Albert Margai could not hang onto power, he was not one to stand back and watch his opponent take it. He encouraged his friend, Brigadier David Lansana to stage a military coup and arrest Stevens and Boston. With Stevens and Boston under house arrest, Lansana proclaimed himself the interim head of state, but his rule did not last.

A group of military officers, led by Brigadier Andrew Juxon-Smith seized control of the government, arrested Lansana and suspended the constitution. They formed the National Reformation Council, chaired by Juxon-Smith. The NRC was itself overthrown by a group of military officers who called themselves the Anti-Corruption Revolutionary Movement, and they were led by Brigadier John Bangura.

Bangura was a staunch democrat. Acting on his principles he invited Siaka Stevens, the winner of the 1967 general election to resume his mantle of Prime Minister. Stevens was reinstated on 26th April, 1968 after spending months in exile. Stevens destroyed what was left of the infant democracy over the next few years and, following in Stalin's footsteps, ensured he could keep his position by executing many of his political opponents. Stevens' response to Bangura's honesty and some might say, generosity in helping him to become Prime Minister was to send Bangura to the gallows in 1975.

Not long after these political musical chairs, George Turhan-Cooper was reassigned, and started to prepare to leave the county. George had thoroughly enjoyed his time in Sierra Leone. He was well liked locally and the fondness seemed to extend to his dog, Bloxam.

George handed over to Andrew Shuster, an individual who could not have been less like him physically. Andy was so tall he became known as the Giraffe, and was renowned for his good looks. George introduced him to all his contacts, including Amadu. When he left, George entrusted Bloxam to his replacement.

Some time later, Andy Shuster was sitting at home one evening, drinking a beer and reading an airmail edition of the Times, when there was frantic hammering on his front door, to which Bloxam responded by barking aggressively. Opening the door, Andy was confronted by three policemen supporting the local Member of Parliament, looking very bedraggled indeed. Pushing the MP towards Andy, the Police Inspector muttered, 'The DC told us to bring him here.'

Offering his hand Shuster said, 'Come in. How can I help you, Mr. Kamara?' Entering the house, the worried and bloodied Kamara replied, 'My car was attacked in Koidu. The police rescued me and took me to the District Commissioner's house. He said I would be safer here.' Andy Shuster was thinking, 'Why, in such turbulent times, would the DC recommend a corrupt MP to be brought here?' but saying, 'So how can I help?'

'Drive me to Kennema,' demanded Kamara. 'Perhaps I could - but why should I?' countered Andy Shuster. 'Because my life depends on escaping to Kennema and safety,' 'That's a dramatic statement Mr. Kamara,' he replied. Andy saw the way his evening was going, but did not want to give up without some sort of opposition. 'Well, it's not very far,' responded Kamara.

In fact, Kennema was approximately seventy miles from Koidu and it was the rainy season, so the bush roads were badly rutted by lorries and punctuated regularly by water-filled potholes, deep mud, and wobbly palm log bridges. Except in a dire emergency, few people would have considered such a journey. Cutting a long story short, Shuster took Kamara to Kennema and dropped him off at a fellow MP's house. Returning to Koidu, the better part of twenty four hours later, Shuster thought nothing more of the episode until a few weeks later he was summoned to Freetown by the Head of Station.

Informed he was to be reassigned, Shuster was extremely surprised at the reason given. Albeit that he had been saved from being beaten, possibly to death, by a mob, Kamara had complained that the treatment he had received in Shuster's hands was beneath his political standing. It was laughable, but Kamara had expected to be medically examined, bathed and found clean clothes before being taken to Kennema in an air-conditioned Mercedes Benz. Kamara had said the rough vibrating journey in a scruffy Land Rover was an insult. But the ultimate insult was he had not expected to be accompanied by a dog which appeared to receive preferential treatment.

The day before returning to London, Andy read a report in the local papers stating that Amadu Jalloh had been ambushed and killed by a rival Kabudu gang. When back in Britain, Shuster spent just over a year undergoing further administrative and firearms training before relocation to the Middle East where he continued to follow the events in Sierra Leone for many years.

Released from harrowing experiences in the Congo, a man called Stanley Clavelshay slipped into Andy's shoes and spent just over a year stabilising the Shipping Agency, as the intelligence waters became ever more turbulent. He handed over to a battle-scarred warrior named Alan Hutton. As the years past, junior Intelligence Officers continued to monitor the political upheavals and file detailed reports all of which enhanced their future prospects.

Siaka Stevens had stood in the 1967 general election on a broadly socialist manifesto, having ruled like a dictator. During his first Parliament he oversaw changes in the constitution which transformed Sierra Leone from a Westminster type Parliament to a Republic. Following his election as the first President of Sierra Leone in 1971, he held the position by hook and by crook until he resigned in 1985. However, he did not let go of the reins altogether as Stevens was able to persuade all serious contenders to step aside in favour of his chosen successor, Army Chief, General Joseph Momoh. He bequeathed to Momoh a state where corruption was now rife, and illegal diamonds were being used to buy anything and virtually anybody. Soon after Momoh's appointment, problems in Liberia affected Sierra Leone. The Liberian warlord, Charles Taylor, escaped from prison and launched an attack on his home-country from the Ivory Coast. He intended to remove the President of Liberia, Samuel Doe, from power, a development which created a new dimension for intelligence gathering in West Africa.

In Sierra Leone, there was mounting discontent over corruption amongst government officials and increasing calls for the return to a multi-party system. Desperate to protect itself, the government placed ministers and Members of Parliament thought to be sympathetic to a multi-party system under surveillance. Then, a Corporal who had been thrown out of the army, Foday Sankoh, with two associates, Abu Kanu and Rashid Mansaray, and with help from Charles Taylor in Liberia founded the Revolutionary United Front. This RUF boasted, "No more slaves, No more Masters, Power and Wealth to the People." For a short time the people supported the RUF and looked forward to free education and healthcare and a share of the diamond wealth. Foday Sankoh reneged on his word, and a significant amount of the money generated from diamond sales purchased weapons for both Charles Taylor in Liberia and for the RUF. The extensive diamond fields held by hundreds of RUF supporters were being plundered and the buying and smuggling of diamonds reached epidemic proportions. These blood diamonds were to fund what became a vicious civil war. Atrocities designed to terrorise the population became commonplace. Execution, brutal rapes, and the hacking off of limbs with machetes were everyday events, as was the burning of homes.

Major-General Joseph Momoh held a referendum for a multi-party system that was endorsed by approximately sixty per cent of voters. General Momoh was replaced by 26 year-old Captain Valentine Strasser in 1992 who was against a multi party system. Soon after seizing power, Strasser arrested nine colleagues for allegedly plotting a coup and had them executed with seventeen other prisoners. Under pressure, due to economic sanctions imposed by Britain and international pressure, Strasser made a commitment for a two year transition to civil rule. But in 1996 Strasser was overthrown by Brigadier Julius Maada Bio; allegedly Strasser would have reneged on his word to hand power over to civilians.

Brigadier Bio kept his word and multi-party elections took place. The elections were undoubtedly violent but they were adjudged "free and fair" by international observers and monitors. In the weeks before the election both the RUF rebels and Government troops were accused of cutting off people's hands to prevent them from voting. Nevertheless, the electorate turned out and elected Dr Alhaji Ahmed Tejjan Kabbah of the Sierra Leone People's Party as their President. Once in power President Kabbah was determined to destroy the RUF.

Then to complicate the situation even further, in 1997 soldiers broke into Freetown prison and released Major Johnny Paul Koromah who was being held for plotting a coup. These soldiers then seized power, after a fire fight with Nigerian soldiers, deployed at State House as part of an arrangement to protect the government and President against the RUF. Dr Alhaji Kabbah was overthrown and escaped to Guinea. Major Koromah assumed power and he invited the RUF with others to form a government.

The prolonged corrupt and brutal political upheavals that blighted Sierra Leone for decades came to a head when a gang of criminals known as the West Side Boys captured and held hostage a group of British Soldiers. The British soldiers were in Sierra Leone on a peace keeping mission under the auspices of the United Nations. The Special Air Service and Paratroopers supported by other arms of the British armed forces took action against the West Side Boys and secured the release of the hostages.

Over the years a selection of Intelligence Officers had survived unscathed, and although it had occasionally been a close run thing, the Shipping Agency had served its purpose and kept London informed. As the situation quietened, Alan Hutton; who had headed the agency for a considerable time, contemplated retirement and not long after the SAS raid he returned to the United Kingdom.

TWO

Over the years, whenever Alan Hutton returned to the United Kingdom on leave or on courses associated with his career, the country had appeared to be getting increasingly greyer and softer. Towards the end of his career he became horrified at what he identified as a rapid decline in the politics of the United Kingdom. He was acutely aware frustrated individuals throughout history had been powerless to change the inherent parliamentary system. He also knew through personal experience that when Britannia ruled the waves and a sizeable proportion of the world, in far flung corners of the Empire, individual administrators had served stoically. Many had died in service, having devoted their lives to programmes that improved the conditions of the indigenous people. In the United Kingdom, with all the modern technology available, what did he see? He definitely did not see an abundance of politicians who were prepared to die for their constituents. However, he did see politicians seemingly prepared to screw the population in various ways. Politics in his opinion was not a vocation, but a profession within a self-regulating organisation obsessed with self-protection, that attracted sticky fingered, money-grabbing illusionists.

Recently retired from the intelligence world, Allan Hutton had ended his career in Sierra Leone, where with others he learnt a great deal about political intrigue, manipulation, bribery and variants of corruption, violence and civil war. The years spent in various African countries taught him and others to recognise and carry out detailed analysis concerning every conceivable facet, relating to political chicanery.

On settling into retirement Hutton devoted a significant amount of time to studying British politics and politicians and during that time he also met and was influenced by a Professor Hector Hicks. The seeds that grew into the movement that influenced the political landscape of the United Kingdom were sown by Hector Hicks in a large Country House in the West Country. Set in several hundred acres, the Country House was not an accredited centre of education, yet over the years it had been used by peace loving hippies and others to air their somewhat oblique religious and political views. The owner of the property, a former Colonel, was happy for the house to be used in whatever way visiting academics required, as the courses generated income that helped with the costs of maintaining the property. Today was another occasion when the house was being used by a group and they were waiting in the library for the arrival of Hector Hicks the eccentric academic.

Bang, bang, bang, the hammering on the door caused several of the people sat at a large table in the library to jump. As the door opened the eccentric Professor Hector Hicks walked in. Approaching sixty with white hair and a flowing beard, H.H. as he was affectionately known, took his place at a lectern and prepared himself to speak. Surveying the eight people looking at him, guessing that none of them was under sixty, HH said. 'Participation is appreciated; through inter-action we should achieve a well balanced appraisal of the subject matter. When interrupting, please mention your name,' and then he said. 'In the beginning God created Heaven and Earth - or at least that's what the scriptures state; however, according to modern scientific research, it's far removed from indisputable fact.'

While those participating nodded their heads in silent approval, HH smiled and then said. 'Perhaps you will agree with this statement. Planet Earth is a mere speck spinning in the vastness of the universe. So how did it get there? Do you think the scriptures are correct when they say: God created heaven and earth?' Before any of the captivated participants could utter a word or make a comment HH continued by saying. 'The next question is - could there be another planet in a distant galaxy sustaining a life form? If there is life in another galaxy, let's hope it's decidedly brighter than humans.' This statement caused a ripple of laughter. After a sip of water HH continued by saying 'Allegedly there was Adam and Eve and look what they started. We humans are convinced we are the superior life form on this planet - compared to what? Who is to say bees or other life forms are not superior? We have yet to communicate with insects or other species to prove our supposed superiority. Have you ever seen a human flitting from flower to flower collecting pollen to fertilize other plants?' Perhaps you have done this with a cotton bud. But are you capable of manufacturing honey and wax as a result of fertilizing the plants with a cotton bud? Of course not! Bees can and both commodities are exceeding useful. So, in my analysis, the question of whom or what has the superior intellect remains contestable. For instance bees are unquestionably more intelligent than the average politician. As an example, bees can be used for detecting mines, prospecting for minerals; they recognise faces and can detect illicit substances. For thousands of years Bees have fed a substantial proportion of the world, while politicians have endeavoured to destroy it. Bees developed air conditioning and democracy millions of years before politicians evolved. Bees also see things politicians can't see as their vision goes into the ultra-violet band and they are better at detecting motion. Whereas politicians who are supposedly human see at a rate (if on a film) of 50 frames a second, bees see at a rate of 300 frames a second. While one bee has less than a million brain cells, when putting their heads together in a colony there are significantly more. However, when individual politicians, who have significantly more brain cells, gather in the Palace of Westminster or wherever, they collectively struggle to find a single brain cell that works properly.'

After a ripple of laughter HH continued by saying. 'How many of you have woken up with ice on the inside of the bedroom windows, a regular occurrence in winter before the onset of central heating? How many of you as children experienced several in the same bed to keep warm? What about double glazing and insulation and who sleeps with the bedroom window open these days? Not many people, if any. Can you imagine life without a telephone and not being able to have a telephone because it's deemed non essential? It used to be like that and nothing was taken for granted – and time in prison was harsh.

'In this day and age the bulk of the population has absolutely no idea what is going on politically, unless of course they are involved in the action. The simple fact is the vast silent majority have been herded and corralled by a vocal political minority, whose political ideals lack reason and balance. The silent majority has been manipulated into silence.' Pausing, HH looked at the six men and two women sat looking him and then he continued by saying

'One day the population will discover they cannot under any circumstances protest, because it's become illegal. Why is this? Well in my personal opinion, a type of Marxism has crept in and I'm not sure if the politicians realise it. As previously mentioned the population has been corralled and is therefore controlled by a minority of some six hundred politicians many of whom have absolutely no hard - nosed practical experience of the struggles the population endure everyday to live. Which brings me to politicians telling the truth and dealing in indisputable facts at all times? Regrettably many appear to fall short of those requirements. Lapses in personal integrity have become graphically clear when information leaked to the media concerning expenses claimed and allowances paid to Members of Parliament have been made public. What happens then? Not much! When caught with outrageous claims, excuses are offered which don't ring true, such as – it was a mistake or I forgot.' Stopping, HH again surveyed the eight people facing him – taking another drink of water he continued.

'To placate public hostility agitated party leaders are prompted to administer a stern reprimand, or even suspend a politician. Of course the public never witness a reprimand or suspension taking place. Politicians are elected by the people and as such are the servants of the people paid by taxes gathered from the people. Misdemeanours should be dealt with by the people and politicians should not hide behind parliamentary privilege and immunity. Should a public committee be formed to recommend scaled grades of punishments covering bouts of public humiliation? Does anyone have any ideas or suggestions concerning a suitable punishment for recalcitrant MPs?'

One of the men introduced himself saying, 'My name is George Turhan-Cooper,' and he continued, 'Parliamentary offenders should be restrained in a cage, located on a plinth in Trafalgar Square; their misdemeanours should be clearly published and the pigeons could assist the public in applying the utmost humiliation. Or even better offending MP's could be brought on in cages at football matches or at the Cup Final for the crowds to scream at. They should also be restrained in sets of constituency stocks with the offence clearly portrayed. Why should these punishments be administered? Quite frankly, in my opinion, most politicians seemingly think they are special, because they are protected. They think they are intellectually superior to the average being. Not so! They eat, drink, urinate, defecate, sleep, yawn, cough and get emotional and die like every other citizen.'

Before he could continue another man introducing himself as, 'Norbert (Nobby) Watson,' said, 'Politicians must be persuaded by whatever means to treat the public with respect and they must cease behaving like medieval barons overseeing the activities of those they regard as inferior and their serfs. Why? Because it appears most politicians have forgotten honesty is an absolute requirement and they have become as slippery as greased snakes.'

Nervously raising a hand, one of the two women present introduced herself as, 'Katherine Brenan,' and then she said, 'Quite unbelievably the population was slimmer and fitter during the Second World War than at this juncture. Why was this? Was it because food was rationed and the population was involved in the physical labour of Digging for Victory to produce vegetables? The meagre meat ration, if available, was supplemented by rabbits, chickens and whatever type of meat a family could produce at home. Put it into perspective, an individual's weekly ration would fit onto a dinner plate and no food could be purchased unless your ration book had sufficient coupons. During that critical period in this country's history, the no nonsense policies were clear and the leadership was dynamic! Fast forward to the present day and the policies foisted upon the public are far from clear and frequently appear muddled. Added to which obesity has become a problem and could the obesity have been caused as a result of too much choice being immediately available? Or could a chronic lack of exercise be responsible? Or is the obesity associated with the proliferation of supermarkets? People drive, park their car and do the shopping, without expending over much physical energy, whereas years ago people walked to the town centre and shopped at specific shops. In this day and age, everything and anything must be immediately available; resulting in laziness, greed and obesity, which adversely affects everyone regardless of gender, age or occupation. The political establishment has not escaped the malaise as it too has been adversely affected by greed and selfishness.'

A man introducing himself as Johnny Mann said, 'The political system is motivated to win elections, which solely benefits the political parties and the politicians. Who for unknown reasons are allowed to vote on their own protection, privileges, salaries, expenses and allowances! There are no simplistic answers to the multiplicity of problems facing the country particularly when politicians consider themselves superior. However after what I've heard this morning, are they really superior to bees?'

As Johnny Mann paused, George Turhan-Cooper, interrupting, said, 'When politicians assemble in parliament for a debate they resemble a cage of demented screeching rhesus monkeys. Whereas bees appear organised and perhaps they would be better at governing this nation and infinitely more honest and better organised than the politicians.' As Turhan-Cooper finished there was a ripple of laughter.

'Yes!' Said a man introducing himself as, 'Alan Warley.' and he continued by saying, 'The options available are becoming ever reduced and perhaps, like an ancient dilapidated building, it's better to demolish the present political system and rebuild something of strength and reliability. Is it now the time for the public to rise in opposition? I would say yes!'

Another man introducing himself as Peter Crawley said, 'Most people will shrug their shoulders in despair, having been convinced by politicians and legislation they are not as tough as their grandparents' generation. How wrong they are! Observe a football crowd, the chanting and rowdiness and the belligerent attitude. The spectators are of the same ilk as those who were steady with Henry the Fifth at Agincourt, with Nelson at Trafalgar or with Wellington at Waterloo. Added to which, the population of the United Kingdom has remained steady during two world wars and recent conflicts. In a nutshell if the population is correctly led, by a physically tough and dynamic leader, the people will prove to be just as resilient and as determined as their ancestors to once again achieve as a nation.'

H.H. then said, 'What can be done to change the system? Perhaps a modern day Robin Hood could be found to resolve the undeniable mess. Politicians are easily identified by their long sticky fingers, which rip the public purse wide open to satisfy their greed for easy money. Unfortunately, present day politicians appear to grab money, like bees collecting pollen, and squander it on inane objects. Perhaps each individual politician, regardless of gender, should be forced to convince a Public Committee and not a Party Committee of their suitability to play a part in governing the country. This should occur before being subjected to the local and party selection procedures. Of course candidates must become familiar with such terminology as leadership, self discipline, single minded determination, a sense of humour and honesty. Those are just a few of the requirements. On reflection bees would probably be significantly superior in all areas!'

George Turhan-Cooper immediately launched into a diatribe against the European Union, when he said, 'The European Parliament should be investigated as the findings would probably fill the newspapers for generations. Because if you think the UK MPs are self – protecting, greedy individuals, the EU gravy train is light years ahead of Westminster. With waste and inefficiency on a massive scale, the incumbent MEPs are milking the EU expenses system somewhat expertly.'

HH then said, 'Let's discuss the war years and Churchill, a leader who had personally experienced war. Having taken part in the Battle of Omdurman in the Sudan, served in the South African War and spent time in the trenches in France during the First World War, Churchill led the multi-party coalition government that saved the nation during the Second World War.'

George Turhan Copper responded by saying, 'Although he had a major hiccup with the Gallipoli campaign, he nevertheless led a coalition government that oversaw a traumatic period in our history. The situation was desperate and the people were suffering bombing raids, food shortages and a lack of utilities and the equipment to fight the war. Food and equipment shipped from abroad ran the gauntlet of German Submarines in what became known as the Battle of the North Atlantic. The life of merchant seaman was a terrifying experience, as the ships were constantly attacked. It is difficult to imagine being at sea knowing it was a virtual certainty to be killed - it was not a case of what if! It was a distinct possibility.'

Nobby Watson interrupted Turhan – Copper by saying, 'When torpedoes slammed into the hull of a ship and exploded, seamen were thrown into the sea or they jumped overboard to escape. When in the water, there was a possibility of their head being cooked by burning fuel oil, while their lower body was frozen by icy waters.'

Johnny Mann then said, 'By 1941 German submarines (U-boats) had managed to reduce the cargo reaching the UK by fifty percent and the country was desperate for food and the raw materials to build the ships, aircraft and weaponry required to fight the war. German submarines were sinking around a hundred ships a month. In one month approximately seven and three quarter million tons of merchant shipping was destroyed.'

Peter Crawley replied, 'To emphasise the severity of the situation, for every seven cargo ships sunk by the Germans, the Royal Navy sank one German submarine. From those figures it's possible to ascertain how serious the situation became and Churchill recognised the threat to national survival. Time, money and manpower were devoted to devising methods to beat the German war machine, which set in motion a technology race. We attacked, aided by sonar and radar. The Germans responded with radar capable of detecting aircraft, providing sufficient time for submarines to submerge. We broke their codes! We built fast Frigates! We invented forward firing depth charges! German submarines were built stronger. Action and counter action and the UK government, regardless of casualties, was determined to keep going, until victory was achieved.'

Alan Warley responded, 'The government and the people at that time were determined to succeed and it's that determination that is lacking at this time. As a result we have a group of weak-kneed, money grabbing, self-protecting, hide behind parliamentary privilege type individuals in power. So is it time for change?'

Not long after that submission a break was called, during which time they consumed tea or coffee and discussed the first couple of hours. After the break they were surprised to be escorted out of the house into woods on the estate. In a clearing HH indicated some lumps and bumps forming rough circles and some of the faces bore frowns of confusion, as they had signed up for a day on Political Development. Brought together in a semi circle facing H.H. they watched him empty a small bag of charcoal and then he said, 'Charcoal is Carbon neutral as it's predominately carbon and during the processes of manufacture the major environmentally damaging gases are destroyed by heat. Therefore when barbecuing use charcoal and not gas from bottles to cook your el fresco meals. Fire was probably the first element to improve the conditions and comfort of early man, along with simple tools and animal hides to keep warm in temperate zones. Then followed stone tools, bows and arrows with flint arrow heads and eventually the Bronze Age emerged making life easier for the partially settled hunter gatherers. With the ever increasing numbers of humans, groups, tribes and nations a more stable existence in huts emerged, life became a little easier.'

Moving off the group continued to wander through the woods talking amongst themselves until coming across some benches and indicating for them to be seated H.H. continued his lecture saying, 'Civilisations began to emerge as the lumps and bumps in this wood demonstrated and they were probably where huts stood and fires burned six thousand years ago. But across the planet other peoples constructed monuments and buildings from shaped stone. In many instances the buildings were aligned with stars. Why was this? Was it a form of homage? We then have marks being made on clay tablets and thereby the first form of writing being created. Now what do think was the most dangerous thing early man did?'

One of the women suggested the creation of fire and another thought it could have been the first spears or bows and arrows. Both theories were slapped down. Leaving them to think what it could be H.H. then said. 'As nation states emerged, we humans trained the horse and invented the wheel to make life easier. Of its time the horse was the ultimate weapon and thereby dangerous. Its speed and carrying capability would have brought terror greater than any human had experienced at that time. Add to that the invention of the wheel and life speeded up and got easier.'

One of the earliest civilisations was Egypt with its Pharaohs who were regarded as spiritual god - like Kings and Queens. These early leaders began to conquer other nation - tribes and started global expansion. The Persians created an Empire, which in turn was conquered by the Macedonian Alexander the Great. Somewhere around this time advisers began to emerge who were supposedly more reliable than the spiritual entities. At this time the advisors were not referred to as politicians. However, historical records mention the trickery and unreliability of some advisors. Taking some papers out of the file he was carrying HH handed a copy to each and read the following to the group. 'Can you imagine working for a company that has a little over 600 employees, yet has the following statistics; 29 have been accused of spouse abuse; 7 have been arrested for fraud; 19 have been accused of writing bad cheques, 117 have directly or indirectly bankrupted at least 2 business; 3 have done time for assault; 71 cannot get a credit card due to bad credit ratings; 14 have been arrested on drug-related charges; 8 have been arrested for shoplifting; 21 are currently defendants in lawsuits; 84 have been arrested for drunk driving over the years. Can you guess which organisation this is? They are members of the Houses of Parliament, that's the same group that produce hundreds of new laws each year designed to keep the rest of us in check.'

As HH concluded his verbal input George Turhan-Copper interrupted saying, 'That was a whole crock of nonsense. That article has been banded around the internet for a considerable time. It has been trimmed and manipulated to fit whatever nation's government and is wholly inaccurate and highly dangerous.'

There was a stunned silence and then HH coughed and continued saying. 'Perhaps that's why the aforementioned was never published or could it have been the deference shown by the press to political stories? Whatever, and this is accurate, on top of their salaries incumbent members of parliament can claim for a second home, including mortgage interest, an office in their main home including extra telephone lines, heating and lightning from an office budget of £20,440 a year; 30 first-class journeys a year each for an MP's spouse, civil partner and children between Westminster and their constituency; £87, 276 to hire staff including members of their family if they chose, provided they are qualified to do the work; 20p a mile for trips by bicycle for parliamentary duties; 40p a mile by car up to 10,000 and a resettlement grant of between £30, 138 and £60,277, depending on age and length of service on retiring or losing their seat and of course they could well be increased.'

Not long after those aspects were presented, the somewhat stunned group returned to the house and the convivial and thoroughly enjoyable meeting ended, and after saying their farewells they left for their respective homes.

THREE

Nobby Watson was a former Warrant Officer in the Special Forces who later became a Prison Officer. Now retired, he was a man with a ferocious reputation. At sixty five years of age Nobby was superbly fit and at five foot ten and approximately four foot across the shoulders, he made various Mr Universe winners look like mice. During their early discussions Alan Hutton was astounded to discover Nobby was quite a sensitive man who was genuinely concerned about the state of the planet. Although having spent years blowing sections of the planet apart, he was worried nobody seemed to understand that the Earth was extremely delicate and in need of protection. A hands on, practical man, Nobby Watson was convinced politicians were doing nothing to prevent the demise of humanity and were only interested in furthering their own rather iffy, seemingly slimy careers.

On becoming a Prison Officer and, as that career developed, Nobby began researching the effect of prison on the young. He discovered many juveniles found prison a useful constructive experience and by no means a deterrent. On release, some committed further crimes to return to prison, to attend a drug detoxification programme, or to obtain an educational qualification. Unquestionably, for most, once over the initial shock of being confined, it was not difficult and some regarded it as a badge of honour. When released, a number became homeless and others found life outside of prison so difficult they preferred the routine and security of being inside.

On that basis, Nobby Watson was of the opinion that prisons were not tough or secure enough to inspire public confidence, particularly when early release to ease overcrowding was taking place. Even more worrying, on the occasions when ladders had been found against a wall or fence to deliver drugs, mobile telephones or whatever, prisoners could have escaped but did not. Added to which prostitutes had also gained access to service clients. To Nobby Watson's horror in some jails, prison officers were no longer in total control, as "no-go areas" had been established by the inmates and violence was rife. Why not send in Paratroopers or Commandoes to restore order? questioned Nobby. He discovered the liberal thinking; weak-kneed politicians did not have the balls to implement such drastic action.

With little or no interaction taking place between staff and inmates, a crisis has occurred and unfortunately, prisons are not vote-winners. When the Ministry of Justice defends the conditions in the prisons by saying, 'Harsh regimes would not lead to a reduction in re-offending.' How is the public supposed to react? In some instances when a prisoner misbehaves their television access is restricted or taken away. Prisoners with televisions pay £1 a week. Why should a prisoner only pay £52 a year to watch television while millions of honest hard working law abiding citizens, including old age pensioners and the disabled, pay considerably more - plus electricity?

Just before retiring from the Prison Service Nobby discovered confinement in a recently constructed top security prison meant a decent bed, with an en-suite toilet facility for privacy, carpet and curtains, four meals a day, central heating, swimming pool and gym facilities. Prisoners could also take advantage of a library, free education up to degree level or to improve their basic educational qualifications. Added to which there were television rooms, with Sky and multiple other channels to select from.

Under European Human Rights legislation, he discovered that, should treatment be required due to drug addiction, a prisoner can expect to receive free heroin, cocaine or whatever and not a substitute. Nobby could not understand why a serving prisoner could be given a fix of heroin or cocaine at tax payer's expense under Human Rights legislation, while a wounded soldier could lose his disability benefit. In reality, it was not a question of a soldier losing benefit; it was the benefits convicted criminals COULD receive.

Neither could Nobby Watson come to terms with a government that under-equips troops, but ensures that junkie convicts can get of their heads on drugs supplied at tax payer's expense. Who deserves support, the prisoner or the soldier? Pocket money is available; and should a prisoner be unfortunate enough to be confined over Christmas or Easter he/she could expect to receive a monetary bonus. Nobby Watson considered the whole situation way beyond farcical.

Nobby had also confirmed what many people thought: politicians considered themselves to be superior and seemed to act as if they were untouchable. Even more worrying to Nobby was that politicians appeared totally unaware of the hundreds of thousands of people in the country, who are educated to a superior standard, possess superior leadership skills and are higher all-round achievers. However, these individuals prefer not to tarnish their image by becoming involved in the stagnant polluted pond that is modern politics. Because the public is weighed down with the incumbent politicians for the foreseeable future, Nobby felt all politicians must be forced to accept they are the servants of the people, paid by the people. Although they hold a privileged position in society many politicians appear to enjoy sticking two fingers up to the public while abusing their parliamentary position.

Nobby Watson was so infuriated by the attitude of some politicians he recommended all politicians, regardless of rank, should live in barrack - style accommodation as generations of the military have had to do. Nobby also felt that, in order to prove their superiority, regardless of gender, health or age, all potential Members of Parliament and maybe even County councillors for that matter, should undergo physical and psychometric selection similar to the requirements needed to enter the Special Forces or Commandos. Applicants should be subjected to a similar physical examination; that should last about a week and with the psychometric tests it should discover an individual's determination to succeed, their moral fibre, and any mental or physical weakness. All prospective parliamentarians and councillors would be required to pass this selection phase before undertaking party or constituency interviews. Incumbent politicians and councillors should be subjected to an annual "fit for purpose" examination. This examination would involve background investigations that looked for any chinks in the armour of the individual. Everything concerning politicians and councillors, and that really means everything imaginable, without any exceptions, regardless of how miniscule it may appear, must be in the public domain. Fail or refuse to submit to the examination, must mean instant expulsion from Parliament or County Council. Politicians should never be able to rescind the requirements for individuals to be subjected to the physical selection test or annual examination.

The selection course should stop politicians considering themselves to be superior and privileged. It was glaringly obvious to Nobby the public was convinced there was a culture of greed associated with politics and that politicians were only interested in feathering their own nests. They state that they stay within the rules. But who made the rules? The politicians did, for their own benefit, the rules created over generations. The public is prevented from learning more due to the fact that members are, selfishly, protected from scrutiny by parliamentary privilege and immunity. As a result, some politicians appear to think they can walk on water, albeit they are nothing special. In fact it was one of several reasons why Alan Hutton was endeavouring to establish a force to bring about change in the political system.

George Turhan-Cooper was next to throw his cap into the ring and he spent time helping Hutton with assessments. Turhan-Cooper along with others knew political conditioning was responsible for convincing the public they were not as tough as their grandparent's generation. However, George convinced Alan Hutton that, if correctly led, the public would prove to be just as robust and determined. Both men concluded weak leadership was responsible for the problems and they, like Nobby Watson, wondered if it could be attributed to the inadequate methods adopted when selecting prospective Members of Parliament.

George Turhan-Cooper's observations convinced him many young men regarded planning as women's work and many young women were beginning to think and behave like men. Some young women appeared even to have picked up men's bad habits. Numerous very young females seemed to be breeding indiscriminately, intent upon living for the moment, contraception being considered "unromantic." Because of low self esteem the plainer the girl, the more likely she seemed to be to sleep with anyone she thinks might want her. Apparently, many young men think it's an achievement to father numerous children by different women, believing it to be a demonstration of their manhood. As a matter of circumstance, most of those children are destined to be tomorrow's underclass, brought up by an inadequate parent, or parents. From day one many will rely on the state for everything and because the state can't provide enough of the good things in life, many will turn to crime. Others will take drugs and consume alcohol to block out the fact they have not got what they wanted from life, thus compounding an ever increasing problem.

George also realized the continuing rise in taxation was unfair as it punished hard-working, home-owning, pension-building, individuals. Meanwhile, the feckless and welfare-dependent in various areas of the country reaped the benefit of increasing state benefits. George's overview of society showed in some areas of the country certain children would have limited opportunities and would achieve little. In turn, they would produce similarly under-achieving offspring.

What had also become glaringly obvious to George, as he carried out his research, was that there used to be an Upper Class, a Middle Class, and a Working Class, all of which had been significantly diluted. In economically deprived areas, there was a generation of under educated unemployed and even work-shy individuals who appeared out of control. This distinct 'Underclass,' appeared unable to see beyond the end of a week and was seemingly bred to gain more and more from State Benefits. Quite worryingly, they expected the government to solve their personal problems and, quite inexplicably, they were fascinated by the cult of celebrity as devised by the media. At one time, a working class youth who was bright, and regardless of ethnic origins, had access to the Grammar school system. For those whose skills were of a more practical nature, apprenticeships were available and a percentage of those went on to university. Can anyone explain what opportunities are available to disadvantaged kids now, the government appearing to care more about illiterate, illegal immigrants, many, apparently, non productive?. A government that has diluted the national character of grit, determination and decency by multi-culturalism and the dismantling of national institutions to such an extent Britons appear to be second class citizens in their own country.

Leaving politics and ideology aside, George Turhan Cooper knew children were the nation's future and what chance did they have when honesty coupled with integrity was effectively extinct. Yet honesty and integrity earns respect. The parents of young children should teach them the difference between right and wrong. Consideration and courtesy are important, as is being aware that success is achieved by working hard. Although some youngsters appear barely able to grunt, every child has abilities and skills and help should be available to every one to develop his /her talents, confidence and self–esteem.

All school buildings, regardless of shape, size or age are inanimate objects and as such are neutral; it's the quality of the teachers and facilities available that determines educational success. In some schools a lack of discipline is a problem with, in some instances, teachers being afraid of their own pupils. With little respect shown to teachers, some schools have policemen within the precincts. In cities, towns and villages, a sizable proportion of youngsters are drunk, rude and ignorant of even basic manners, as they push and shove past people with never an 'excuse me'. While certain sections of the population, struggle to obtain social goals, through purchasing consumer goods or by earning a significant amount of money, others posses the desire but don't have the means to achieve what they want and resort to an alternative method of achieving their goals – crime?

Alan Warley, a retired 'Donkey Walloper,' or in reality a former Cavalry Officer who was used to commanding Armoured Units, was next to give his support. Warley was of the opinion Members of Parliament should be charismatic and inspiring, as apposed to appearing like guilt-ridden, liberal - thinking intellectuals, with little or no hard nosed, close quarter back street work experience. Warley also felt liberalism was responsible for the United Kingdom being thought of as a Terrorist Haven. What a magnificent title! Could that be due to weak-kneed politicians who, lacking moral fibre, denigrate the country and its history? So, who really has the charisma, the leadership skills, the integrity, and the balls to lead this country? As apposed to the greedy specimens of sub humanity with the personalities of boiled carrots, found wandering within the precincts of the Palace of Westminster.

Alan Warley was convinced the first seeds of resistance were scattered onto extremely fertile ground, several years previously. As a result of the acutely embarrassing spectacle of a British Prime Minister, endeavouring to deliver a politically motivated speech to the apolitical Women's Institute? Did the howls of derision, the slow handclap and a partial walkout by some of the countries steel backbone, register? It most certainly did! The rows of steel eyed, stony-faced silent women, who remained in the hall facing the Prime Minister, produced a clear picture of resistance. On television in front of millions, the PM appeared self-conscious and embarrassed and, unbelievably, the Prime

Minister faltered. Most of the women present went home to husbands, partners and families, where they discussed the episode and verbally scattered the seeds of resistance. For generations the population had trusted those in government and those in command, convinced those representing them were knowledgeable, experienced and bursting with integrity.

The more Alan Warley studied politics, collected and collated the available information, the more alarmed he became at the political ineptitude discovered. It was scandalous, as the nation's politicians appeared detached from, and totally unaware of, the realities and struggles of everyday life. Their mind-set towards the population was questionable, as they looked down from Ivory Towers provided by the tax payer; their attitude and inherent traits associated with self-preservation and greed were worrying. Whatever, in Peter Crawley's assessment, politicians appeared incapable of focusing on the key questions of what makes a good politician? Which are? If they fail to recognise and espouse a culture of service, honesty, kindness and selflessness, they are beyond being effective and should be regarded as being worthless sludge suckers.

Professor Johnny Mann, a mathematician and statistician, was the next to join the group and he was convinced that politicians, in whatever guise, were soft and delicate and incapable of accepting the realities of real life. He also felt that strong leadership, with an exceptionally dynamic, tough person leading the government, was required - someone not afraid of upsetting world opinion. It's this country that matters to the citizens and what this country can achieve on the world stage. It most certainly is not a case of how much money politicians can obtain by manipulation and pulling the wool over the electorate's eyes. He felt the population could cope; even though politicians have created crippling stratas of insignificant nonsense and wasted billions of pounds during the process. Johnny Mann was also of the opinion that the circumstances relating to party and constituency selection should be reviewed, because an individual who has received a Public School education, culminating in an Oxbridge degree, should not be considered superior and have a distinct advantage. These Oxbridge graduates may well possess superior intellect but their intelligence does not always transfer easily to aspects of everyday life. Nor should an Oxbridge and Public School background be regarded as superior to the individual who has practical hands on everyday work experience in whatever discipline, with a traceable promotion trail. Neither in his opinion should anyone under the age of forty or over sixty five seek election to parliament or stay elected.

The next to enter the inner sanctum of the group was a former Airborne Forces Officer named Peter Crawley. He knew there was a cross section of motivated and highly trained ex military personnel, both male and female, who were prepared to act, if correctly led, to change the political system. In many instances, the skills they possessed surpassed almost anything available on the streets. If and when these components were brought together and detailed planning was at hand they could form a cohesive resistance capable of almost anything. Should they function at only fifty or even thirty percent of their potential efficiency, the national pot could be brought quickly to the boil. Many of those who became involved had sworn allegiance to the Crown and they remained loyal subjects of the Monarch as Head of State. Many had also signed the Official Secrets Act. However, the time had come when political dogma, and weak kneed policies, had become meaningless.

One major element of concern amongst some of those who were contemplating involvement was the supercilious attitude of many MPs, and they wanted one last throw of the dice against this bumbling, less than charismatic, self-protecting sub-species. Crawley felt political parties were detached from local people's lives as decisions regarding the selection of potential candidates to stand for a constituency were taken at Headquarters. Particularly in Parliamentary by-elections, where the national party machine was more interested in preserving the image of the Party Leader than listening to the requirements of the local people. It also appeared to Peter Crawley that the Annual Political Party Conferences lacked rock solid debate and only satisfy media requirements concerning the Party Leader's major speech. Policies were frequently formulated through 'focus groups', checking opinion polls to understand what the media considered an issue. Unquestionably, in Crawley's opinion, newspapers are responsible for dictating what aspects of politics the general public read and hopefully discuss. Then there were the Party Leaders maintaining control of MPs through parliamentary Whips, which indicated most MPs are nothing more than canon fodder, programmed to enter the lobby to vote when the Whips order it.

The next to join the group was a John Ballard who had been in Marketing for most of his working life and he was convinced politicians thought they were s a new elite or even a new type of aristocracy, which, to Ballard, indicated the majority was being controlled by a minority seeking to increase their power, wealth, prestige and their political survival. In other words, an Oligarchy had crept in and Ballard was convinced politicians had evolved into nothing more than bottom feeders, in the cesspit of UK politics.

John Ballard knew that, in the past, the British were capable of being brutal; after all they used to hang people for murder. When the death penalty was abolished it was stated 'life' would mean 'life,' prisoners now appealed against their life sentence. We also used to flog people, including soldiers and sailors, and use press gangs to fill the ranks of the Navy. Why was this? Well historically, we British were engaged on a programme of world conquest, which also involved slavery. On that basis alone, what present day politician has the balls to recommend the reinstatement of capital punishment for murder or hard labour, chain gangs, the cat o` nine tails, the stocks and no- nonsense regimes? Is it due to those aspects of our past history that it appears difficult for some politicians to promote British Pride? But what is British Pride? Is it a crowd brandishing placards that propose the beheading of infidels?

Those involved with Alan Hutton in forming the movement had, at various times, expressed concern about the amount of uncertainty associated with politics and the problems caused by the unelected invisible, faceless and nameless beings operating behind the scenes. They were convinced politicians did not run things; it was the unelected think tank types, the civil servants, political advisors and spin doctors who influenced the politicians. Some Members of Parliament appeared to have been swallowed by the system and were easily identified, as when regurgitated they had a sponge for a brain and long sticky fingers. These behind the scenes, virtually invisible entities, have been, and are, guilty of producing political policies – which when analysed are far removed from rock solid and understandable. The nation's political parties, wandering in a mindless political wilderness, are now suffering the effects of a self-induced bureaucratic quagmire. It would appear politicians don't have the faintest idea or viable contingencies to sort out the mess they have created and as a result there is deep-rooted uncertainty, voter suspicion and election apathy

Taking a break from meeting people and his continual study of politics and the state of the country, Allan Hutton was relaxing by pottering around his garden and thinking how satisfied he was with the support, advice and assistance being provided by associates. The support and information obtained so far had helped him formulate a plan on how to further the cause and implement the first stage. Returning to the house Alan Hutton sat in the lounge enjoying a drink and after supper he showered, and going to bed stone cold sober, a very happy man – he died in his sleep.

FOUR

As an atheist, George Turhan-Cooper decided not to attend the Church service to commemorate his late colleague. Arriving at the cemetery before the religious aspect of the funeral commenced, George decided to loiter beneath the branches of an ancient Yew tree. After fifteen minutes, he watched the pall-bearers extracting a basket-work coffin with dignity from the rear of the hearse. Eased onto the shoulders of the pall-bearers, all was progressing well, until the front left pall bearer slipped and brought down another bearer with him. When the coffin hit the tarmac, the lid came off and out popped the body of Alan Hutton, looking somewhat paler than when Turhan-Cooper had last set eyes on him. Shocked horror reigned for what seemed an eternity amongst the mourners, before the silence was shattered by a woman hysterically screaming.

'You should be ashamed of yourselves.'

Amid frantic scenes, several degrees of decorum were re-established when the undertakers eased Alan Hutton's body back into the coffin. Wielding a wheel brace collected from the hearse, one of the pall bearers beat some buckled and twisted basket-work back into shape and fastened the lid with several heavy blows. After which the pall-bearers lifted the coffin onto their shoulders and entered the church. During the shambles it was self-discipline that prevented George Turhan-Cooper from laughing, although he suffered suppressed giggles.

The cemetery was a less than stimulating place to linger and at the conclusion of the burial procedures, whilst others were berating the undertaker and pall-bearers, Turhan-Cooper surreptitiously left. Returning to his car, he departed and while driving he thought about his past and chortled at what he had witnessed, knowing full well Alan Hutton would have howled with laughter. As the journey progressed George was tut-tutting in response to someone on the car radio, explaining that in the name of 'cohesion' Imams should be allowed to teach the Koran to all school children, when he noticed a road diversion sign. Obeying the sign, he instinctively became wary and a little later realised he was in unfamiliar territory and was convinced the diversion signs had been moved. Slowing down to try and recognise the area, he realised he was entering the notorious St Spiro estate, when he recognised five tower blocks. Although it had a tarnished reputation, in the early evening light and with the tint of his Mercedes Benz windows, the estate did not look particularly bad.

Noticing a convenience store Turhan-Cooper pulled into a parking space behind the store and stopped, with the intention of getting directions from the shop keeper. Speaking with the young female shop assistant he received clear and precise instruction on how to get back onto the main road. Leaving the shop he turned the corner to where his car was parked and there, before his eyes, his car was being vandalized. A group of mostly hooded, seemingly drunk youngsters were kicking the car and urinating against it. The most upsetting aspect as far as George was concerned, was that approximately half the group appeared to be young knife-wielding, hooded females.

When George began remonstrating with the group, there was a barrage of loud insults and foul language from the obviously intoxicated youngsters. A youth, creeping up behind George, felled him by hitting him over the head with a length of wood. The jeering drunken louts accompanying the attacker then lost any semblance of civilised behaviour they may have possessed, when they crazily pounced on the unconscious man. While two yobs kicked at the inert form, others searched for his watch, wallet, money and car keys and, while using knives to cut clothing away, they stabbed George several times. In possession of the car keys, two youths and three girls excitedly left the near naked blood soaked old man and got into the Mercedes Benz. Starting the car, the yobs drove off, the rear wheels screaming in smoking protest.

The young woman in the convenience store, who had spoken to George, witnessed the assault, summoned the authorities and watched an ambulance crew and the police arrive. The medics professionally recovered the virtually naked, blood splattered, unconscious elderly man and then the Ambulance left for the local Hospital with its siren blaring and lights flashing. On arrival the patient was examined in the Accident and Emergency department and was then rushed to an intensive care unit, where procedures for saving his life commenced.

Six days after the attack, in the intensive care unit, the haunting voices echoing in Georges head were divided in their insistence: one group was screaming, 'Give in to sleep', whilst other voices shouted, 'Wake up!' As he began to regain consciousness, his eyelids flickered and then there was a change in his breathing, followed by the merest movement of his head. After blinking several times, his eyes finally settled on the unfamiliar light fittings in the ceiling. Turning his excruciatingly painful and pulsating head carefully to the left, George saw the metal-framed light-green screens and detected a strange smell. Moving his equally painful right hand cautiously across his chest, he felt the covers and realized he was in bed. Then he realised why he could not move his left arm or hand: drips were attached. While wondering how he'd got there he heard strange low intensity voices. Turning his head slowly and painfully to the right George saw a policeman and a male nurse standing at the bedside. Forcing words from his dry, sore mouth, he hoarsely croaked, 'Why am I in hospital?'

'You were found unconscious in the street,' answered the Policeman. He continued, 'Why on earth would anyone of your age confront the louts, wasters and drug dealers haunting that particular neighbourhood?'

With difficulty George said, 'How long have I been here?'

'Just under a week, and how are you feeling?' responded the nurse.

'I'm thirsty and my head, chest, left thigh and right arm hurt like hell.'

'Can you recall anything?' asked the policemen.

'Not much, beyond getting lost because the traffic had been diverted and finding myself in unfamiliar territory. Having decided to stop to ask directions, my only recollection is that, on leaving a shop, I saw my car was being vandalized. A group of mostly hooded, seemingly drunken, youngsters were kicking the car and pissing against it. The most upsetting aspect being that about half the group appeared to be girls! When remonstrating with the brats, there was a barrage of insults and foul language from the obviously drunken, insolent youngsters and I've woken up here.'

The policeman then said, 'It's amazing that you can remember anything. It's glaringly obvious someone on the St Spiro Estate mischievously or maliciously moved diversion signs. According to the Press there are areas within St Spiro that we the Police will not patrol on foot and at certain times of night, will only patrol in Transit vans. The St Spiro Estate is multi-racial and many of the inhabitants only come out at night. The estate is full of drug pushers, pimps, prostitutes and every other kind of villains, hanging around in groups. Little English is spoken and there are several fast food outlets and late night off licences, all of which do a roaring trade. Your utter stupidity or perhaps outrageous bravery in confronting the yobs has been featured in several national newspapers and made the front page of some. There have also been a couple of television news reports and we have been informed you are an ex-Military man.'

'How old are you?' asked the nurse.

'Almost sixty five and what happened to my car?'

'It's been recovered, Sir. Fortunately it's only slightly damaged.'

A major consequence of confronting the louts, who had been abusing anyone in what they considered their territory, was the press coverage, which eventually had far reaching effects. The hospital staff dealing with the deluge of mail eventually established the patient was Lieutenant Colonel George Turhan-Cooper; and while in hospital he received hundreds of letters. However, amongst the overwhelming number of sympathetic letters and get well cards there were a couple that actually threatened him, his family and his home.

The Colonel, as he was universally referred to in hospital, had never been in the forces and he realized somebody in the intelligence world had provided a suitable cover story. Whatever the reason and whoever produced the military aspect, Turhan-Cooper's identity was secure and he was a man who understood the meaning of honour, honesty, and integrity and every other moral standard.

Born in Essex and an only child, his early life was impoverished and for most of the time, while young, he was a bare-footed, snotty-nosed ragamuffin, with his backside hanging out of his trousers. His Father was supposedly a skilled printer and a talented artist, but according to his Mother, his father had formed an affectionate relationship with alcohol. With an unreliable husband who brought little or no money home, the family struggled in an atmosphere of poverty.

George's first memories were of himself in a cot in his mother's bedroom and apparently his father had either died or left his mother by then. After a couple of years of struggling against hardship, his mother pushed him off to an aunt in Lancing, Sussex where he stayed for several years. Later in life he would say he had no affection for his family apart from his aunt who occasionally took him to London, where they visited the Lyons Corner House in Leicester Square.

When visiting his grandfather, George would spend time with his Aunt sailing on the River Lea near Broxbourne. As for his grandfather, his aunt used to say he abused his official position with the Council to condemn houses and he would then purchase the houses and, after a few repairs, would resell them at a profit. Later in life, his mother informed him his grandfather had once been a member of Oswald Moseley's "Blackshirts." His Grandmother, on the other hand, was intensely religious, which meant George was sent to a Catholic school, which he detested, having been christened a Catholic at the insistence of his grandmother.

The boy George was exceptionally bright and mischievous and one particular prank resulted in a severe beating and fondling of a sexual nature from the local Catholic Priest. Early one morning, George had slipped into the local Catholic Church and put red dye into the Holy Water and, hiding underneath the pews, he began giggling as he witnessed the faithful, solemnly making the Sign of the Cross. The red spots on foreheads and clothing convincing some of the older women a miracle had occurred.

Recognising a prank, the Priest, who was not amused, crept up on the boy, who was squeaking and snuffling in delight. Grabbing George by the ear, he frog marched the eight-year-old to the vestry. Removing George's trousers, the Priest spanked his bare backside and fondled his private parts. Frightened and not understanding what was happening, George wet himself and as the Priest jumped away in disgust, George pulled up his trousers and, with tears streaming down his face, ran from the Church. He never mentioned the episode to his aunt and because of what happened he grew to detest all forms of religion and all Priests and became a convinced Atheist.

At the age of eleven, George developed an interest in boxing and as a result of coaching and a strict training regime, to which he happily adhered; he learnt the secret of self-discipline eventually becoming a schoolboy boxing champion. Then, without an explanation from his mother, George was shunted off to a friend of his grandmother's in Tottenham, as his aunt had given birth to a son. George had absolutely no idea how his grandmother and Mrs Collins ever met or knew each other. Mrs Collins and her husband lived in a two up and two down house near Tottenham Gas Works and he lived there, quietly unhappy.

Never in a position to earn sufficient money to find somewhere else to live, George eventually moved back with his mother in New Southgate, North London, where he stayed until leaving for Durham University where he gained a first class honours degree in Islamic Studies and Arabic. Later he also attended Shemlam in Lebanon (the spy school) and studied Turkish at the school of Oriental and African Studies London, and in Istanbul.

Following the intensive care received, George Turhan-Cooper was eventually declared well enough to be transferred to a normal ward. In the ward there was a schoolteacher, a South African factory manager with an unpronounceable name, and there was also George Partridge, an ex-Army man in his middle eighties. During the Second World War he'd been in North Africa and then taken part in the invasion of Sicily and ended up in Trieste after taking part in the battle for Monte Casino. There was also another elderly man called Frank Moorland who was in his late eighties and had taken part in the Normandy landings on 'D Day' the 6th of June 1944 and ended the war in Germany on the border with Denmark. After a couple of days getting to know his fellow patients, it turned out to be, for a short time, one of the funniest periods of George Turhan-Cooper's entire life. Fortunately, the Doctors and Nurses handled the humour with dignity and on many occasions they left the ward giggling. Most of the humour came from the South African, who did not pull any punches.

The seemingly anally-retentive teacher was preoccupied with hygiene and ward cleaning and the numbers of people who came into the ward. In one day he recorded twenty-seven different people entering the ward and none of them were visitors. Most of the people wore normal clothing, sold newspapers, brought food around or were doctors. The teacher also monitored the cleaning process and over several days a series of different cleaners entered the ward and gave it a lick and a promise that barely touched anything.

As a result of the teacher's observations there was serious criticism concerning patches of dried blood and cobwebs, which had been in situ for days. When the subject of cleanliness was raised with Nurses, they blamed contract cleaners which prompted George Partridge to say that his barrack rooms during the War were cleaner than this ward. That remark resulted in a hospital manger visiting the ward. On entry the manager was heard muttering about cleanliness and the teacher took it upon himself to indicate the patches of blood. Bending to look closely at the spots of blood and the cobwebs, the manager then stood erect and rather superciliously said, 'Is that what all this fuss is about?'

'Its called basic bloody hygiene,' shouted Frank Moorland, the oldest on the ward, from a chair at the side of his bed. 'Years ago I spent time in the Cambridge Military Hospital in Aldershot. The treatment received there was far superior in all aspects to what I have received here or in any other NHS hospital since. The QARANC nurses, or for your benefit the Queen Alexandra Royal Army Nursing Corps, at every stage made the stay as pleasant as possible. It was an era of starch and cleanliness and the ward Sister was a veteran tyrant who ruled with a rod of iron. She would have flogged the cleaners and ripped the heads off the nursing staff responsible if dirt and dried blood was found on her ward.'

Interrupting Moorland, the hospital manager said in response and in a rather condescending tone of voice, 'Oh, my goodness you were in a Military hospital in a different era and subjected to strict discipline, Sir.'

Before the manager could utter another word George Partridge, who had no intention of taking prisoners, shouted, 'Two of us in this ward have thrust the bayonet at the Hun and others for your freedom. You may ridicule and mock the elderly, but believe me you are about as effective as a split condom. In fact, you are probably less effective and obviously have never heard that cleanliness is next to godliness. Even in hospital patients are not safe from contracting some type of M.R.S.A. or a virus or variants thereof. Added to which, and quite unbelievably, some patients have been neglected or sent home to die, go blind, or are refused treatments as not being "economically viable" because the drugs are expensive. What about pride in your work and a determination to succeed and organize and monitor staff discipline? You are a tosser sir, a first rate tosser.'

On the receiving end of the loud and extremely poignant lecture, in unfamiliar territory and not knowing how to respond to the onslaught, the middle-aged manager looked embarrassed and hurriedly left. Incidentally, the ward was scrubbed and disinfected from top to bottom the following day.

A few days after the cleansing incident, the South African left and was followed not long after by George Partridge, Frank Moorland and the teacher, and as new patients arrived and left, the ward settled down to a rather mundane routine. As time passed, oh so slowly, George was horrified to learn that his house had been looted and trashed because his address was found in his stolen wallet. He also learnt one of his attackers had hit him so hard over the head with a wooden fencing stake that it broke and, when he was knocked to the ground, the yobs had kicked and stamped on him.

To add insult to injury, George was more than disgusted to learn that his attackers would not be brought to justice. They considered themselves above the law. The police arrested the hooligans whose names were provided by well-wishers and the Police charged the drunken scum with violent disorder. However it turned out that nobody could, or was prepared to, identify the attackers in an identity parade or provide information. As a result, the case was dropped and the most infuriating aspect as far as George was concerned, was that having escaped conviction, the feral, swaggering, insolent, drunken and mindless yobs were still causing trouble in the St Spiro neighbourhood.

One afternoon, while seemingly snoozing on his bed, George was engrossed with a radio discussion he was receiving through headphones. The broadcast concerned the MOD and the Treasury having been caught out with their attempts to 'save money' in the long term by getting rid of pension commitments through redundancy; and apparently the Government had got away with it at the end of the First Gulf War. The supposed 'scam' was to make Senior Non-Commissioned Officers (NCOs) redundant, as it was, to all intents and purposes, the end of the Cold War. Some of the men received redundancy notices on the road to Basra from Kuwait as they chased the Iraqi army, which was in full retreat with its spoils of war. Anyone, particularly those serving in a Corps and who had up to 15 years' service, was given a 'package' that would have cut the future wage bill and severely reduced future pension rights. Mention was made of the attempt to sneak in something similar to make many Ghurkhas redundant after 14/15 years service, One correspondent involved with programme said, 'Despicable' is too moderate a word to describe this behaviour.' Then an interviewee said, 'The Ghurkhas who serve in our Armed Forces should be given the opportunity to stay in this country when their service ends if that is what they want and those who stay would certainly contribute to our society.'

Somebody else then said, 'When in the Far East in the sixties, British soldiers were disgusted to discover the Ghurkhas were paid about a quarter of what we were paid when serving with them in Borneo. We were told it was due to an agreement with the Indian Government. When Indian independence was declared, half of the Ghurkha regiments went to the Indian Army and half to the British. In Borneo they absorbed a huge amount of the strain during that successful campaign. We found them to be great comrades and friends.' Another correspondent said, 'When attending the School of Infantry, Signals Wing, where we did our Regimental Signals Instructor (RSI) course, we spent time helping the Ghurkhas. Their weakness was in written and spoken English, not ability, and we were pleased and honoured to be of assistance. They were absolute aces at Morse and helped us in mastering Morse and, as a result, some of the Ghurkhas ended up speaking with strange English accents.'

Having spent almost three months in hospital, George Turhan-Cooper was eventually released into a residential nursing home to complete his convalescence. Shuffling into the comfortable well-polished lounge, George's steps lacked the spring of his youth and his clothes hung off his body. Although his body was frail, it was his bright shining eyes feeding information to his brain that mattered. Easing into his favourite armchair, the property of the nursing home, he looked around. Without exception, his fellow residents ensconced or, more truthfully, slumped in the lounge, were either asleep or in a dribbling, twitching state; well out of it, mere much-soiled commodities in the pursuit of profit. Physically and mentally alert enough to operate the remote control, he switched on the television and contentedly watched one of the morning property shows. Later the same day George received yet another letter redirected from his house, which was almost ready for re-occupation after several windows had been repaired and re-decoration completed This letter was one of many from his wife who, luckily, knew nothing of his adventure, as she was visiting her youngest sister near Melbourne, Australia. On several occasions while in hospital he'd been asked about his next of kin and his family and he'd refused point blank to talk about them.

FIVE

As a result of the intense media coverage concerning the attack on Turhan-Cooper, Nobby Watson decided to do something about it. Contacting several ex Special Forces men he knew were fed up with self-indulgent, money grabbing deceitful politicians. He was pleasantly surprised as, without exception, they all offered their services and unbeknown to the authorities they commenced monitoring, planning and evaluating possible targets. The group led by Nobby Watson had been monitoring the habits and activities of the young thugs who attacked Turhan-Cooper on the Saint Spiro estate. Although getting on in years, these highly trained individuals were responsible for compiling a series of detailed reports and knew to the second the optimum time to pounce. On the other hand the feral youths fuelled by drugs and booze were unaware of their vulnerability and blatantly flouted the law, joy riding in stolen cars and generally behaving outrageously.

The ten oldies working with Nobby were all ex-Special Forces including two former (Cabbage Heads) Royal Marine Commandoes. All had been expertly trained and would fight to win. Without exception they were skilled in unarmed combat and several had Judo Black Belts. Binge drinking or drugged youngsters running amok causing mindless havoc, or even stone cold sober youths, who tried to fight these "old men," would have a problem.

On completion of his surveillance shift on the Saint Spiro estate, Nobby Watson had enough time to enjoy a midday pint in a local pub and kept his counsel while overhearing a conversation between several men, concerning the political situation. The man nearest to him said, 'MPs are nothing special.'

Another man replied, 'They like you to think they are. Politics is not an occupation for honest citizens. At the moment parliament appears full of individuals seeking to milk the system of substantial amounts of money. Without doubt they are an utter disgrace and should be dealt with.'

'MPs seek fame or could it be notoriety?' responded another.

Nodding in silent approval, Nobby took an appreciative swig from his glass while listening and thinking about the motivated men not far away. Men trained to carry out tasks, without question. Men, who did not run from trouble and to a certain extent, who have been treated with contempt by successive governments. Yet governments were totally ignorant of the power and collective skills available across the country. To say it was a powerful force would be gross understatement, as it possessed the skills and determination to fulfil any challenge. Reinvigorated and shaken from their slumbers, some of these men would be operating tonight. Then Nobby Watson's thoughts were interrupted by another man saying, 'When Members of Parliament appear on television some look like fat- faced overweight zombies, with the personalities of flies, programmed to fiddle expenses.'

Then another said, 'The rich get richer while the workers get shafted.'

Checking his watch Nobby left the bar as action was scheduled for tonight and not only did he have to get ready, but above all he had one very important telephone call to make. At 2230hrs on the evening of Friday the 12th of June, approaching from different directions three men were pushing wheelchairs each containing a man wrapped in blankets and wearing a black balaclava. While proceeding to their allocated positions these men suffered ribald abuse from drunken yobs about being 'big babies' and 'useless fat sponging cripples.' While abuse was being hurled at the wheelchair unit, a red Ferrari 355 was cruising the Saint Spiro estate. The two men in the Ferrari were observing the groups gathered in or near bus shelters in what seemed clearly defined gang areas. By the numbers of youngsters drinking from bottles or cans it was obvious the Off Licence or Convenience Store had been busy. The noise of the Ferrari engine, boosted by the driver revving whenever they came across a group, gained the youths attention. While the youths focused their attention on the Ferrari, an Ambulance and a Ford Transit van eased into the vicinity undetected. Inside the Ambulance Nobby Watson with others in the Ford Transit were preparing to capture several of the drunken and abusive youths.

Easing into a parking space behind the Convenience Store, the now stationary Ferrari's engine was occasionally revved and the nearby youths became totally focused on the engine noise. Meanwhile inside the Ambulance and the Ford Transit ten men, dressed in black overalls, wearing black balaclavas, black rubber soled boots and black gloves, were waiting for the order to move. After checking his watch, Nobby dialled a number on his mobile telephone and when a male voice said, 'Hello' Nobby tapped the body of the telephone three times with a coin and within seconds the lights in the area went out. In the all enveloping darkness the wheelchair group eased into action and strolled towards the first group of youths aided by penlight torches. The group of surprised youths were overpowered and quickly restrained and, while that was going on, men from the ambulance and Ford Transit eased into action and overpowered more youths. Two yobs, who tried to encourage Staffordshire Bull terriers to attack, were thrown to the ground and had their arms and ankles secured with nylon rope and plastic ties. Left on the ground those youths wriggled, struggled and shouted, the barking dogs were released from their leads and they ran off. The captured youths were unceremoniously thrown into the back of the vehicles, having been forcibly restrained and silenced with gags. Inside the vehicles they were then bagged up – with sand bags over their heads. Although there had been loud screams and shouts of protest, all the yobs appeared to have been stunned or traumatised into silence. Maybe that was the result of drink or drugs. After the wheelchairs were thrown into the Ford Transit and with everyone accounted for, all three vehicles left the area.

After the lights went out the whole operation had taken less than three minutes. When out of the immediate area, Nobby Watson, in the cab of the Ambulance used his mobile again and tapped it three times. When finished he took the telephone to pieces and over a distance of several miles he threw the battery out of the cab. After removing the SIM card, which he cut into minute pieces and scattered as they drove, he threw the body of the telephone out of the window. While this was going on, the lights on the Saint Spiro estate came back on. In the rear of the ambulance and the Ford Transit the conditions were crowded and uncomfortable, and with men in black sitting on the restrained youths, the shouting was kept to a minimum.

Pulling into a lay-by the ambulance and Ford Transit stopped and the men involved with the wheelchairs got out, climbed into the rear of a canvas covered Long Wheelbase Landrover and were driven away. With more room now in the vehicles, the journey continued for over an hour. Arriving at a barn on a remote farm, the youths were brought in one at a time and systematically searched. Four mobile telephones were found and three of the youths were found to be carrying knives. There were also some spliffs and an amount of cannabis. Bagged-up, gagged and restrained, these youths were frogmarched into another barn, where they were forced onto chairs and further restrained. While this was going on all the mobile telephones were switched of and disabled by having both their SIM cards and batteries removed. Without occupants now, the ambulance and Ford Transit were parked and their correct number plates refitted. After which both vehicles were steam -cleaned to remove any trace of the event.

At 0230 hrs the secured and blindfolded yobs were subjected to a speech delivered by Nobby Watson who said in a strong loud voice, 'Your heads will be boiled for breakfast. Trouble is, when your skulls are cracked open, there'll be a whooshing sound as the air rushes into the empty space! We are used to the foul smell and very occasionally we find an oversized brain cell which is quite tasty when fried with garlic.' Walking away Nobby spoke to one of the men keeping an eye on the youths saying. 'They will want to eat and drink and use the toilet. Under no circumstances give them anything or release them. Let them soil themselves and they will learn the hard way not to mess with their elders!' During the night, accompanied by a great deal of grunting and wriggling, several chairs were tipped over. When the youths hit the floor, there were subdued moans of pain, but they were left in situ to contemplate their situation. One thing that became graphically clear to those observing the yobs was that once they tried something and it failed, how devoid of initiative they became. When daylight finally seeped into the building it was not long before Nobby Watson returned to stir the pot. Dressed in black and wearing a black balaclava and gloves, he walked over to the first chair, where, ripping the sack off the yob's head and removing the gag, he shouted, 'Name and age.'

Much to his surprise the young man replied, 'James Underwood aged nineteen. Could I please go to the toilet?'

The emphasis on the word please registered with Nobby who replied, 'Of course,' and acting the nice guy, Nobby indicated for two of the guards to untie the youngster and escort him to the toilet. This naming and ageing process continued for over an hour and all went to the toilet. When the details of the eleven youths had been completed, they were again gagged and bagged-up. While escorted to the toilets several had complained about being thirsty and hungry. Two in particular were significantly more stressed and agitated than the others and when questioned they admitted to using heroin.

Early the following morning, on the Saint Spiro the restrained youths and the dogs were found and after hearing about the men in black, people began asking questions and worrying about the missing youngsters. Some parents had tried to establish contact with their offspring by mobile phone and having failed to do so, they then contacted the police, who began asking questions. When the police referred to CCTV cameras in the area, they saw a couple of wheelchairs and discovered the cameras had failed to function at the critical time due to a power cut. However, when they checked the number plates of vehicles seen in the area before the lights went out, they discovered the numbers on three vehicles belonging to police cars operating in Newcastle, Scarborough and Liverpool.

The Media had been investigating the mysterious disappearance of nine young men from the Saint Spiro Estate and were having a field day with supposition. Particularly, after interviewing the two youths found bound with their dogs wandering nearby, who could only talk about men in black. Individual photos of each missing youth with extensive stories were featured in every newspaper, their families had also been featured on television and although the police were fully involved, they were mystified.

Meanwhile, in the barn, the re-education programme continued, and for the most part, the yobs decided to corporate after attempts to act tough through abusive speech and shouting had been ruthlessly crushed. Not by force, but by the use of psychology and demonstrations, by two of Nobby's aides ,of unarmed combat technique and a demonstration of breaking tiles and lumps of timber with their bare hands. What really got to the youngsters, who proved to be squeamish, was the practical demonstration by Nobby of killing, plucking and gutting chickens and geese for the pot.

Later, Nobby, while looking at the dejected sorrowful specimens of yobish humanity sat facing him, still restrained, said, 'I was born and brought up on one of worst estates in East London and only a small number of those living on the estate committed most of the crimes. You specimens would know all about that and about the others who stand up to you. Of course crap on the streets attracts further crap, which goes around in gangs. You don't do things as individuals because in gangs you can act hard to boost your egos. I've been there and done that. Why are you here? That would be telling, but it's revenge for attacking someone who spent an extended time in hospital. You may also have noticed two of your number have disappeared.'

Two yobs, who admitted to heroin addiction, and who tried to prove they were hard by refusing to cooperate, had been pitted. Pitting involved being restrained in a pit filled with cow and pigs` dung a couple of feet deep. After less then an hour they were screaming to be let out, but, after several buckets of cold water were thrown over them, they went silent and were later found sobbing. When checked they pleaded to be released. 'No chance and you will be spending at least a week in there,' they were told by the guard.

'What about food and drink?' screamed one of them.

'You will receive raw meat and a bottle of urine to drink,' the reply.

The following morning, and not far away, carpenters known and trusted by Nobby Watson had been busy constructing several sets of robust stocks that would spread the message. Having received a telephone call from the carpenters, Nobby Watson drove a horse box, minus its partitions, to collect the carpenters` endeavours. On arrival ,Nobby, assisted by the staff, loaded eight large wooden posts, followed by sixteen planks with holes in, a selection of smaller planks and a box of nuts and bolts for assembly.

On completion of the loading, the foreman said to Nobby, 'Everything is marked, so all components marked with an A go together and it's the same with B.C and D. Hopefully they will do the trick.' Shaking hands with the foreman, Nobby thanked him for his assistance and climbing into the cab, began the drive back. On arrival at the farm, the components were unloaded and laid out, according to the letter grouping, in one of the outbuildings.

The following morning, Alan Warley, Peter Crawley, Johnny Mann and Nobby Watson were involved with four teams, five men to a team, including themselves. Each team started the process of assembling and taking apart the lettered components. It was essential each team did this until they were familiar with the process, as they would be assembling the items in the dark. While the rehearsals were underway, Nobby also inspected sets of printing to check the plastic weather proofing, as they would be mounted on wooden frames. When satisfied with the assembly procedures, the teams loaded the components, along with the printed work and frames, into Transit Vans.

At around 2200 hrs, the first of the struggling, sacked up, gagged and bound youths was brought to the outbuilding and forced into Transit vans. Climbing into the back of the vans, four black clad men settled down for their journey while another drove. One man in each group was carrying a .22 Rifle. This procedure was repeated until all the youths were loaded and by 2230 hrs all the vans had left for their areas.

The Transit van, carrying team A led by Nobby Watson, arrived in the vicinity of the Gainsbar roundabout, which, although about a mile away, leads directly to the M5. Team B, led by Alan Warley, parked near the Secbar roundabout that also leads to the M5. While Team C, led by Peter Crawley, drove to the vicinity of the Ketstate roundabout and Team D, led by Johnny Mann, made for the vicinity of the Nallot roundabout. Both these roundabouts were on roads leading to the M4 Motorway and none of the roundabouts were monitored by CCTV Cameras. Arriving at their allotted areas and taking advantage of the darkness, accentuated by clouds and available cover, black clad men checked the traffic flow. With the traffic flow easing in all areas, the teams set about preparing for their construction tasks. Although all the roundabouts were well illuminated, in the surrounding darkness men crept to pre selected fire points and with silenced .22 Rifles aided by telescopic sights, they shot a series of lights out at each roundabout. With the areas in almost total darkness the men carrying the rifles returned to the vans and waited until satisfied they could carry out the next phase of the operation.

At the Gainsbar roundabout Nobby Watson said, 'OK let's do it after the next car, as there is now a substantial gap between vehicles.' With two men on each gate post , they placed the posts in position and keeping their eyes open for traffic they returned to the Transit van for the planks and fittings. In all four areas they managed to construct four sets of stocks in an average of four minutes. Dragging struggling, grunting youths over to the stocks at the roundabouts, the four yobs were forced into position and secured with heavy chains and huge padlocks. After removing the sacks, gags and blindfolds, the youths were left shouting their heads off. Supported on posts above each yob was a poster stating in six inch red letters. '*This yob with others beat up stabbed and hospitalised an old man.*' Having completed their tasks without being challenged, each team left the scene. On the return journey at random places, a further five youths were forcibly removed from the vehicles and dragged to trees or lampposts in quiet country areas. Those youths who were restrained against trees, lampposts or similar, suffered the additional indignation of having treacle poured over them and then feathers from a torn pillow being scattered over them. As a parting shot, the men in black threatened, 'Should we meet again we will rip your heads off.'

As the night progressed all nine youths in the various areas became damp, cold and lost the urge to scream and shout. Unable to move they were frequently highlighted in the headlights of passing vehicles. Having noticed the youths and printed notices in their headlights, passing motorists, without exception, laughed and ignored the captives. The yob held in the stocks at the Ketstate roundabout was noticed by a passing journalist, who, after taking a series of photographs and making a short film, informed the police. When the police arrived, they immediately began to interview the youth saying. 'Who did this to you?'

'No idea but they are tough bastards,' the response.

'What do you mean you have no idea?'

'They were dressed in black and wearing masks.'

'What's your name and where are you from?' asked a Constable

'Terry Chambers, 3 Spinners Road, Saint Spiro Estate, Moorefield.'

'You're not far from home then.'

'Set me free,' pleaded Chambers while struggling and he was answered by a Sergeant saying, 'We don't have the tools and have called for assistance.' While waiting for the assistance to arrive, the two officers heard over the police radio, that another youth had been found in stocks at the Nallot roundabout and a couple more youths had been found chained to trees. When released by members of the Fire Brigade with cutting equipment, in three of the four cases ,the yobs ran away. Not one of them possessed sufficient intelligence to realise they had provided their names and address to the police when first found.

In the meantime, the journalist who taken the photos, had informed other journalists who were now asking questions. The photos taken and the short film made at the Ketstate roundabout, were circulated to the media and posted on the Internet. Within twenty four hours the story of the captured youths was blasted all over the newspapers and featured on television news and spread across the internet. The major question being asked was why this had happened, which, to some, was glaringly obvious from the printed material. Whatever, many people wanted to know who was responsible. However, as time passed and the incident gained international notoriety, whenever questioned, many of the randomly selected people thought it was an appropriate punishment.

SIX

Stanley Clavelshay, a retired, former Intelligence Officer, was slowly drying out and at times, as a reformed alcoholic and heavy smoker, he felt lethargic. In an attempt to counteract the lethargy he consumed copious amounts of coffee, cranberry juice and, quite unbelievably, mineral water too. Then to further complicate his existence, having initially kept a weather eye on his elderly father, the old boy had died. Upset by his father's passing, his general demeanour was not lifted by the complexities within his father's Will, which was supposed to secure his son's financial future. The problem was the value of the estate, as the bequeathed property and investments were substantially greater than the ceiling, before inheritance tax at forty per cent, kicked in. The thought of giving money, and thereby losing money, to the Exchequer, was irksome and after a Probate Court ruling, Stanley Clavelshay considerably more than reluctantly settled the full amount of what he considered an outrageous tax.

Financially secure, he pursued a desire to become self sufficient and devoted a substantial amount of time to gardening; finding the hours of hard work therapeutic. His intention was to pay an absolute minimum per year for services, and to that end he already had a borehole supplying his water and a composter that turned the waste products from the toilet system into clear water. A wind turbine had been installed as had electricity-generating Solar panels, and he was already in the envious position of having the electricity company pay him for the surplus electricity his equipment fed into the national grid.

Starting work early in the mornings, he enjoyed the seclusion of the garden and the accompanying birds singing their hearts out. As the work progressed he lost weight and in keeping with his new image he shaved his beard off. Feeling infinitely fitter, he was sleeping like a baby for the first time in many years. The large garden was fenced to prevent rabbits consuming the vegetables and the chickens were producing more than sufficient eggs. After purchasing four greenhouses, he dug the foundation and built a three brick high wall to set the greenhouses upon and then he assembled and glazed each greenhouse. The hardest work was mixing the concrete and wheeling it to each greenhouse to concrete the interior floors and with that task completed they were producing tomatoes, melons, cucumbers and peppers. Later he had solar panels, to produce hot water, fitted on the roof of his residence and a ground source heat pump was being installed after several hundred yards of tubing had been buried in the large garden. Extra fruit trees to supplement those already in existence were planted. Then in late September and October a war of attrition began between himself and the local squirrels, who were convinced all the walnuts on a huge walnut tree in the garden belonged to them.

After some time Clavelshay re-established contact with his former colleague and subordinate, Chris Slade, who, also retired, was, in the main, concentrating on beekeeping.

Clavelshay had, as a result of meeting and talking with Slade, decided to keep bees. Slade had supplied Clavelshay with a top-bar hive of the type Slade had first encountered in East Africa, where he developed his initial interest in bees. The great advantage as far as Clavelshay was concerned, was the bars from which the honeycombs were suspended by the bees were at waist height, a boon to a stiffening back. Slade persuaded him to use this method of beekeeping as he didn't relish the thought of stacking heavy boxes of honey as required, if he adopted the conventional beekeeping method.

The problem about being taught beekeeping by Slade was that he was an enthusiastic home brewer, and, not realising the anguish he was causing his friend, constantly plied Clavelshay with samples of honey beer, cyser and mead. For Clavelshay, one drink was too many and two, not enough. It was a test of will- power not to succumb to more than the samples offered. Stanley Clavelshay didn't even dare to think about trying home brewing himself.

When not tending his garden, Stanley Clavelshay scoured the press and absorbed the news bulletins on radio and on television. The saturated coverage made him wonder why according to the media the country was teetering on the brink of so much uncertainty. Then to his utter amazement, Clavelshay read about the unprovoked attack on George Turhan-Cooper, whom he knew extremely well from his dark and murky past. The story and broadcasts about the attack held his attention and he eventually wrote a letter addressed to the hospital. Subsequently, he read, listened to and watched the news concerning the treatment of the youths from the Saint Spiro Estate.

As a result of the vicious attack on Turhan-Cooper, Clavelshay endeavoured to discover why there were so many stabbings and killings amongst the young? Why were the elderly ridiculed and frequently treated with contempt? What was happening to the civilised society to which he had grown accustomed? After studying the situation, he concluded the problems disturbing significant numbers of the population, could be attributed to social deprivation, breeding apathy, resentment and a desire to lash out. It was glaringly obvious there were significant gaps between classes and the types of accommodation available and above all, the areas in which the less privileged were required to live. Millions suffered from a lack of opportunity to advance their lives and Clavelshay concluded the method of government was weak and the country was suffering as a result of the ideals of do-gooders and liberalism gone mad. Added to which, it appeared that many people were sick and tired of the suited brigade dictating through the media how an individual should live. The manipulated control through taxes, the collapse of the financial system, the price of food and fuel, brought about by bad management and institutional greed, were significant problems.

Sat drinking a chilled elderflower cordial in the summer house, Clavelshay was listening to a portable radio and reflecting on the political situation, while examining the figures associated with elections. On analysing the electoral system he had produced a paper covering a multitude of election results going back generations. For example one recent entry said. *For generations the population has been manipulated and due to the frailties of the electoral system they have been deceived into believing the system is trustworthy. When in fact its not! For example! The Crewe and Nantwich election results and many others proved more people voted against the election winner - who poled - 20,539 votes. When added up, the votes against amounted to – 20,959. More people voted against the Conservatives winner than for. Now examine the electorate eligible to vote of 71,963 and the turnout of*

41,498 which indicates by taking the turnout figure away from the electorate figure 30,465 people did not vote - add that to the 20,959 + 30,465 = 51,060. So how can the winner represent a constituency when 51,060 out of 71,963 or 70% of people in the constituency were against or did not vote?

The aforementioned situation was mirrored in many constituencies; it was beyond ridiculous and time for a change. But would parliament be willing to change the system? It was decidedly doubtful, he thought, as many incumbent MPs would lose their seats. Perhaps, in reality though - would that be a bad thing?

Although concentrating on the figures and listening to the background music on the radio, he heard the faint crunch and rustle of a vehicle approaching up the gravel drive. After crossing the main lawn and approaching the car he was astonished to see a man, whom he immediately recognised, getting out of the car. Moving away from the car and offering his right hand, Alan Warley said, 'You appear to be in bloody good shape these days.' Then he added, 'Stanley, it's good to see you are fighting fit. Incidentally, I'm visiting at the behest of Andrew Shuster who wishes to broach certain subjects with you.'

Andrew Shuster, Andy to his closest friends, had now become one of the leading lights of the secret world of intelligence gathering. During his diverse career he had, after leaving Sierra Leone, mainly operated in the Middle East. At various times he'd been based in Jordon, Kuwait, Iraq, Cyprus, Bahrain, and Saudi Arabia, which made it possible to follow current events in the Middle East from a ringside seat, so to speak. He said those days had been the best in his career: with little or nothing to worry about.

While ushering his friend towards the summer house, Clavelshay said, 'Any idea what Andy wants to discuss?'

Alan Warley replied while settling into a comfortable chair, 'Not the faintest idea!'

Clavelshay was about to reply, offering his findings on the statistics concerning the election figures he'd been working when he heard a car moving up the drive. Excusing himself, he left the summer house and saw Slade getting out of his car. He shouted a greeting acknowledged by a wave. When Clavelshay reached Slade and while shaking hands he said, 'What brings you here?'

'Nothing beyond having a peep at the bees, to make sure everything is functioning and the bees are behaving themselves. At least you are here this time, when I called several weeks ago there was no sign of you.'

'Oh, I seldom leave the place. Perhaps you called when I was doing the shopping or some such similar mundane task in town to stay alive.'

'The mind boggles at the thought of *you* shopping,' replied Slade.

'Incidentally Chris, I have a friend sitting in the summer house'

'Male or female and anyone I know?' questioned Slade.

'Male and you may have heard of Alan Warley?'

'I've heard of him in the distant past, unfortunately he will have to wait, as the bees are infinitely more important and it won't take long,' replied Slade as they walked to the rear of the house where the long hive sat on a trestle on a sunny bank. As they arrived Slade said, 'Do you still smoke your filthy old pipe?'

'On occasion,' replied Clavelshay, who had more or less given up smoking, limiting himself to a single post-prandial pipe when sat in the garden or in the conservatory, unwinding in the cool of the evening as the sun went down.

'Perhaps you might like to light it up in a minute or two as that should be good enough to keep the bees under control on a nice day like this.'

'I'll pop back to the house to collect my pipe and baccy,' and on that he left, returning a minute or so later. It required little to persuade him to light up in a good cause. The bees were busily entering and leaving from the circular entrance hole and they were able to see plenty of yellow pollen going into the hive being carried on the bees' hind legs; a sign that all was likely to be well within.

At Slade's direction, Clavelshay enthusiastically wafted a few puffs of smoke around the entrance and then he donned a hat and veil. Slade didn't bother with these as his long experience with bees kept in this type of hive proved that, given gentle handling, they were normally more docile than in conventional hives, which inevitably disturb the bees significantly more when opened. Working from the rear of the hive, they first prised up and removed one bar to create working space. Clavelshay again puffed smoke in the gap. Gradually working their way through the hive from back to front ,they gently lifted each bar out for examination. The first few had little on them but then they came to one on which the bees were drawing fresh wax honeycomb, clustering together to create extra warmth to help the flow of the wax from the glands on their abdomens and to shape it into the hexagonal cells for honey storage.

The next comb was a good deal bigger and contained quantities of fresh nectar as well as some capped honey at the top. The bees had started to curve this comb a little off line and Slade was able to carefully realign it with his hive-tool, a combined scraper and lever. The following three combs contained much more sealed honey and then they came to one which had lots of stored pollen – bee-bread. 'This is the edge of the brood nest', said Slade as he removed the next comb, which was more thickly covered with bees. Holding the comb vertically with his left hand, resting the right hand end of the top bar on the top of the hive, he used the back of his right hand gently to pat the bees on the comb. They moved aside, enabling him to see the tiny eggs and larvae in their cells. Their presence told him that the hive was queened right and by their appearance they were probably healthy. Replacing the bar he moved onto the next one where he saw lots of sealed brood and caught a glimpse of the queen as she retreated to the other side of the comb. She had a blob of yellow paint on the back of her thorax applied on his last visit; making her easier to spot and obvious if she had been replaced by the bees.

Looking at two more combs there was no sign of queen cells to indicate swarming preparations and they didn't disturb the remainder, although Slade did ease them apart slightly with his hive tool. The displaced bars were moved up almost to their former positions and Clavelshay pointed out to Slade that he had replaced them too loosely and there was no room now to replace the first one. 'There's a reason for that,' said Slade. 'The bees will fill the small gaps I've created with propolis and we can harvest that the next time I come.'

'Propolis – what's that?' asked Clavelshay.

'A sticky brown substance the bees gather from plants to stop up small holes. It is remarkable and it's been used for hundreds of years for medicine and other things. Stradivarius used it in the varnish on his fiddles. It was used as a wound dressing long before antibiotics. It is anti-biotic, anti-fungal and anti-viral and is the reason why the inside of beehives, which, although warm and moist and full of sugars, are generally healthy, and not the medical hell-holes you'd expect. If you have a sore throat for instance, chewing a piece of propolis will ease it in no time. If you make a tincture it's great for putting on small nicks and scratches as well as for gargles etc.' expounded Slade, patiently.

'How do I make a tincture, then?'

'Use a small amount of neat alcohol from your still...' started Slade before he was interrupted somewhat indignantly by Clavelshay:

'How do you know I've got a still?'

'Oh, come off it, you've always had a still around the place somewhere, even when we were in various areas of Arabia! Remember?'

'Oh, alright then,' admittedly Clavelshay grudgingly, 'It's tucked away in the back of the barn, gathering dust. It's not been used it for ages as I've given up the booze. I suppose I could get a brew going though, purely for medicinal purposes. How much would be required?'

'Half a pint will be ample to dissolve the propolis from one hive,' advised Slade, 'and that will last a year and leave plenty to give away. You only use a few drops at a time.' On completion of the hive inspection Slade said, 'Incidentally, how did you learn to produce such high quality spirit?' Clavelshay replied as they began walking to the summer house, 'When in the Southern Sudan a Norwegian friend, who paid his way through University by running an illicit stile, taught me the best water, sugar and yeast mixes. But the real distillation ace was a Dutchman who had been one of the leaders of the Dutch resistance during the war. He performed miracles with a discarded tractor fuel tank, broken glass and galvanized pipes, when plumbed into the shower unit.'

In the summer house, having apologised for neglecting his guest and introducing Slade, they settled into an enjoyable ten or so minutes of reminiscing, before Slade broached the subject of politics. Not wanting their enjoyable chat to turn too dry, Alan Warley chimed in, Slade having reminded him of an old Australian joke.

'Two Crocodiles were lounging at the side of the Yarra River. The smaller one of the two turned to the bigger one and said, 'I can't understand how you can be so much bigger than me? We're the same age; we were the same size as kids and I don't understand why.'

'Well,' said the big croc, 'What have you been eating?'

'Politicians,' replied the small croc.

'Where do you catch them?'

'In the car park, near the Parliament Buildings.'

'Same here' replied the big croc adding, 'how do you catch them?'

'Well, I crawl under one of their cars and wait for one to unlock the car door. Then I grab it by the leg, shake the crap out of it and then eat it!'

'Ah!' replied the big crocodile, 'Your problem is you are not getting enough real nourishment. It's a well known fact that by the time you finish shaking the crap out of a politician, there's nothing left but an asshole and a briefcase.'

As the laughter subsided Alan Warley said 'Australians also refer to politicians as fence post turtles.'

'OK,' answered Clavelshay, 'What the hell is a fence post turtle?'

Alan Warley replied, 'When driving through the bush you may see a turtle balanced on a fence post - that's a fence post turtle. Confused? Here's the explanation. You know it didn't climb there. It doesn't belong there, it doesn't know what to do, and you wonder what type of idiot put it there.'

After the laughter subsided and warming to the subject matter Slade said, 'What about the value-systems for the young, advanced through various television programmes, or the miscellaneous magazines directed at them, that sow the seeds associated with gaining celebrity status? Straightforward uncomplicated integrity amongst the young is extinct, yet integrity eases an individual along the path of life. Personal integrity, good manners and punctuality gain the respect of others and in turn achieve happiness. However, that could be an alien concept to the groups of unruly drug and drink confused, hooded lesser beings found shuffling around our cities, towns and villages, the kind who attacked George Turhan-Cooper.

Warley said in response, 'Consideration and courtesy are important, as is understanding, to advance in life. They ought to know you don't have to get drunk, use drugs, shoot, stab, and punch, scratch, kick, and spit or swear at strangers. Each child in most instances is special to their parents. There are, of course, uncaring parents and thankfully they are in the minority. Unquestionably, a major objective for future politicians should be the provision of strong policies that assist and guide the young to develop their confidence and self-esteem.'

Before he could add another word Clavelshay interjected with, 'The majority of the population supports a return of execution for certain types of murder. The response by politicians is their individual conscience, or perhaps it's even their collective consciences, won't allow them to support such a proposal. Or is it human rights legislation? What utter tosh! Members of Parliament are not going to personally hang the individual concerned. Somebody else will gladly perform that duty and who gives a toss about the rights of child murderers?'

Warley responded by saying, 'Whatever their personal conscience, Members of Parliament must be fully accountable to the electorate. Which, at this point, they are not! So is it time for a change? In a word, yes! But how do we achieve change? Whatever, there is an indisputable requirement for a strong parliament led by a charismatic individual, who will put the Great back into Great Britain and fill the publics hearts with renewed pride. The only exercise most modern politicians undertake is the production of inconsequential hot air, which has surrendered the nation to the overbearing, politically correct, spaghetti brained, and potty left. As a result, weak- kneed political do-gooders have gained the high ground but they have failed to demonstrate clear leadership and communication skills that benefit the whole nation. The options available are becoming ever reduced and a strong leader is required who should not be afraid of world opinion and should take the hard nosed decisions to benefit this country and this country alone'.

' The population should not be advised through the media and politicians that this country is a modern day melting pot of mixed humanity. Indisputably and historically, foreigners did settle here in the middle ages and before and they did help create our culture. A force is required that can defend the property and people in the cities, towns and village, the world that matters to the individual. We require a society that whole heartedly accepts and agrees that citizens are responsible for all their actions. So how do we as a nation overcome such problems and once again march with our heads held high? Discussing whatever situation in the House of Commons at this juncture, only produces theorist- driven, indecisive hot air, whereas perhaps direct action is the only option'.

'A modern day Churchill is required. So what to do?' questioned Slade.

After a few more minutes of chatter the visitors decided to leave, seen off the premises by Clavelshay. Lighting his pipe Stanley Clavelshay sat thinking and wondered if the first ripples of revolution were about to expand across the pond of the United Kingdom. While relaxing he was wondering what Andy Shuster could want as he was forced to wait for a letter.

SEVEN

Relaxing in the well appointed lounge of his home, Stanley Clavelshay was listening to the radio while reading a circular. On reaching the end of the circular, he was pleasantly surprised by the postman arriving early. Collecting the mail and opening the letters, the fourth letter was from Andrew Shuster. It was brief in the extreme, saying, 'Here, 20th of June at 0900hrs.' 'Mind you' Clavelshay thought, 'the London post mark is an obvious decoy, as Shuster did not live anywhere near London and nothing could be gleaned from the message.'

Early on the morning of the 20th Clavelshay began the drive to the country property Andrew Shuster had inherited on the passing of his father. The journey was pleasant enough and after the initial fifteen minutes, it was mostly countryside, and, as a consequence, many of the traffic jams associated with the morning rush hour were avoided. The rolling, sparsely wooded countryside was particularly pleasing and within four miles away from the property he was driving along a Ridgeway with spectacular uninterrupted views. Andrew Shuster had said the location of his property was only known by locals from the farming and hunting community, as the mail was left in a box at the entrance to the drive.

In fact College House, as the property is known, is a large country house standing in about a thousand acres of woods and agricultural land. Although the house name indicates a site of education, it has never been an accredited seat of learning nor had anything to do with education.

Entering through the impressive stone archway supporting the huge main gates, Clavelshay drove towards the house. On the occasions he had previously visited, he'd been impressed by the mature Oak trees lining the drive, and as he passed under their canopy he was amazed at the shaded beauty. Passing the main entrance he drove into the stable yard and recognized a Mercedes Benz parked there. Getting out of the car he registered the crispy clear chirping sounds of birds singing and was stunned by the wonderful hanging baskets filled with flowers adorning the yard. About to set off for the house, he heard a metal door scraping open and, turning towards the sound, he saw the imposing figure of Andrew Schuster.

'It's nice to see you in such good shape and ready for action so to speak,' said Andrew, shaking Clavelshay's hand before ushering him across the cobbles into the porch. 'Never thought I would see the day that you were retired … it must be bloody dreadful! Let's walk to the front door where the memsahib should be with the dogs.'

Entering the more than spacious porch, inside accompanied by several excited Jack Russell's was Mrs Christine Shuster. The memsahib as Andrew referred to her was resplendent in a Tweed costume, with blue stocking, brown brogue shoes, with a headscarf covering her white hair. Using a towel to dry the dogs off, after collecting the mail, Christine Shuster stopped what she was doing and handed the letters to her husband. Turning to face Clavelshay she said, 'please go in, you know where the summer lounge is. I will bring tea and biscuits in a couple of minutes after extricating myself from the dogs.'

Taking his leave, Clavelshay crossed the expanse of the tiled entrance hall accompanied by Andrew Shuster who then peeled off to the left and proceeded down a corridor, leaving him to enter the lounge. There he found George Turhan-Cooper enjoying the room, with its antique furniture, oriental carpets and glass fronted cabinets full of silver and porcelain trinkets. Shaking hands with his former boss Clavelshay said, 'nice to see you up and about again. It was a bloody terrible thing that happened to you Sir.'

With the portraits of previous Shusters staring into the room George Turhan-Cooper took a letter from an inside pocket and opened it, 'It was one amongst many, but it was significantly more meaningful than most. Thank you for your thoughts Stanley.'

'Don't mention it George. Needless to say I would love to get my hands on the feral louts.' While they were talking and looking out over the manicured lawns they heard the lounge door open and in came Christine Shuster carrying a tray with cups and saucers and the required accessories for tea and biscuits. Placing the tray on a table Mrs Shuster said, 'milk and sugar gentlemen. Incidentally, Andy will return in a minute or two.'

Selecting chairs the two men eased into them and each accepted the exquisite china cup and saucer offered and helped themselves to a teaspoon of sugar and some milk when proffered. Relaxed and enjoying the delicate flavour of the tea without knowing what type it was, it occurred to Clavelshay he'd probably ruined a specific flavour by adding milk and sugar. Nevertheless, finishing the tea he was placing the cup and saucer on a small table, when the door opened and in walked Andy.

Glancing around the room as if searching for someone Andrew Shuster then walked over to the bay window, where he stared at the garden for a few seconds, as if he were collecting his thoughts. Turning to face the two men, he said, 'Having just received the telephone bill, I will admit to seldom looking at it. However, today my attention was drawn to the fact British Telecom has decided, in their overwhelming wisdom, to instigate a Payment Processing Charge of £4.50. My attitudes may be old fashioned, but surely British Telecom was established to provide a service to the public. The public are not there to provide services for British Telecom. Why should we be charged for using cheques? I do not have a mortgage and have never had one. I do not have a credit card and never will have one. I have a Maestro / Switch charge card and that's my only submission to banking modernity. I have never instigated a standing order for whatever. On occasion the Telephone bill is taken to the Post Office for payment and sometimes I post a cheque with the Bill and now they want to charge extra for paying by cheque. What nonsense! Sorry, it has really annoyed me.'

'You must excuse him, he gets irritated with certain aspects of modern life,' remarked Mrs Shuster while gathering up the tea cups. While moving away from the window Shuster said, 'George, what are your intentions regarding the cretins who caused you so much damage?'

In reply Turhan-Cooper said, 'I want to kick the shit out of them.'

'Understandable,' replied Andrew Shuster, laughing at the remark. 'Many young people have drug and alcohol problems, which in some instances stem from dreadful childhoods. Some are from single parent families, others have two parents and both parents are inadequate. Others are from families where the parents have drug or alcohol problems. Some were abused during childhood or come from broken homes. Others ran away from home at an early age and yet, not all are from underprivileged, deprived or broken homes.'

Turhan-Cooper heard Clavelshay say, 'Some of the worst culprits are from privileged, well balanced family backgrounds with reliable parents. Nevertheless, significant numbers of the young, from whatever background began experimenting with drugs and alcohol at an early age and there are many instances of drunk eleven and twelve year olds. Incidentally, I support your intention to get even.'

Andy Shuster continued the theme by saying, 'The younger generation have attitude problems inasmuch as; patience is not a strong point, nor is the ability to put up with any type of hardship. They expect to be happy all the time, which is unrealistic and virtually unachievable. The alcohol, drugs, promiscuity and stealing are a means of easing their stress and making them happy. It's a method of insulating themselves from fear, anxiety and anger, the everyday emotions we have all experienced at some time in our lives.'

Christine Shuster interjected by saying, 'from my understanding a sizeable percentage of youngsters have no perception of other people and everything is me, me, me. We want it and we want it now and most think they deserve it. With low self esteem they believe they are rubbish. Many are not prepared to work hard, to save, to wait, to struggle; it has to be an instant fix. They don't know how to set goals. What ambitions they do have are unrealistic; they want to be celebrities, pop stars, racing drivers or a lottery winner. In all probability the overall drug and alcohol situation is far worse than the government admits and it's highly likely politicians don't actually register the reality of the situation or realize how bad the problems really are.'

Then in utter contrast to what they had been discussing Andrew Shuster suddenly said, 'Christine, my dear will you escort Stanley away from here and entertain him in the conservatory while George and I discuss certain sensitive aspects. In fact, I wish to speak to each of you in confidence on differing subjects. You may well wonder about the relaxed security procedures and why I did not provide different times to meet with you? Well, in all honesty I thought it would do George good to meet and talk with Stanley for a few minutes.'

Getting to his feet Stanley Clavelshay nodded in response saying, 'no problem,' and, relieving Mrs Shuster of the tray of cups and saucers, followed her out of the room. After the door closed Andrew Shuster said, 'who was the best operator you ever came across serving or retired? And I do mean the very best'

Thinking for a moment George replied, 'John Vialls.'

'Came to the same conclusion,' responded Shuster adding, 'what's he doing now? Someone told me he's married with kids and farming in Dorset.'

'That's a fact,' replied Turhan-Cooper.

'Is he contactable?'

'Yes, but it would be a brave man that approached him.'

'Are you brave enough George?'

'It depends on what it's about, because if it failed to fire his imagination he is more than likely to ram a fence post up my backside and stand me in a field as a scarecrow.'

'Interesting, never worked with him myself, although I do recall an episode in the Sudan Club, when on a stopover in Khartoum some years ago. If my memory recalls it correctly, a fellow who had worked in the Sudan for years and who'd been a Glider Pilot at the battle of Arnhem during the war, boldly declared that nobody had ever pushed or thrown him in the pool. Apparently many had tried. Within seconds he was in the water, having been picked up and thrown in by Vialls, it was all good natured and accompanied by howls of laughter. However, like many, I'm aware of his Neanderthal reputation. On that basis would you be prepared to contact him?'

'Depends very much on the content of what you divulge.'

'You may recall when working in Sierra Leone all those years ago a deceased citizen of Mali called Amadu Jalloh.'

'Of course, having worked with him - when he suffered snake bite I took him to hospital. Having handed control of him over to you… I think I know exactly what you are going to talk about and its rather unnerving.'

'This matter concerns recovering some gold.'

'Gold,' responded George somewhat incredulously.

'You have a problem with Gold, George?'

'None whatsoever, however I feel Stanley should be present. Exactly how much Gold are we taking about and where is it?'

'I can produce satellite imagery photos of the area where the gold is located for your perusal. It weights about three kilos. At the present we are short of sufficient funds to advance Alan Hutton's proposed programme and three Kilos of gold would help.'

'It would be expensive to recover by whatever method you are contemplating. Get Stanley in here; and as of this moment the proposal to contact Vialls is a complete non-starter. He would not be interested.'

Leaving the room Andrew Shuster soon returned carrying a briefcase and with Stanley Clavelshay in tow. Putting the briefcase on a table he motioned for the others to join him and then he produced a series of satellite imagery pictures from the briefcase which he spread on the table. Looking at the images George Turhan-Cooper picked up a couple and concentrated on them, while being observed by the others. Placing the pictures back on the table George then said to Andrew Shuster, 'so where is the gold?'

Picking up an image Andrew Shuster drew a circle on the picture with a pencil and said, 'it's in a place called Hospital Swamp which is North West of Koidu.'

'I knew the area very well and doubt it still exists,' replied George adding, 'this is purely speculation. Amadu Jalloh told me something similar years ago and the area has been fought over and been heavily mined both legally and illegally for years.'

In response Shuster replied, 'the programme requires funding and the gold would produce several thousand pounds. Do you think the proposal is a fool's errand?'

'Absolutely, and Vialls would castrate you and mince your testicles for sausage meat if you approached him. However, it may be possible to save you.' Picking up the images he had previously been looking at he said, 'on this picture is the rough location of a clay pot. The buried pot contains a significant quantity of large top quality diamonds. I was taken to the location by Amadu for saving his life, and he said that if anything happened to him they were mine. '

'But it was it was forty years ago George.'

'Yes ,and so was the gold that Amadu told you about.'

'What's the value?' asked Clavelshay.

'Millions of pounds if sold in the correct market'

In response Clavelshay said to Andrew Shuster, 'If you could offer Vialls

substantial remuneration for his services, which could be in cash or in an investment fund that would pay a pension for the rest of his life, he might be somewhat interested. Where is the action?'

'Sierra Leone and that's all I'm saying at this juncture!'

'Sounds challenging and I will approach him,' replied Clavelshay.

'We would appreciate you doing so, Stanley'

'Do I detect an official mission?' replied Clavelshay.

'It will be given very serious consideration Stanley.'

'Is that it then?' enquired Clavelshay.

'Just about, let me know as soon as possible.'

Leaving the summer lounge Clavelshay followed Andrew Shuster to the front door where they shook hands and that was that. Clavelshay returned to his car in the stable yard and left the estate.

In the house Turhan-Cooper followed Shuster along a ground floor corridor where Shuster opened a nondescript door and the two men descended steps into an arched cellar. Passing under four arches and then opening a steel door they descended more steps into a large whitewashed concrete chamber, which was brighter than day, due to fluorescent ceiling lights. One aspect George Turhan-Cooper noted as they moved across the chamber to yet another steel door was the number of different coloured cables attached to the walls. Opening the door they descended more steps and moved along a corridor accompanied by a low density humming which he thought was probably the sound of air conditioning. At the next door they entered what could only be described as an underground theatre, where, in George Turhan-Cooper's estimation, he registered around one hundred tipping seats. None of which were occupied. Turning to face Shuster, Turhan-Cooper said, 'what the heck is this place?'

'During the war this house was used by a branch of the intelligence services,.We are standing in what is, was, an area headquarters for wartime resistance fighters, constructed at the beginning of the war on Churchill's orders. My father was an area Commander in the resistance, established to cause mayhem if and when the Germans invaded. After the war this unit was kept operational until the late eighties and then it was written off. Not a penny has been spent on it since the war and it's still in good nick.'

Looking around and nodding appreciatively, George Turhan-Cooper responded by saying, 'apparently there are several such units scattered around the country, the selected people who manned the establishments were to harass the enemy. So why have you brought me here?'

'From here, in all probability, will be launched actions to counteract the crime on the streets and at the same time form a viable resistance to the method of government foisted upon us. This centre can once again become a regional or even a national centre of resistance. Alan Hutton was well into the planning and implementation phase when he died. Fortunately yours truly was aware of most aspects and inherited the mantle of responsibility. Incidentally, yours truly shares the bitterness discovered by Alan during his research over what he saw as attempts to destroy this nation. As a result this facility is being prepared and at this juncture the only problem that could possibly be noticed is the consumption of electricity, if used for a lengthy period. It's not a question of paying the bill, but the amount of electricity suddenly being consumed that might cause subtle enquiries.'

'Why not install a generator?' replied Turhan-Cooper.

'We probably will. Incidentally, there are people working in the woods sorting out some smaller underground bunkers. Although a rural community, protecting it during the war was a priority and therefore in the woods, there are several anti-aircraft gun pits and emplacements and shelters for searchlight batteries. There are barns and a couple of stable blocks that can be utilized.'

Having left house they strolled to a specific area of woods, where George Turhan-Cooper was surprised to see an old intellectual he knew as Johnny Mann, speaking to a group, that included Slade, David Warley, Peter Crawley and Nobby Watson. All of them would have a profound effect on the movement as it expanded and carried out what became known as the Internal Security Operations.

EIGHT

Whilst driving home Stanley Clavelshay thought about how to contact John Vialls and decided to use the telephone and the best method to adopt would be to be absolutely direct, 'no prisoners' as Vialls would say. Satisfied with the method of approach he'd decided upon, and just a little nervous about making the call, Clavelshay arrived home and after parking his car he entered his house. Going into the lounge he decided to sit down. Picking up the telephone he dialled the number, after ringing six times, there was a click and then a distinctive female American accented voice said, 'hello.'

'Hello Maureen, Stanley Clavelshay speaking.'

'Oh my God, we were only taking about you the other day.'

Relaxing slightly Clavelshay replied, 'I hope it was complimentary.'

'We were actually wondering what eventually happened to you.'

'I'm retired and a teetotal non smoker now, is John there?'

'Yes, hold on and I'll drag him to the telephone for you.'

He listened for several seconds of background noises, and wondering what sort of accent Vialls would now have, after years of farming in Dorset. He found out almost immediately when Vialls growled down the telephone, 'so what do you want, you old bastard?'

Aware of security and not knowing if the telephone was monitored he replied, 'would you like me to buy you lunch next Thursday at 1300hrs in that Dorset establishment we dinned at during our last get-together. I'm not saying anything, beyond it could be financially rewarding and an explanation will be provided if and when we meet, have a meal and perhaps go for a stroll.'

'Sounds reasonable, responded Vialls, the cogs in his head suddenly set spinning as he tried to figure out what this could all be about.

'OK see you at the establishment on Thursday.'

The county of Dorset is steeped in history with unparalleled vistas. Snuggled into the county's ample rolling green breasts are ancient villages that have been at peace with the world for generations. The establishment referred to for lunch is in the village of Plush. The 'Brace of Pheasants,' which is raised, sentinel-like, overlooking the village, is a thatched and beamed country pub. Towering above the 'Brace' as it's affectionately known used to be several magnificent beech trees forming a green canopy when seen from the surrounding hills.

Arriving at the Brace Clavelshay parked his car in the field that was indicated and somewhat shocked at the lack of Beech trees, he walked to the entrance. He was recalling the last occasion he'd visited and once again nodded his approval of the idyllic village. Casting an eye over the small triangle of grass with its off-centre signpost, Clavelshay climbed the remodelled steps and entered the 'Brace.' Once again on entering the beamed bar he appreciated the welcoming atmosphere. Moving up to the bar Clavelshay ordered a celebratory lunchtime pint, the first for months, and on receipt he took a couple of long appreciative draughts. Turning away from the bar he noticed the inglenook fireplace they had previously occupied with the table inside. Noting it was unoccupied he made his way there. Sitting down and placing his pint on the table he allowed fond memories of the previous occasion to seduce him into relaxation.

Hearing the door open he saw Vialls, the last Neanderthal on earth, enter the bar where he was welcomed as 'John,' a regular, by the barman. When served, Vialls turned away from the bar and, while swigging bitter, made his way to Clavelshay sat inside an inglenook. He joined Clavelshay, placing his pint glass on the table and ducking beneath the lintel. 'So why are we here?'

'Andy Shuster has information concerning diamonds in Sierra Leone. He says should you be interested in the task, whatever it involves, you will be financially rewarded. Outside of that you will have to discuss the subject with him, as on this occasion I'm acting as a go between.'

'From rumours dating back years and with no personal experience of working with Andy, he has a reputation somewhat similar to a greased condom.'

'He's a big cheese now and if you are interested contact will be established and on receipt of a response, you will be supplied a contact point or an address that's mutually agreeable, if that suits you. Let's eat.'

Laughing Vialls said 'Situation normal. Do you fancy another?'

'No thanks, believe it or not that pint was the first for months.'

'Maureen mentioned you are now teetotal.'

'In all honesty *almos*t, as I have the odd beer with Slade.'

'Christ that's a name from the past! What the hell is he doing?'

'He took early retirement and visits occasionally to check the bees he supplied'.

While eating the topics broached were diverse in the extreme. Some topics were humorous causing much laughter and others were deadly serious reflecting on their past experiences. Vialls concluded by saying. 'Get the leaders of all concerned on the phone right away and I will explain in more detail…ok.

Clavelshay responded by saying, 'sometime in the future you should compare theories with George Turhan-Cooper. He is a rampant atheist and expounds the theory that all members of the church, whether they are a Pope, Cardinal, Archbishop, Bishop, Cannon a ground floor priest or a vicar should be arrested for spouting utter nonsense and living off immoral earnings.'

'He sounds my type of man. How is he these days, after the assault on him by yobs? There was prolific coverage in the media when it occurred. Figuratively speaking he was 'Captain of the ship' during our last outing.'

'Saw and spoke with him recently and he appears to be in fine fettle.'

'Give him my regards if you see him again.'

Settling the bill after their excellent meal they moved out of the 'Brace,' and standing in the car park decided against a stroll. Before getting into their cars, a few words were exchanged on how long Clavelshay thought it might be before he made contact again. Clavelshay said he would contact him within a week and then they climbed into their cars and went their separate ways.

Vialls received a telephone call six days after the lunch at the 'Brace,' from Clavelshay, asking him to meet Andy Shuster in the lay-by off the A361 east of Lyng and below the Athelney memorial in Somerset. Athelney was an island in the Somerset levels or swamps, where King Alfred the Great took refuge from the Danish invaders, in AD 878. When at his lowest point and hiding on the isle of Athelney, the King went unrecognised by his people. It was there Alfred is said to have burned the cakes he was asked to supervise by an old woman. It was also from Athelney he later emerged to defeat the Danes at the battle of Edington. Later Alfred the Great founded an Abbey at Athelney to commemorate victory against the Danes.

Arriving early Vialls set about reading the potted history boards and was mystified at the tatty brick memorial on the hill to commemorate such a significant event in English history. Sat in his car Vialls was preoccupied with his thoughts, thinking of the future as he gazed across many miles of unremarkable flat land. Vialls saw Andy Shuster's car easing into the lay-by and getting out of his car he saluted a mock acknowledgement. Stopping behind the car driven by Vialls, Andy Shuster got out and they shook hands with Shuster saying, 'The last time I saw you was in the Sudan Club in Khartoum, how are you?'

'I'm in pretty good condition from farming and bursting with curiosity.'

'Nothing will be divulged here and therefore might I suggest we go to the pub in East Lyng. We can then enjoy a beer and have lunch? Should you be in agreement, follow me.'

'Who's paying for the privilege?'

'Me,' replied Shuster.

'Sounds good to me,' replied Vialls moving towards his car.

Driving off they soon arrived at the nearby Rose and Crown on the summit of the hill in East Lyng, a village overlooking the Somerset levels. After parking the two men entered the bar and after asking about a table for lunch and ordering a couple of beers, they were then shown to a table situated to the right of the fireplace. While Vialls was perusing the menu and preparing to order, Andy Shuster was unlocking the briefcase he'd carried from his car. Selecting several A4 sized Satellite Imagery photos he placed them face down on the table and picking up a menu he too selected what he wanted for lunch. After a young lady collected their lunch orders and left their table Vialls took advantage of her heels striking the flagstone floor and quietly said, 'Why and what's at stake?'

'When starting my career my first operational assignment was to Sierra Leone. Cutting a long story short, a friend who was successful in the diamond industry was killed. Some time before his death - and this is the absolute truth -he informed an agent that, should anything happen to him, a clay pot containing a quantity of large top quality uncut diamonds and some gold were his.' Indicating the photos he continued, 'these recent photos are of the area where the pot is located. The agent was taken there years ago; the tallest cotton tree is within paces of the pot's location.'

Picking up the top photo Vialls turned it over and immediately noted an area of forest surrounded by what looked like masses of gravel and hundreds if not thousands of holes, pits and larger excavations. The substantial area of desolation appeared to be dissected by the remnants of a river or a water course. Picking up another photo Vialls noted a bush road reasonably near to the diggings and a couple of nearby villages and areas that had been cleared for agriculture on both sides of the road near the villages. Noting the canopy of several very tall trees John Vialls looked directly at Shuster and said, 'Two questions. Where is this? What is the scale to judge distances?'

Pausing while their lunches were delivered Andy Shuster replied as the young woman's heels again struck the flagstones with a distinctive clip, 'Approximately one centimetre to one kilometre.' Then, somewhat suspiciously, he appeared to be checking for potential eavesdroppers when he whispered, 'Kono district Sierra Leone.'

'With gold and diamonds, a metal detector would be an asset for locating the supposed hoard.' Pointing at the second photo Vialls said, 'a PC-6 turbo prop aircraft could land on that road which appears within spitting distance, if the scale is correct.'

While they were eating Shuster replied, 'is that the aircraft manufactured by the Swiss?'

'Yes, the Pilatus PC-6/A2 Turbo-Porter, the 1971 version. The PC-6 has a Short Take Off and Landing capability on virtually any terrain, plus it's possible to haul it up in less than 200 yards and land in around 100 yards with a payload of around 3000 pounds. Test pilots drop it in about 65 yards. It's a wonderful aircraft, holding the record for the highest landing by a fixed wing aircraft, at 18,865 ft, on a glacier in Nepal. With a cruising speed of around 125 knots and a range approaching 800 miles - extra fuel could be carried to enhance the range due to the payload capacity.'

'Landing on the road might not be possible due to wingspan and trees.'

'Not a problem,' replied Vialls. 'Look at the satellite images. Alongside the road, there are several cleared areas and it would be possible to land and take off.'

'I bow to your superior observations.'

Both men were wondering about the reaction to the proposed situation as they ate their lunch in brooding silence. Vialls was the first to break the silence when looking out of the window at the passing traffic. 'Is it an *official,* assignment?'

'It could be made so,' replied Andy Shuster.

'In writing,' responded Vialls.

'By your response can it be assumed you are interested in or are prepared to undertake what has been very roughly outlined?'

'On receiving the proposed assignments in writing and after the logistics involved have been discussed, it could be interpreted as positive.'

Pushing his plate aside Shuster said, 'What logistics?'

'Could a PC-6 aircraft be made available? Who will fly it? Can it be stripped out and have long range fuel tanks installed? Short wave radios are required for communication, as the aircraft would only drop me and when the mission has been completed a means of recalling the aircraft would be required.'

Interrupting Shuster said, 'use Mobile telephones.'

With a smile on his face and with laughter in his voice Vialls replied. 'It's glaringly obvious you are not the brightest button in the box. In simple terminology, Mobiles may not work in the area. Therefore, small hand-held short wave radios would be the best option, with a supply of fully charged batteries. Even you must realise it won't be possible to charge batteries. Added to which, where will the aircraft be located after dropping me?'

'Who is to say you will get the use of an aircraft?' replied Shuster.

'No aircraft, no mission. It's that simple,' replied a serious Vialls.

Registering the tone of voice and turn of phrase Andy Shuster was becoming agitated, as he was not used to subordinates dictating terms or raising aspects concerning equipment and logistics. Grateful the meal was coming to an end he took leave of Vialls and going over to the bar settled the account. Returning to the table having had a few seconds to think he decided discretion was probably the best route and capitulating he answered Vialls with. 'You will receive an outline as it concerns you in writing. Regarding equipment for the operation, an investigation will be carried out by me. Does that satisfy you?'

'So far so good,' answered Vialls getting to his feet. 'I'm off now, tell your minions to use Clavelshay for telephone contact and absolutely nobody else. Don't send anything through the post. When documentation is ready for signature tell Clavelshay and he can contact me and we'll arrange a meeting. Does that ring your bell?'

'Sort of,' replied Shuster.

As Vialls turned to walk away he suddenly stopped and said loud enough for everyone in the bar to hear, 'Close up aerial photos of the road will be required, as the local council will require the information.' With that he walked out of the bar and within seconds he was driving away.

Smiling somewhat inanely and nodding in response at the few people in the bar who had undoubtedly heard Vialls, Shuster got to his feet. Picking up the satellite imagery photos he put them in his briefcase and left the premises for his car.

NINE

After the meeting with Shuster, John Vialls felt optimistic about committing to something more adventurous than repairing post and rail fencing surrounding a sand school. The reason for his efforts outside of the normal farming requirements was Maureen, his American wife, was horse crazy. Not only did Maureen and their two children compete in western riding events, but she also bred Appaloosas and Quarter horses. Horses, coupled with school fees for an up market Prep School and a well know Public School, were a bigger drain on financial resources than could ever be imagined. Particularly when most of their dairy herd had recently been slaughtered after testing positive for Tuberculosis (Vialls suspected the local badger population.) As a result, Vialls needed to find a way of supplementing his farming income and diversification did not appeal. However, he was all for culling every badger for a hundred miles, but Maureen had talked him out of it, primarily because badgers are protected.

While working, he thought about the equipment he would require for assisting in the recovery of the supposed diamonds and gold from the approximate location indicated on the satellite imagery. Knowing the area would be plagued with Malaria, he set about producing an effective mosquito repellent from tobacco mixed with water in plastic bottles. When shaken vigorously, a stinking liquid was produced, and when applied to the skin it was guaranteed to keep mosquitoes and most animals away.

Although John Vialls enjoyed farming he was fully aware his life was sedentary in comparison to his previous career. A little excitement was generated during the winter and early spring when he and Maureen took part in the Sunday evening Piddle Valley Quiz League with two other people. The four of them represented the Halse Arms which enabled them to visit pubs in the area and in the process have fun and get to know people. Not being a family addicted to television, during the summer months the family attended and competed in various equestrian events that John Vialls enjoyed watching and helping with.

****

In London Andrew Shuster had been in contact with the Royal Air force about the possible use of a Pilatus Porter and after some enquires he was informed the RAF knew where two PC-6's could be made available for use if required. Sat facing Shuster across his desk, was an RAF Wing Commander called Paul Chapman, who unbeknown to Shuster, was more than familiar with flying specialist secret missions. He was saying, 'The PC-6 is an aircraft constructed for short take-off and landings, which means it can operate easily in environments predominantly inaccessible for almost any other type of aircraft, added to which it can be quickly converted for a variety of uses.'

Warming to Chapman, Andrew Shuster said, 'could it be landed on a dirt road edged with trees at last light or at first light in a West African country, after flying from this country?'

'Yes, but we must know the payload as that could effect the range. For instance if heavily loaded we could land enroute, say in Gibraltar, to top up the fuel and again say in Marrakesh or elsewhere to keep the fuel level high. The final details can be ironed out later.'

'By the way you are speaking it sounds as if you will be flying the aircraft and the payload will be a single male specialist to be dropped off and to be collected later when he sends the signal. After the drop the aircraft should be located nearby but out of the country. If there is a screw up that would mean you would not be implicated. In fact we agree to whatever you RAF types want or desire. All we need to do is drop off and pick up a specialist.'

'Will he carry much equipment and what's the waiting time?'

Thinking for a couple of seconds Andy Shuster replied, 'the man concerned is a top grade survival expert and he would carry minimal equipment. Say less than a hundred pounds weight. Can't say how long, but you will probably hang around for a couple of days. He would of course let you know.'

'When is the clandestine drop scheduled for?'

'About fourteen days' time, we will confirm the date,' replied Shuster.

'What area of the country is the man coming from?'

'The West Country – why?'

'Primarily to save as much fuel as possible, if it's the West Country we could sneak in and utilise the old Second World War RAF Churchstanton fighter base at Culmhead in Somerset. It's now partially a business park and the disused runways are cracked and weed infested, but for a clandestine mission there is more than enough room to land and take off. Or perhaps we could use the hilltop airstrip at Compton Abbas in central Dorset. If you could obtain the required permissions we could utilise the facilities to be found at the Royal Navel Air Station Yeovilton, which is know as HMS Heron. My preference would be Compton Abbas.'

At the conclusion of the meeting with Shuster, Chapman possessed a little more information but nothing specific concerning the exact location and he knew precisely zero about the specialist and did not expect to know. However, he had been requested to inspect a PC-6 and, if found suitable, he was authorised to requisition the aircraft. This was something Chapman had never done before and he was authorised to carry out any modifications deemed necessary. Furthermore he possessed the documentation signed by goodness knows who, to back him up.

The PC-6 located by Shuster was flown to Shoreham airport in Sussex, where Wing Commander Chapman watched it coming in to land prior to his inspection on behalf of Shuster. During World War Two, Lysander aircraft operating from Shoreham dropped off and picked up secret agents in various parts of Europe. Chapman commenced his inspection by reading the paperwork which told him the aircraft was a Fairchild PC-6/BIA-H2 manufactured in 1968. Total airframe hours from new, 9,724.8. Engine type and model Pratt and Whitney PT6A-20 and hours since new 5,155.5, propeller type and model Hartzell 3 blade and hours since overhaul 1,707.9. Avionics VHF Com, Garmin SL 30, VHF Nav, Garmin SL30, Transponder Garmin GTX 327, Audio Control System Garmin GMA 340 Audio, GPS Garmin 530w/2-Glide Slope Localisers, Traffic Avoidance Avidyne TAS-600. Satisfied with his inspection and the documented evidence on condition and servicing records Chapman handed the requisition paperwork over to the pilot representing the owner and he was pleasantly surprised how well it was received. With the field of play now clear, so to speak, Chapman flew the PC-6 to an RAF maintenance unit. The following day, having informed Shuster they now possessed a PC-6, Chapman began his supervision of the conversion of the aircraft from a ten seat passenger carrier. With the seats stripped out and any excess weight removed, a special fuel tank was installed internally, which meant the range was dramatically enhanced when used in conjunction with the underwing fuel tanks being fitted.

On completion of the maintenance work Chapman flew the PC-6 from the maintenance unit on a test flight over Compton Abbas in Dorset where he checked and noted the navigation coordinates of 50'58'00.82North and 2'09'15 15' West. He then flew onto the old Churchstanton RAF station in Somerset, where the number 2 Polish Fighter Wing operated from during World War 2. On the flight he skirted the Royal Naval Air Station 'HMS Heron' at Yeovilton and then skirting the Mendips, he kept his eyes open as he knew the area was saturated at times by low flying Chinook and other helicopters as well C 130 Hercules transports and various jet aircraft. Picking up the M5, he followed its route keeping to the east or on the left while flying south. Avoiding Taunton, Chapman flew the PC-6 over the Wellington Memorial and the wooded Blackdown hills, before circling above the airfield where he noted the criss-cross layout of the runways, with what looked like a business park with a windsock in the middle. Checking the navigational coordinates for the location he read and noted them as 50'55'52.04 North and 3'07 34.35 West. On completion of the test flight Chapman was satisfied all was well with the PC-6 and on landing and after some further checks it was certified as fully airworthy and parked ready for the operation.

****

Stanley Clavelshay received a package via a motorcycle courier with a covering letter saying the package was for John Vialls and would Stanley please make sure Vialls received it within twenty four hours. Using the telephone Clavelshay called Vials and told him to meet him in the 'Brace of Pheasants' at lunchtime the following day.

Arriving at the 'Brace' Clavelshay once again parked his car in the field and strolled to the entrance accompanied by the sound of pigeons cooing and birds singing. Entering the bar he ordered himself a half of bitter and made for the table in the alcove. Only a couple of minutes elapsed before Vialls walked in and after ordering a beer for himself he strolled across the room and joined Clavelshay. As Vialls sat down and made himself comfortable and took a swig of beer, Clavelshay pushed the package across the table to him saying, 'read it and sign it and give it back to me. I don't want to know anything about the content.'

Opening the package Vialls spent a couple of minutes reading the contents, which he found particularly interesting. In essence, he had a contract, the terms of which he was familiar with from his past career. What pleased him was the following statement: 'Should the diamonds and gold be successfully recovered, when sold you will be entitled to a ten percent commission that could be paid in cash, or if it's a substantial amount it could be invested on your behalf into a pension fund or split into whatever you desire.'

Included in the package were the navigational coordinates for the landing site in the Sierra Leone bush, which he placed in his pocket. There were also instructions for him to inform Clavelshay to take him to the airstrip at Compton Abbas. The pick-up time will be 0445 hrs on the 10th of June, in six days time. Looking at Clavelshay Vialls said, 'have you got a pen?' Reaching into his jacket pocket Clavelshay handed a pen to Vialls who signed and dated the documents in the required places and after putting the documents into the package he handed it to Clavelshay, saying, 'I need to be within spitting distance of Compton Abbas airstrip for 0415hrs on the 10th of June.'

'Do you want me to collect you or shall we meet on neutral territory?'

'Firstly, as far as I know you don't know where I live. Telephone number yes, location no.' remarked Vialls. 'Should you pick me up? Lets leave that decision until later; mind you nobody would inadvertently stumble across us at that time of the morning.'

'Fancy a quick reconnaissance from here?' questioned Clavelshay.

Taking a swig of beer Vialls then said, 'That's probably the best suggestion. I know how to locate the airstrip via Sturmister Newton through various lanes. It's located on top of the hills, with incredible panoramic views of the countryside for miles and miles. There is a need to find a hidey hole and preferable, a quick shufti will pay dividends. I don't want to be fumbling and stumbling around in darkness very early in the morning. '

'Ok then, lets get the show on the road, your car or mine?'

Vialls replied while getting to his feet, 'I will ask if it's OK to leave my car here for an hour or so.' While Vialls was seeking permission to leave his car in the field, Clavelshay left the bar for his car and waited. Getting into the car Vialls said while indicating, 'go down the lane past the Sign Post, that way will lead us through the lanes to Sturmister Newton.'

While driving Clavelshay noted such place names as Mappowder, Hazelbury Bryan, Rivers Corner, Manston, Bedchester and Melbury Abbas before reaching the airfield at Compton Abbas. On arrival they noted the parked aircraft and the various buildings and radio mast from the car park. Looking behind them they noted the woods which particularly interested Vialls as a hiding place. Leaving the car park they drove down the lane noting the thick hedge demarcating the airstrip and it occurred to Vialls he would have to get through the hedge and for that he would require some secateurs. Before leaving the vicinity of the airstrip they went further down the lane and carried out an inspection and decided the best way onto the airstrip would be through the hedge. Turning the car around in the concrete drive of a farm entrance they left for the Brace. On the way back Vialls said to Clavelshay, 'no need for you to pick me up, I will get Maureen to drop me off nearby and then leg it to the site.'

'I'm glad of that as I don't live locally,' replied Clavelshay.

Arriving at the Brace they talked for a couple of minutes and then Vialls left and got into his vehicle and drove away. On his way home Clavelshay stopped in Dorchester and, at the Post Office, paid for the package to go by Next Day Special Delivery to a Post Office Box address in London.

The following morning, on receipt of the documentation concerning Vialls, Shuster was somewhat concerned about adopting a totally clandestine operation by operating illegally from private or disused airfields. Having contacted the military authorities he was assured permission would be granted for the PC-6 to use the Royal Navel Air Station HMS Heron at Yeovilton, which is just north of Yeovil in Somerset and only eleven miles from where Vialls lived, and therefore much easier to get to. The passes and permissions required arrived in Shuster's office the following morning and were immediately despatched by motorcycle courier to Clavelshay for Vialls and directly to Chapman.

Signing for the package addressed to Vialls, Clavelshay immediately contacted him by telephone. They agreed to meet at the entrance to the Public Library at midday in Dorchester. That RV was chosen for the ease of parking and the convenience as each would have about half an hour to drive from different directions. The first to arrive in the car park was Clavelshay and after parking he made his way to the library and when only half way to the entrance, he saw Vialls arriving. Aborting his intention of getting to the library entrance, Clavelshay changed direction and made for the car being parked by Vialls. At the car he handed over the package and watched Vialls reading whatever and pocketing a couple of what looked like passes. Looking up Vialls said, 'that's far more sensible. Maureen can take me there. Thank you very much for your assistance. Hopefully, we will meet again in the foreseeable future.' With that Vialls nodded and turning he got into his car and drove away with a mock salute and wave towards Clavelshay.

TEN

At 0300hrs on the morning of the 10th of June not only was it dark, but it was also drizzling. On the farm Vialls checked his watch and decided it was time to get moving. Wearing camouflaged trousers, smock, faceveil, and jungle boots, he placed a camouflaged bergan, with two metal detectors attached, into the rear of the Landrover. Getting into the passenger seat, Vialls turned to Maureen and said while fastening his seat belt, 'lets get the show on the road.' While Maureen was driving to the rendezvous location, his mind was turning over every facet of his preparations for the mission.

Not many miles away a Royal Navy Lieutenant Commander was briefing four Marine Commandoes. 'We will arrive at the RV just before 0400hrs where we should find a man with equipment, who will be escorted to the Air Station. No names, no pack drill, and I have absolutely no idea what the equipment consists of. He will prove his identity by producing the required passes and we will fulfil the escort mission in total silence. Any questions will be asked or answered by me; we provide his protection, any questions?'

'No' replied a Sergeant.'

The rendezvous location was a gravel filled lay-by used by road maintenance gangs just off the Podimore roundabout on the A303, near Yeovil in Somerset. The location of the RV was approximately a hundred yards beyond the entrance to the twenty four hour fuel station and truck stop that borders the roundabout and only yards short of the village of Podimore. Having negotiated the roundabout Maureen headed for Podimore. Slowing down, she knew there was not far to go. Then, on seeing three yellow lines on the road illuminated by the headlights, Vialls said while pointing, 'slowly slowly there's the entrance to the lay-by.' Easing into the lay-by entrance Maureen stopped and turned the headlights off. Turning towards her husband she gave him a kiss and, as he was leaving the cab to collect his equipments she told him 'take care and remember I love you.' As Vialls hefted the bergan onto his shoulders Maureen turned the headlights on and after reversing out of the lay-by she headed for home.

Creeping into the shadows, assisted by the occasional vehicle lights as they passed behind the hedge on the edge of the A303, Vialls found a suitable place and sat on the bergan. Shrouded by bushes Vialls looked at the luminous dial of his watch. There were twelve minutes to wait until it was 0400hrs when he hoped somebody would arrive to escort him to the PC-6.

While checking his watch again he detected the distinctive noise of a Landrover approaching from the direction of the village. Vialls was not surprised when it began slowing down and then turned into the lay-by on sidelights. From his position Vialls watched the vehicle being turned around to provide an easy exit with the engine running and with the driver in position. In the slowly expanding light of the dawn Vialls detected the outline of four men who appeared to be armed. Checking his watch he waited until it was exactly 0400hrs and in the reflection of passing vehicle lights on the A303 he approached the group of men. Stopping in front of the group, Vialls watched as the Naval officer saluted and asked him to produce his passes.

Rummaging in the left hand pocket of the smock Vialls produced two small plastic cases containing cards and handed them to the officer, who checking them by penlight said, 'thank you sir, we will keep these for now. Would you be kind enough to follow us?'

Doing as requested Vialls removed the bergan from his right shoulder and pushed it into the rear of the Landrover. Climbing into the vehicle accompanied by the officer and the armed men, Vialls began to relax as they moved off. In less than five minutes they approached the highly illuminated Royal Naval Air Station. Looking out at the surrounding security fencing and lighting, Vialls was surprised at the various gates that opened as if by magic until they reached the side of hanger. Not a word had been spoken until the officer said, 'we will wait here until a Royal Air Force PC-6 arrives. Its ETA is in about three minutes. We will escort you to the aircraft and then our responsibility ceases, unless something goes wrong with the aircraft before take off.'

'Many thanks,' replied Vialls, detecting the sound of an approaching aircraft. On seeing its landing lights and the ghostly outline of a PC-6 drifting onto the runway Vialls followed it as the pilot manoeuvred it towards the side of the hanger. As soon as the PC-6 was turned broadside, there was a ripple of laughter and even in the early morning light the registration letters FU2-UP-U2 were clearly visible on the camouflage painted fuselage. 'Now that's not a recognisable international aircraft identification,' Vialls heard the Naval Officer mumble. Then he heard him say, 'some RAF ground crew are probably laughing,' as he and others were. Then

Vialls caught a glimpse of the pilot standing at the fuselage door. He had difficulty believing what he was seeing as he thought it was Paul Chapman. When the pilot descended from the aircraft and walked over to the group it was a case of instant recognition as they solemnly shook hands and said nothing. Shaking hands with the officer, Vialls said, 'thank you very much,' and followed Chapman to the aircraft. After climbing aboard Vialls spent a few seconds securing the bergan before easing into the co-pilot's seat. Handing Chapman the coordinates for where he wanted to land he said, 'it's in Sierra Leone.'

'Luckily, I've flown to Sierra Leone several times since we last flew an aircraft together and having been best man at your wedding all those years ago. How the hell are you? It's been a couple of years since we last met.'

Watching Chapman carrying out the pre-flight checks Vialls waited until he had finished before saying, 'quite bad, I'm back in harness due to tuberculosis wiping out most of our dairy herd which has caused financial problems.'

Chapman replied, 'OK let's get moving it's a long way. The flight plan, formulated only a few seconds ago, is to land in Gibraltar to top up the fuel and in a couple of other places.' Chapman then released the brakes and as the aircraft started to roll forward, Vialls heard a Scottish voice say, 'You are cleared for take off.' Increasing the power Chapman eased the PC-6 onto the runway and in no distance the aircraft lifted into the air and almost immediately it was on course and heading for Gibraltar.

The airport on Gibraltar is a Royal Air Force station owned by the Ministry of Defence which is shared with civilians. It's probably the closest international airport to any town in the world. Bringing the PC-6 into land was straight forward and Chapman enjoyed floating the aircraft onto the tarmac of the fortress colony. To Vialls, visiting Gibraltar for the first time, it appeared as if the whole area was taken up by military installations. While closing the aircraft down Chapman said, 'The climate is mild and pleasant. Do you have any clothing other than the camouflage you are wearing?'

'Why?' questioned Vialls warily.

'Dressed as you are, you will scare the natives, and we don't want that do we? We will be stopping over in Marrakech and probably somewhere else as we won't be completing the flight in one leg.' Noting an Iberia Airbus A319, parked nearby Vialls said, 'that's unusual, when did - Spanish flights begin to utilise Gibraltar?' Chapman replied, 'restrictions on Spanish civilian flights and the prohibition of flights over Spanish territory from Gibraltar ended recently.' While they were talking an RAF fuel Bowser arrived and Chapman then became involved with the procedures for refuelling the PC-6.

On completion of the refuelling Chapman signed for the fuel and stood talking with the driver who expressed his astonishment at the type of aircraft Chapman was flying. What became graphically clear to Vialls was the aircraft registration of FU2-UP-U2 was recognised and specifically associated to aircraft flown by Chapman. After refuelling procedure both men climbed back into the aircraft and while communicating by radio to the tower, both men heard a clear voice saying.

'You are cleared for take off.'

Watching Chapman easing the power on, it appeared to Vialls a longer run than normal was being used…and then Chapman eased the PC-6 into the air and set course for Marrakech. As they flew over the narrow stretch of the Mediterranean Sea, known as the Straits of Gibraltar, towards the North African coast Chapman said, 'The area we are flying over has historically been referred to as the

Pillars of Hercules and on the North African coast is the Spanish enclave of Ceuta. There are also several small islands whose ownership is disputed or claimed by both Morocco and Spain. Added to which the straits are widely used by smugglers and illegal immigration to gain entry to Europe.'

Marrakech, also known as the 'Red City,' is capital of the mid-southwestern economic region of Marrakech-Tensift–Al Haouz. Looking down from the aircraft it was glaringly obvious to Vialls they were close to the foothills of the snow-capped Atlas Mountains. After receiving permission to land Chapman was constantly checking for other aircraft as he held the PC-6 on a flight path towards Menara Airport.

On landing the plane was directed to a parking place, where Chapman again supervised the refueling procedures before leaving for a Hotel. Having eaten and consumed a couple of beers at the bar, both men retired to their allocated rooms. Meeting at 0630 hrs the following morning, Chapman said on seeing Vialls. 'How was your overnight stay?' 'Not too bad and I must admit to enjoying the food and drink.' On returning to the airport Chapman carried out his normal pre take off checks and when cleared for take off, Chapman eased the PC- 6 into the coolest air of the day. This could be the most difficult leg and while edging Algerian airspace with the Atlas Mountains below, and on their left they flew on until, before them, lay the seemingly endless Sahara Desert.

The Sahara is the world's largest desert at over 9,000,000 square kilometers or 3,500,000 square miles, and every square mile is screaming hot. In fact, the Sahara covers most of North Africa, making it almost as large as the United States of America or the continent of Europe. The desert stretches from the Red Sea to the Atlantic Ocean and to the south, where it meets the semi-arid savannah areas where the sand encroaches like a gigantic Python that slowly swallows everything as it expands.

Using Taoudenni in northern Mali as a means of establishing or knowing they were on course for Timbuktu, the vastness of the Desert was mind blowing to Vialls who, while perspiring profusely, was looking down from the cockpit, onto an area that resembled a First World War battle field. Chapman said in response to Vialls pointing and saying, 'what the hell is that?' 'Salt has been mined in the area since time in memoriam and what you see are thousands of hand-dug mines. Taoudenni is slowly migrating and the people move to a new location when the nearest salt deposits are exhausted.' Chapman also said after a few seconds of radio communication in French. 'There was once a Mali Army Post in the area but it is now closed. People used to be exiled for being political dissidents, debtors, and petty criminals. Temperatures reach in excess of 140 degrees during April to September. During that period most people cannot live in the intense heat and they leave Taoudenni in droves.'

The transparent cockpit of the PC-6 in the cloudless sky with the suns rays burning like a furnace, made it extremely uncomfortable. Even with a cockpit side window open, they sweated profusely as they flew towards Timbuktu. Occasionally, while trying to ease the discomfort and boredom of the flight Vialls noted high flying vultures. Then, in the middle of thousands of miles of sand dunes and hundreds of miles from anywhere, Vialls saw men with columns of Camels.

Timbuktu in Mali is famous for being remote and is prestigious as an intellectual and spiritual centre long involved with Islam. Timbuktu is situated just north of the Niger River. The location has caused it to become a meeting place for West African peoples who, long ago, established trading links far and wide, including Europe. In the western world Timbuktu is a metaphor for exotic places particularly when people unconnectedly say 'from here to Timbuktu.' However, very few western people realise the significance of the contribution made to Islam and world civilization. Timbuktu is thought to have established the first University in the world. Even in this day and age local scholars and collectors still speak of, and maintain an impressive collection of, ancient Greek texts.

Speaking in French, Chapman requested permission to land. Almost immediately they were cleared to land at Timbuktu's airport, where after landing he negotiated the refuelling of the aircraft. After completing the refuelling phase Chapman spent time checking oil and thoroughly inspecting other aspects concerned with the airworthiness and reliability of the PC-6. Satisfied all was well, both Vialls and Chapman obtained something to eat and drink and while talking they mutually agreed to sleep in the aircraft. Speaking with officials in French, Chapman said, 'would it be OK for us to sleep in the aircraft?'

'No problem provided you shift the aircraft to a safer location.'

Early in the morning, after a good night's sleep, food and drink, they set off for Bamako. Following the course of the Niger River for a significant amount of the journey, Chapman pointed out the dirt airstrip at Niafounke. Now enjoying the challenge of conversing in French, Chapman obtained permission to land at Seno airport Bamako, and while approaching they left behind clear skies and encountered heavy cloud. While refuelling the aircraft they experienced light rain, and on completion they obtained clearance for take off, and prepared to head for Faranah in Guinea. In the air again and experiencing light rain they noted the Dabola Tinkisso Hydro Electric Dam's airstrip.

After a cooler, shorter, more relaxing day at the controls Chapman brought the PC-6 into Faranah in Guinea. Speaking French he obtained information concerning fuel and accommodation. After securing the aircraft they left in a Peugeot car for the Hotel de Niger, which they reached after driving over a bridge that spanned the Niger. Although still warm, it was significantly cooler in Faranah than when they were flying across Mali. After eating a meal and drinking both men went for a swim in the Hotel's pool. Now within spitting distance of Sierra Leone compared to the distance already travelled, they sat talking for a couple of hours planning the next move. Driven from the pool by rain and before going to bed both men ensured the short wave radios and other electronic devices were fully charged inclusive of spare batteries.

ELEVEN

In Faranah, a town that was once a French Colonial outpost, both Vialls and Chapman were enjoying breakfast and planning the next phase of the flight. The plan was to depart before dawn the next day and to arrive at the destination just as dawn was breaking, sufficient time to provide Vialls with an opportunity to get organised, and theoretically, disappear into the bush. While finishing his Coffee, Chapman said.

'I suggest you take a couple of bottles of water with you.'

'I've already taken care of that,' replied Vialls.

Outside it was hot and it was also the rainy season. As a precaution they took a taxi back to the airport, where Chapman checked the PC-6, assisted by Vialls. After preparing the aircraft for the next phase and checking the gathering clouds, they decided to wander around a nearby market. With Chapman translating the mainly French language in use, they followed the trading for rice, cattle, palm oil and kernels. While acting the part of tourists they also wandered around Faranah noting the hospital, the Catholic mission and learnt that the surrounding area was inhabited by the Dialonke people.

Returning to the hotel by taxi just before a monsoon type downpour began, they were surprised by the amount of surface water failing to drain away. Chapman became anxious about the weather conditions, as being within the same climate zone, the landing site in Sierra Leone could be saturated, making landing and take-off difficult, if not impossible, due to mud.

Later in the day they relaxed at the swimming pool and enjoyed an extended period of cloudy sunbathing and the occasional swim. Leaving the pool, they returned to their rooms, before taking an early supper and getting a few hours sleep. Rising at 3 a.m., and having packed their belongings, they made for the hotel reception desk, where, after settling the account, they waited for a taxi arranged by the hotel. They followed the headlights of a vehicle as it entered the hotel precincts, its lights emphasizing the rain, which fortunately turned out to be their taxi. Getting in, after placing their baggage in the boot, it did not take long before they crossed the bridge over the River Niger and arrived at the airport. Getting out of the taxi into lightly falling rain and darkness, Chapman paid the driver and picking up their baggage they made their way to the PC-6. Within a few yards of the aircraft they were suddenly challenged with a loud,

'Halt!' accompanied by a very bright torch being shone in their faces.

Instantly obeying the order, and while standing still they produced documents, that proved their identity to the armed guard overseeing the security of the PC-6. Allowed to proceed, they unlocked the aircraft and after stowing their baggage, climbed on board and entered the cockpit.

Sat in the left hand seat watched by Vialls in the right hand seat, Chapman began the pre-flight checks and when satisfied he started the engine and turned on the landing lights. After checking the instruments and the function of the controls Chapman released the brakes and taxied the PC-6 to the runway and checked by radio to see if any clearance was required. Without any response after several attempts, he released the brake. With the wipers operating Chapman increased the power and as the PC-6 moved forward and gained speed the aircraft lifted off and climbed away from Faranah.

Turning off the landing lights and setting course Chapman continued to climb as he knew of mountains in the area that reached to around 6000ft. After about twenty minutes, Chapman said, 'We should be near the Loma Mountains in Sierra Leone. The highest peak is Mount Bintumania which reaches 6,400 feet. The whole area is protected and hunting is prohibited. Within a few minutes we should be approaching the area for which I have the co-ordinates.'

'Try not to hit the mountain,' replied Vialls, laughing.

Throttled back above the clouds and cruising, there was no requirement for the wipers, and Chapman was determined to keep the PC-6 at altitude until there was sufficient light to carry out a landing. Sunrise was estimated at 06.30 hrs and after circling for a time until the sun peeped over the rim of the world, Chapman began the descent. Descending through clouds Chapman brought the wipers back into use and from the right hand seat, Vialls identified the town of Koidu. Other features of the surrounding area became clearer as they flew including the forested hills and valleys, the River Sewa, tracks, roads, huts and houses. What Vialls took to be the surface of the Moon was in fact the illegal diamond mining areas that appeared as acre upon acre of heaps of whitish sand surrounding water filled holes, craters and pits; the whole surrounded by forested hills.

Constantly checking the coordinates, Chapman reduced power and brought the PC-6 lower and lower. Finally satisfied a landing could be carried out; Chapman glided the aircraft in to land on the bush road within yards of over-hanging trees. As the aircraft slowed, Vialls tapped Chapman on the shoulder and after giving him a thumbs-up, he left the cockpit and picking up the bergan and a bag he waited for the aircraft to stop. Opening the door he threw the bergan and bag out and then dropped to the ground, where, turning to face the fuselage, he slammed the door shut. Grabbing the bergan and bag, Vialls ran into the bush, from where he watched the aircraft slowly gaining speed beneath overhanging branches. In the aircraft, when sufficient clearance became available, Chapman eased the PC-6 into the air and set a course for Conakry, the capital of Guinea, situated on the Atlantic coast.

Hidden by six foot high elephant grass, Vialls was applying his homemade insect repellent. While applying the repellent and above the noises of the bush Vialls detected some very faint shouting and wondered if it indicated IDM digging for diamonds. Satisfied he was alone in the immediate area Vialls picked up the bergan and shrugged it onto his shoulders. Carrying the bag in his left hand Vialls moved cautiously, and after a few minutes, with the shouting slightly louder, he was positive the large cotton tree was near. Identifying the remnants of the wrecked suspension bridge on the edge of the illegal diggings, Vialls then found the cotton tree and was about to take the bergan off when he heard some nearby voices.

Surviving in the African bush was second nature, to Vialls and creeping to the remains of the suspension bridge, he slid down the bank into the remnants of the river. Crouching as he moved, Vialls negotiated a route through the heaps of soil, sand and water-filled excavations. Finding an old Maraka pit, he took the bergan off and dropped it and the bag into the pit, followed by himself. By standing on the bergan and the bag he was able to peer over the edge, where he saw, about fifty yards away, a group of six uniformed and armed men creeping towards the diggings. Unbeknown to Vialls, they were a group of policemen, about to launch an attack against Kabudu gangs, who were fighting over the illegal diggings.

When several shots rang out, the police took cover behind the piles of sand and soil and returned fire. With a fire fight raging, two of the policemen were hit by shots being fired from their left rear, and one of them was screaming in agony. When Vialls saw several, almost naked, armed men, creeping up behind the policemen, he was torn between shouting a warning and giving himself away. Deciding to remain silent he watched the cold blooded execution of the policemen. Some of the policemen were not dead, and Vialls witnessed the brutal mutilation of them by members of a Kabudu gang. Shouting abuse, they beat the screaming policemen to death with shovels. Then, having stripped the uniforms from the dead policemen, three men, wielding machetes, causing blood to be splattered everywhere, hacked off the dead policemen's heads.

From his location Vialls, watched a member of the Kabudu force one of the policemen's heads onto a stick, which he then carried over his shoulder, while others threw the mutilated bodies into Maraka pits. Satisfied with their victory over authority, and with the sun well above the horizon the Kabudu moved off, leaving a shocked Vialls surveying the scene.

Constantly checking the area from his position, Vialls eventually shrugged off the bergan and bag and pushed them over the lip before climbing out of the pit. Making his way back to the cotton tree, an extremely cautious Vialls un-slung the bergan and unpacked the metal detectors. Preparing the more sensitive model while carrying a trowel, Vialls began the process of scanning the area began.

Screened by stunted trees, some clumps of bamboo and elephant grass, Vialls stopped frequently to listen and check for any unusual sounds in the surrounding area. As he continued, suddenly and quite unexpectedly, he got a clear response indicating metal. Scraping and digging in the soil, Vialls uncovered a rusting machete with a broken handle. Casting it aside, a few seconds later he again got a reading, and digging, recovered the rusting remnants of what he took to be a bicycle pump. In a period of just over an hour, with further intervals to check for noises in the area, Vialls uncovered a further four articles which included two coins, an empty ammunition clip and a meat skewer.

Feeling the heat and not daring to take his camouflage smock off, Vialls returned to the cotton tree. After taking a drink of water and resting for a few minutes, he picked up the detector and recommenced the search. Perspiring profusely in his camouflage smock and trousers, he suddenly received a clear indication of metal. Digging and scrapping, his heart skipped a couple of beats when he uncovered the neck of a clay pot. Being extremely cautious and making sure he was alone, he extracted two clay pots, one of which weighed considerably more than the other, and returned to the cotton tree.

Quickly checking the inside of the pots, Vialls was satisfied they contained what he was seeking. Before pushing the pots into the bergan, he tore up a shirt and stuffed it into the pot necks, then, picking up the bergan, Vialls made for the bridge. Once there, he took the metal detectors, and any other equipment he no longer required and dropped them into the mud of the river. After placing the bergan on his back he stamped on the equipment forcing it into the mud.

Making his way back to the Maraka pit Vialls was determined to find a better hide for the next twenty four hours, from where he could contact Chapman in Conakry. Looking around the area, he selected an area of trees about two hundred yards away on the edge of the illegal mining area, and made his way there. On reaching the shelter of the trees, the first thing Vialls did was check his watch and he was astounded to realise it was only five minutes past nine. Looking up at the clouds he thought it would rain and while looking at the clouds he noticed that several palm trees in the vicinity had gourds attached for collecting palm oil. Moving off, Vialls soon found a Maraka pit, and was pleasantly surprised to realise it was inter-connected to another pit by a small tunnel. Taking his time he pushed the bergan and bag into the tunnel and then wriggled into the cool atmosphere which was wonderful when compared to the rising temperature above ground.

A little later, a considerably less tense Vialls took the opportunity to inspect the area from the safety of the pit, and, while doing so, he suddenly heard someone whistling and singing. Checking in the direction of the sound, he was not surprised to see a young man with a rope around his waist, climbing a palm tree. Watching the young man changing the gourds and climbing down the tree, Vialls watched him move to another tree further away and then it started to rain.

At first the rain was just above a drizzle, but then it slowly and steadily turned into a downpour that began to create pools around the area, merging and making larger pools. Sheltering in the tunnel, Vialls thought he was reasonably protected, until water began to trickle into the pit. With water beginning to soak into the sandy base of the pit, he thought he might be forced to move. Looking over the rim of the pit Vialls saw the young man, who had been collecting palm oil, sheltering under a nearby tree, and he waited until he left.

Satisfied he was reasonably secure, Vialls took the plastic bottle out of the bag and reapplied more of the liquid insect repellent to his face and hands, as he had no wish to be irritated by hoards of insects. Checking his watch, it was almost eleven thirty and the first radio transmission was due to take place at twelve o'clock mid-day. Removing one of the shortwave radios out of a side pocket in the bergan, he checked it ,and prepared to make the first transmission and just before twelve o'clock Vialls switched the radio on, and holding it clear of the pit, at precisely the allocated time, he called Chapman saying.

'Foxtrot Uniform Two. How do you read me, over?'

To his surprise Chapman replied, 'Loud and clear over.'

Vialls then replied, 'Mission accomplished and awaiting pick-up, over.'

'Roger,' replied Chapman, adding, 'Move up to the road junction. Sunrise is estimated at 0635hrs; will arrive at around 0600hrs tomorrow, out.'

Switching the radio off Vialls placed it back in the side pocket of the bergan and prepared himself to get wet while walking to the road junction at night. As the time passed oh so slowly and dusk finally turned into total darkness, Vialls, the hood of his camouflaged smock pulled up for protection, prepared to move off. Although it was raining less intensly, it was still hot and humid and an hour passed before Vialls finally decided to climb out of the pit and make his way towards the elephant grass a short distance from the road junction, where he arrived without experiencing any problems. As the hours passed, Vialls was struggling to resist the temptation to continually check his watch. Then quite suddenly the wait became interesting, when he detected the noise of people approaching. Helped by the torches they were carrying, Vialls made out a group of men carrying all manner of equipment, including shovels and a type of sieve. As they moved towards the moonscape of diggings, Vialls was preparing himself mentally to move off again, when another group of men carrying torches came clattering along the track. When one of the torch beams was shone in his direction, he caught a glimpse of a large snake moving about six feet from him. Looking like a camouflaged log he thought it was probably a python, as he'd only seen it for a fraction of a second. Remaining in the prone position for several minutes while mosquitoes buzzed around his head, he was acutely aware of the snake's proximity. Easing onto his hands and knees, he maintained that position for a few minutes, then he moved out of the grass, and slinging the bergan onto his shoulders, he made his way to the edge of the road junction.

As the night progressed the sky cleared, and with the moon casting its eerie light over the road junction, from where he was hiding Vialls could clearly make out various star constellations and even a couple of the planets. Although that was interesting, he also saw several shooting stars streaming across the sky, and suddenly a major concern was a vehicle moving on the road in a blaze of headlights. Thankfully, it did not stop. As the night progressed he remained alert to counter any actions that might occur.

Then something occurred for which there was no answer, and which forced Vialls to move yet again, and that was a column of ants. The first indication was being painfully bitten on the hand. Fumbling for a pen-light, which he shielded very carefully, he saw thousands of ants surrounding him. By the time he moved, his face had been bitten by the ants that had crawled over the camouflaged clothing. Later, having escaped the ants and settled down, he saw several lights going along the road accompanied by the clatter of equipment as further groups of men moved to or from various diggings.

Finally, with the eastern sky beginning to lighten, Vialls decided to move to the edge of the road and prepared himself to signal Chapman. Checking his watch Vialls estimated he had about ten minutes to wait before he would hear the sound of an aircraft, when he suddenly heard the subdued sound of the PC-6 approaching. With the bergan at his feet and ready to move in any direction should it be necessary, Vialls flashed the pen-light skywards three times and within seconds he saw the PC-6 drifting over the trees. As the aircraft touched down and approached his position, Vialls moved to where he could be seen. As Chapman brought the aircraft to a halt, Vialls ran over, and opening the hatch, he threw the bergan in, climbed aboard and then shut the hatch. Before Vialls was even in the co-pilots seat Chapman had the aircraft roaring and turning as he operated the controls and increased power. Roaring back up the road in the same direction from which the PC-6 had landed, they lifted off and began the return journey. The first stop would be Bamako in Mali and from there they would stop again before flying across the Sahara.

As they settled into the journey, Chapman concentrated on flying the aircraft while Vialls sat thinking about what he had witnessed. As the flight progressed, Chapman altered course to avoid a huge sand storm rolling across the Sahara. Preferring to carry more than sufficient fuel for each leg of the flight plan, the PC-6 was topped-up a couple of times before arriving in Marrakesh. After securing the aircraft the two men utilised the facilities at the Airport hotel and at no time did Vialls relinquish possession of the bergan.

The following morning after a good night's sleep and breakfast, the flight to Gibraltar commenced, and just after leaving the North African Coast, Chapman contacted Royal Air Force (RAF) Gibraltar and received clear, precise clearance, approach and landing details.

Situated on the Southern tip of Spain, Gibraltar is fondly referred to as the Rock by the British. The climate is pleasant and tourism is important to the local economy with many people arriving to see the Barbary Apes. The Rock has been a British Military fortress and base for around two hundred years and a substantial area of the Rock is covered with Military installations, and the airport is part and parcel of the garrison. Britain gained sovereignty over the Rock under the Treaty of Utrecht in 1713. The United Nations supervised referendum, held in 1967, confirmed the wish of the population to remain British. Nevertheless Spain continues to claim sovereignty and the border was closed between 1969 and 1985. In 1989, the British reduced the military garrison by around fifty percent with only elements of the Royal Navy and Royal Air Force remained in situ.

To Chapman bringing the PC-6 in low over the Mediterranean on its approach, the Rock of Gibraltar stood out like a mountain towering over the surrounding territory and sea. After landing, Chapman followed a Landrover that came over to the aircraft, directing the PC-6 towards the side of the Control Tower. After closing the engines down, Chapman and Vialls left the cockpit. and were saluted and greeted as if expected. An RAF Flight Lieutenant informed that that he had been briefed to expect a PC-6 aircraft with that registration and nobody knew when or if it would even arrive. Looking at Vialls, who had not shaved for a few days and was dressed from head to toes in mud stained camouflage combat clothing with a bergan slung over his right shoulder, the Flight Lieutenant asked if there was anything he could do to assist.

Chapman replied, 'The plan is to fly to the UK tomorrow. Can accommodation and food be provided?'

'Plus a couple of beers and a bath,' remarked Vialls.'

'Gentlemen, please be good enough to get into the Landrover.' Doing as requested, they were driven away. En route, the Flight Lieutenant said, 'You must have influence in high places due to the instructions received concerning your protection.'

'What do you mean by protection?' questioned Chapman.

'We were instructed to ensure the aircraft and its crew were fully protected and comfortable for the duration of the stay,' replied the Flight Lieutenant, who continued, 'You will be staying at the Rock Hotel, which is something of an institution on Gibraltar.'

Arriving at the white edifice that is the Rock Hotel, they were escorted to the reception desk by the Flight Lieutenant and were booked in, without even a second look at the strange way Vialls was dressed. Before leaving his two charges, the Flight Lieutenant said, 'What time do you contemplate leaving tomorrow?' Looking at Vialls, Chapman replied, 'is it possible to get us to the aircraft for 0900hrs?'

'No problem gentlemen,' and, giving them a card with telephone numbers on, he said, 'If you have a problem or wish to see a little of the Rock ,give me a call,' and with that they shook hands, and he left.

After going up their rooms and bathing, both men made for the bar, and even then Vialls had the bergan with him. Having enjoyed a couple of beers, they then consumed an enjoyable meal, laced with convivial conversation, afterwards retiring to their respective rooms. Deciding to watch television before going to bed, Vialls became totally engrossed in an audience participation discussion taking place, with one of the panel saying, 'I would consider retribution and revenge to be a normal aspect of humanity, particularly after people have been abused, assaulted, robbed and generally ill treated.'

In response, another panellist replied, 'There is a distinct possibility a weak society could be responsible for allowing inadequate punishments to be carried out against criminals, which in turn could bring about groups of vigilantes and lynch mobs. But what is the alternative to the lenient sentences handed down these days?'

Another panellist responded, saying, 'In the sixties, the liberal fraternity, against the death penalty, were placated by being assured that life sentences handed down would in fact be life. However, it's abundantly clear some prisoners are being released after serving only partial sentences. If those who commit murder are allowed to live, then life sentences must mean life, even though the financial burden on the tax payer will be enormous.'

A member of the audience responded, 'What's wrong with hanging? It's more economical than providing accommodation and three meals a day,' which was greeted by a round of applause.

Turning off the television, Vialls prepared for bed, and grabbing the bergan, he forced it under the bed near to where his head would be resting on a pillow. Some eight hours later he woke up and proceeded to the bathroom. Looking in the mirror, not having shaved for a few days and without the means to do so, he washed his hands and leaving the bathroom, got dressed.

Pulling the bergan from below the bed, Vialls opened it and removed the clay pots. Now, for the first time, he really examined the diamonds and gold. Just after placing the clay pots back into the bergan, there was a knock at the door and when he opened it, Chapman was standing there and it was obvious he had shaved. Slinging the bergan over his right shoulder, Vialls accompanied Chapman to the restaurant for breakfast, where they indulged themselves until satisfied. While preparing to leave their table the Flight Lieutenant walked in and said, 'There is a vehicle outside ready to take you to your aircraft, if you would like to follow me gentlemen.'

'What about settling the account?' asked Vialls.

'Already taken care of sir,' replied the Flight Lieutenant.

Getting into the Landrover, it did not take long before they were next to the PC-6, and after getting out of the vehicle, Chapman opened the aircraft, which allowed Vialls to push the bergan onboard and climb in. Chapman entered the aircraft and settled in the cockpit. After strapping himself in and making himself comfortable, Chapman begun the procedures to leave Gibraltar. On starting the engine, he received the clearance to taxi the PC-6 to the required location, and on stopping, he received permission to take off. Opening the engine up, the aircraft proceeded down the runway and upon achieving sufficient speed, Chapman eased the PC-6 into the air.

Chapman concentrated on the flying and, as the flight progressed and time elapsed, Vialls began to relax and enjoyed looking down on the Pyrenees, while thinking about the last time he had flown over the same area in a Russian bomber. He enjoyed looking down on the various areas they were flying over, then, suddenly; they left the coast of North West France and flew across the sea. Traversing the English coast, the PC-6 flew over the rolling hills and patchwork countryside of the West Country as they flew towards HMS Heron.

With Chapman speaking almost constantly over the radio, they eventually drifted over the runway and the PC-6 landed at the Royal Navy Air Station. Taxiing behind a Landrover, they were guided to a hard standing, where Chapman closed the PC-6 down. On leaving the aircraft they discovered, from the same Lieutenant Commander who had picked up Vialls from the lay-by, that there was nobody to meet them. Somewhat surprised at having arrived unexpectedly, they both concluded the authorities in Gibraltar had not as yet informed the authorities in the UK, and they assumed, at this juncture, that they had been more or less abandoned. Assured by the Lieutenant Commander that Chapman could continue the flight, Vialls and Chapman shook hands with Vialls saying,

'Keep in contact and many thanks.'

Escorted to a Landrover, Vialls requested to be taken to the lay-by he was picked up from a few days previously. On arrival and just after getting out of the Landrover, Vialls saw the PC-6 flying off and with the bergan over his right shoulder he made for the service station to use a telephone.

Dialling his home number, and after it had rung out three times, Maureen said,

'Hello'

'Can you collect me from where you dropped me a few days ago?'

'Of course, I will be there in about half an hour.'

After successfully contacting Maureen, Vialls walked back to the lay-by and waited for just over half and hour during which time he watched the traffic on the A303. When Maureen arrived, Vialls placed the bergan on the rear seat, climbed into the passenger seat and relaxed as they headed for the farm.

Arriving home Vialls went into the lounge and while maintaining watch over the bergan, he relaxed for the first time in several days. Going upstairs, he forced the bergan under the bed, and after taking a shower, shaving, and changing into more suitable clothing, he decided to do absolutely nothing beyond relaxing and enjoying a home cooked meal and a couple of beers, until the following morning.

TWELVE

Landing the PC-6 back at base, and while taxing to a hard standing, Chapman was preparing himself to complete the administrative procedures. Stopping and closing the aircraft down, Chapman collected his personal effects, and on leaving the aircraft, he got into a Landrover. Looking forward to a couple days of relaxation, his dreams were shattered by the letter handed to him by the driver. Perusing the letter, while being chauffeur-driven, he read, "Contact me at this telephone number," and was signed, Andrew Shuster. Only a few minutes had elapsed since landing and Chapman was in the process of dialling the number. After ringing five times someone said, "Hello.'

In response Chapman replied, 'I was instructed to telephone this number in a letter given to me after landing a PC-6 aircraft.'

'In that case you must be Chapman. My name is Andrew Shuster.'

'How can I be of assistance?' replied Chapman.

'I presume Vialls is back and the mission was successful.'

'No idea, however Vialls was left at the Royal Naval Air Station.'

'Thank you,' replied Shuster putting the telephone down.

A slightly bemused Chapman looked at the silent receiver for a couple of seconds and then replaced it on the cradle. With that, he set about getting himself cleaned up. While Chapman was concentrating on the task of sorting out his personal effects, and planning a couple of days off, the telephone in the Vialls house in West Dorset rang and Maureen Vialls answered it saying, 'Hello.'

A voice she did not recognise said, 'Is your husband there?'

'Who is this speaking?' asked Maureen Vialls.

'Andrew Shuster,' the reply.

Recognising the name, Maureen said, 'Please hold on and I will get him,' and, with that, she walked over to her husband. Thanking his wife for the information, Vialls strolled over to the table where the telephone was located. 'Hello,' he said.

Shuster responded, 'Did you get my diamonds?'

'Your diamonds,' replied Vialls, adding, 'Something was recovered and I'm not convinced it's specifically yours. In fact, getting Clavelshay to contact and meet with me would be my advice. We will then discuss the situation.' Vialls replaced the receiver and walked away. Barely thirty seconds elapsed before the telephone rang again and this time it was Clavelshay asking to speak with Vialls, and after exchanging pleasantries, Maureen signalled for her husband to come to the telephone, while mouthing, 'Clavelshay.' Taking the receiver from Maureen, Vialls smiled at his wife and pre-empted Clavelshay, saying, 'I suppose because I upset Shuster, you are about to try and arrange a meeting.'

'Something like that,' replied Clavelshay adding, 'He really is miffed.'

'Good, in my estimation he is about as effective as a split condom.'

'Full of admiration for your superiors,' replied Clavelshay.

'OK what about a meeting,' replied Vialls.

'The Brace, at mid-day tomorrow, if that's ok with you?'

The following morning Vialls placed the bergan into his car and made his way to the Brace of Pheasants at Plush. After the surprise of parking in a field he lifted the bergan onto his right shoulder. Looking around, he was stunned to realise the beech trees that had provided a screen, had disappeared. The car park was a building site, and it looked like drainage was being installed. Leaving the field he walked to the entrance and was disappointed to find the brick steps had been concreted over. Climbing the steps Vialls entered the pub, where he noticed Clavelshay already sitting at the table located in the fireplace alcove. Ordering a beer at the bar, Vialls made his way to the table and, sliding the bergan in first, he then slid into position facing Clavelshay and said, 'Good afternoon and how can I help you?'

In reply Clavelshay said, 'There appears to be some contention concerning who actually owns what I presume is in the bergan. Having been present at the initial briefing, Shuster was only informed about gold being available at hospital swamp. Whereas, Turhan-Cooper was taken, in person, to the rough location of the diamonds, by the man who buried them, the reason being that Turhan-Cooper had once saved his life. Rest assured the probable contents of the bergan belong to George Turhan-Cooper.' Taking a swig from his glass, Vialls heard a noise at the entrance, and turning towards the sound, he nearly dropped his glass on recognising George Turhan-Cooper who stumbled into the bar. Waving a walking stick, Turhan-Cooper acknowledged both Clavelshay and Vialls, before he set about ordering a drink. With a glass in his hand, Turhan-Cooper came over to the table and eased next to Clavelshay, and while placing his drink on the table, said, 'Good afternoon gentlemen.'

Nodding in response, Vialls said, 'What's with the walking stick?

Turhan-Cooper replied, "I sprained my ankle a couple of days ago.'

Vialls responded, 'I must apologise for apparently upsetting Andrew Shuster. However, to be absolutely honest, I don't trust him. He may be big in the corridors of power, but from my knowledge of him, he is somewhat slippery.' Laughing, Turhan-Cooper replied, 'Your assessment is reasonably accurate. With significant financial problems, brought about when he inherited College House, and the inheritance tax he had to pay, he has become very greasy.' Laughing, and feeling somewhat relieved by Turhan-Coopers response, Vialls, looking around to see if anyone in the bar was close by, said, 'Would you like to see a couple of samples?' Delving into a jacket pocket Turhan-Cooper produced a small magnifying glass and said, 'It may surprise you both but I have some knowledge concerning serie diamonds. In response Clavelshay said, 'What on earth are serie diamonds?' While Vialls was rummaging in the bergan, Turhan-Copper replied," There are two types, the serie and the bort. In simple terms the serie is the jewel diamond and the bort is the industrial. Or the serie is like clear glass and the bort is like opaque stone.' Having extracted five diamonds out of the pot in the bergan, Vialls placed them on the table, producing an audible gasp from Turhan-Cooper. Picking one up and examining it through the magnifying glass, Turhan-Cooper exclaimed, 'Bloody amazing and of the highest quality,' and after examining all five, he exclaimed, 'Bloody fantastic ,and if the others are like that, we are in possession of millions of pounds.'

In fact when in Sierra Leone, George Turhan-Cooper had visited the separator house on several occasions, where the various processes in the recovery of diamonds, were explained to him. He was fascinated by the separator house and intrigued by the bull mills, the gravel passed through before dropping onto the hot grease - covered, rolling vanners to which the diamonds stuck. Later he had met and spoken with several mining engineers and geologists, who explained the colour of diamonds, which range through perfectly white, extremely white and very white, white, almost white and faint yellow, plus further colour variants. Then there were the flaws, both internal and external, and the inclusion within the diamond. What George Turhan-Cooper had so far seen were, as far as he was concerned, flawless and perfectly white. He was also aware the marketing or selling of rough uncut diamonds was a mine field that had to be negotiated extremely carefully.

Clavelshay said, 'What's the next move?'

'I would like to take the five I have seen to test the market. I suggest Vialls takes care of the remainder until the situation is sussed. Incidentally, how many of them are there?'

'Fifty one,' replied Vialls, adding, 'There is also a pot of gold.'

'Bloody hell! I thought the five were probably the majority.'

'From my observations all 51 are similar,' remarked Vialls.

Looking at Vialls, Turhan-Cooper said, 'As far as I'm concerned you can keep the gold and do as you wish with it. Let me pocket these five and you can take the rest home with you, I will establish contact through Stanley and keep you informed of developments. Further more, are we going to eat or end this meeting here and now?'

'I'm all for eating as soon as possible,' replied Clavelshay.

Getting up from the table Vialls picked up the bergan and placed it over his right shoulder, saying, 'That's ok by me and I'm off to the toilets.' Looking at Vialls and the bergan, Clavelshay said, 'You don't trust anyone to look after it then, John?' In response Vialls said, as he moved away, 'I'm responsible for its security and it will be done my way.'

After enjoying an exceedingly good lunch, and having settled the bill, the three men moved out to the car park, where they stood talking for a couple of minutes before shaking hands, and after entering their cars they drove away. Out of curiosity Turhan-Cooper went down through the village and up past the church just to see what was in the area. Turning around he drove back to the Brace and then headed down the Piddle Valley. What he noticed on the hills, covered by a few bushes, was that the trees appeared to gain in height as the valley decreased in size. All in all in his opinion, one of the most beautiful areas of England he had ever driven through.

Vialls, on the other hand, drove straight home, the security of the diamonds occupying his thoughts for most of the journey. On arrival at the farm he parked his car in its normal place, and, taking the bergan containing the two pots, he entered the house. In the kitchen he placed the bergan on the table and removed the pot containing the gold. Picking up the bergan, Vialls took it upstairs and pushed it under the bed. Returning to the kitchen, he brought the kitchen scales to the table and began the process of weighing the gold, pouring the gold dust and the small nuggets into the pan until there was a kilo. Having weighed the kilo, he placed the gold into a large cooking pot and carried on the same process for just over four kilos. Placing the gold back into the clay pot Vialls than grabbed a calculator and worked out that he had, in his possession, 144.53 ounces of pure gold. But knowing precious metals were traditionally sold and purchased in troy ounces. he decided to check on his computer and discovered a troy ounce is approximately 10% heavier that the standard ounce He learned that 1 troy ounce = 0.0311 kilograms, or, put another way, 32.1507 troy ounces equal one kilogram, whereas 35.5 ordinary ounces = 1 kilogram. Therefore, on that basis, Vialls prepared himself for some hard nosed negotiations when he eventually found out to whom he would be selling the gold. Anyway, it appeared he was sitting on something like £100,000 pounds worth of gold.

While Vialls was estimating his potential monetary gains, George Turhan -Cooper was continuing his drive to London. While driving, Turhan-Cooper was thinking about whom he should contact, with reference to selling the diamonds. He was fully aware of the Diamond Corporation and of Harry Winston, from his days in Sierra Leone. But other names like De Beers and Cartier kept entering his mind and he knew they were mostly retailers of jewellery. So he decided to approach a couple of people, who he knew operated in Hatton Garden, and who travelled regularly to Amsterdam. The area around Hatton Garden has been associated with London's jewellery trade since medieval times. The ancient history of London states specific streets and areas were dedicated to various types of business. Over generations, craftsmen working in Hatton Garden have achieved an international reputation for superb jewellery and it's where London's diamond trade is located.

Early the following morning Turhan-Cooper telephoned Ep Vanderven, who he knew was involved in the diamond industry. After a rather incredulous conversation with a disbelieving Vanderven, Turhan-Cooper agreed to meet for lunch at the Bleeding Heart and booked a table. In possession of the five sample diamonds he set off for the lunch rendezvous, parking his car not far from the Bleeding Heart restaurant in Grenville Street. On arrival Turhan-Cooper noticed Vanderven at a table and on approach he nonchalantly produced a diamond and slipped it across the table, saying, 'Nice to see you again Ep.'

The atmosphere within the historic and sophisticated, wood-panelled restaurant, adorned with pictures, was shattered, when Ep Vanderven, almost screaming with excitement, exclaimed, as Turhan-Cooper was sitting down, 'Where the bloody hell did you get that from?'

Removing another diamond from his jacket pocket and placing it on the table, Turhan-Cooper said, 'You had difficulty believing me on the telephone and now you are boiling with excitement.' Having stirred the atmosphere in restaurant to such a degree it caused other diners to focus on their table, Vanderven whispered, while picking up one of the diamonds, 'These are worth millions. They are the very best diamonds I have ever seen. Where did you get them from?'

'It's a long complex story: they originated in Sierra Leone. When you hear the next piece of information, please endeavour to remain calm and collected. We don't want curious staff and others coming to this table to investigate the source of the commotion do we?'

'George, I promise to remain calm.'

Pointing at the diamonds Vanderven was holding, Turhan-Cooper said, 'I'm glad, as there are fifty one diamonds in total. A significant number are bigger and brighter, than those.' With his Dutch accent becoming more pronounced, due to his extreme excitement, Vanderven replied, 'Bigger and brighter, they must be worth millions upon millions.' In reply Turhan-Cooper said, 'Give those back to me.' Accepting the diamonds and placing them in his jacket pocket, he continued, 'If you're interested, you can examine the remainder. It will take a couple of days to arrange, and I stress they are not located in London.'

'Yes, I'm more than interested and would like Tom Rosecrans and Hodding Kooyman to accompany me. They are experts and have entry to the wholesale diamond market.'

'That's perfectly acceptable and I suggest we order lunch. After we depart, I will make the arrangements and let you know where to travel. Incidentally, it's about a hundred and forty miles west of here.' Vanderven replied, 'Fine, the names just mentioned will be approached and warned of the journey and I will provide an outline to stimulate their interest.'

After enjoying a superb lunch, in one of the best restaurants in London, the two men went their separate ways. When he arrived home, Turnham-Cooper immediately contacted Stanley Clavelshay. Saying, 'I have just returned from a meeting with a diamond specialist. Could you arrange for Vialls to bring the diamonds to the Brace?' Clavelshay replied, 'When do you want him there?' 'Mid day, in forty eight hours,' was the response, followed by, 'You had better come too.' After they ended the conversation with a 'Goodbye,' and, 'See you at the Brace,' Turhan-Cooper then contacted Vanderven and explained the location of the Brace of Pheasants in Dorset, the time, and the best route from London.

Having been briefed by Clavelshay, Vialls set about taking precautions and went out and bought a selection of newspapers. With the headlines and dates clearly visible, he placed groups of diamonds on different papers and took a series of photographs. After recording that the diamonds had been in his possession on a given date, he loaded the photos into his computer. Then placing a black plastic bin bag in the sand school, he positioned the gems on it, the glittering diamonds clearly emphasised, and with the farm house in the background, Vialls took more photos. He took a photo of the diamonds, again on a black bin bag, in front of his Landrover, clearly displaying the registration number. Satisfied with what he termed a security phase, Vialls returned the diamonds to the house and, after secreting them and the bergan, he proceeded with his normal farming routine.

On the morning of the meeting Vialls made sure his digital camera was charged as he intended photographing those he did not know. Arriving in the field car park of the Brace before the others, Vialls prepared his camera and waited. Only a couple of minutes elapsed before a Dutch registered Bentley eased into the field, and when the three men got out, Vialls obtained photos of the men and the Bentley. As Vialls was preparing to leave the Landrover, with the bergan Clavelshay and Turhan-Cooper arrived. As they got out of their vehicles, Vialls wandered over and said, 'The Dutch contingent has arrived and has already entered.' Clavelshay responded, 'I see you have your pet bergan over your shoulder.'

Climbing the steps they entered the bar, and Turhan-Cooper, on recognising Vanderven, greeted him with a handshake and all were introduced to both Hodding Kooyman and Tom Rosecrans. Ordering a variety of drinks at the bar, the group settled at a table, and, while waiting and talking, Turhan-Cooper eased two diamonds in his possession onto the table. The reactions of Kooyman and Rosecrans on picking up the diamonds were electrifying, which caused Vanderven to say, 'You have seen nothing yet.' With the drinks about to be delivered, calm was restored and Turhan-Cooper pocketed the diamonds as the drinks were placed on the table. While drinks were being consumed Turhan-Cooper said, 'May I suggest that, after drinks, we leave the bar and inspect the diamonds elsewhere?' Vanderven replied, 'The Bentley is large enough to accommodate all six of us and I suggest we utilize it.' Vialls responded, saying, "I will sit in the drivers seat, and the reasoning is, it will prevent anyone suddenly driving away.' 'Kooyman in a heavy accent said, 'You don't trust us.' 'You are correct,' replied Vialls.

On leaving the bar, the six men walked the short distance to the field car park. With the sunshine accompanied by the sound of pigeons cooing, it was an idyllic scene as they looked over the village. Unlocking the Bentley, Kooyman, with a sweep of his right hand, invited Vialls to occupy the driver's seat. Placing the bergan on the seat, Vialls removed the clay pot and handed it to Turhan-Cooper, who was sitting between Kooyman and Rosecrans with Vanderven on a fold down seat in the rear. Clavelshay, occupying the front passenger seat next to Vialls, watched him checking a digital camera, and turning to face the men in the rear, Vialls said, 'For security reasons, I require photos of you, while you inspect the diamonds.' Looking towards Vialls, Rosecrans replied, 'Feel free as I would do exactly the same.'

In the rear of the Bentley, as the diamonds were being inspected with magnifying glasses, the excitement was growing. Passed from man to man, they were assessed, and so far the diamonds were in the colour range perfectly white, extremely white and very white, which is the highest category. When it came to internal inclusions they were flawless, and with no internal or external flaws, making them very rare and very expensive. Using a minute set of scales, Rosecrans was weighing the diamonds and his findings were startling. So far, not a single diamond had been below 100 carats, and even though they were not as yet cut, they were extremely valuable.

Speaking to Turhan-Cooper, Rosecrans said, 'The four C's are important and these are Cut, Colour, Clarity and Carat weight. All those elements have a direct effect on the price of a diamond, and from what I have seen, these diamonds, although not as yet cut, are extremely rare and virtually priceless.'

One aspect worrying Vialls, who was listening intently, related to rough uncut diamonds before cutting, and he said, 'When sent for cutting, these stones could be swapped for lesser quality diamonds by the cutters.' Vanderven replied, 'You have a valid point, and it does happen.' In response Vialls said, 'So how do we protect these diamonds?' Vanderven replied, 'My suggestion would be submitting them one at a time, without anyone knowing how many require cutting. They could be distributed to several cutting businesses, one at a time.' Vialls replied, 'What would be the percentage of weight loss when the stones are cut?' Looking up from examining a diamond, Kooyman answered, 'Its dependent on size and shape, and a well shaped rough diamond, sawn to a good shape, will lose up to approximately 48% of its weight. There are dramatic variations and some lose up to around 70%. However the loss with these diamonds will in all probability be significantly less.'

More than satisfied with what they had examined, the Dutch contingent, after counting all fifty one diamonds back into the clay pot, handed it back to Vialls. Then Vanderveen said, 'What exactly do you want to do?' Turhan-Cooper replied, 'We want to sell them for as much money as possible.' Rosecrans replied, 'If you are prepared to hand them over, I would deal with all aspects concerned to raise as much money as possible and the amount should be in tens of millions of pounds.' Having placed the clay pot back in the bergan, Vialls said to Clavelshay and Turhan Cooper, 'Gentlemen, could we have a discussion outside and away from the vehicle.'

Getting out of the vehicle, the three men walked passed the Brace and down past the signpost and thatched cottages, while discussing what to do. The main train of thought, put forward by Vialls, concerned the security of the diamonds as the estimated value would be temptation for cutters to make substitutions of lesser quality diamonds, when out with their control. On the way back to the Bentley Turhan-Cooper said, 'I'm prepared to go with Vanderven and his group. We should photograph each individual Dutchman, and as a group, and the diamonds should be signed for. Turhan-Cooper and Clavelshay sat in Clavelshay's vehicle preparing a document for signature and then returned to the Bentley, while Vialls made directly for the bar of the Brace, where he ordered a bottle of Champagne for a minor celebration. When the others re-entered the bar Vialls opened the bottle of Champagne and poured each man a glass. Turhan-Cooper proposed a single word toast of, 'Success', and every one repeated the word 'Success,' then consumed their glass of Champagne. Having done that, they left the bar, and in the car park, Vialls very nervously pulled the clay pot out of the bergan and handed it over. Then he said, 'Ok, let's have some photos of all you guys for the record.' and everyone obliged, without even the slightest hint of an objection. Having signed the document, which was nothing more than a sheet of paper, the satisfied Dutch trio got into the Bentley and drove away; leaving the others to contemplate what had occurred. While Clavelshay and Turhan-Cooper were discussing various aspects of the proceedings, Vialls returned to the bar, expecting to see the champagne glasses still on the table. Picking up the glasses used by the Dutch, with his handkerchief, Vialls gave the barman ten pounds for the glasses which he accepted. He left the bar and now back at the car park, he said, 'Not only do we have photos but we also have fingerprints and probable lip prints.'

Standing around admiring the village and the area, after discussing aspects of the business they had done, they then got into their respective vehicles and left the area. While driving home in his Landrover Vialls began to think about dealing with the gold.

THIRTEEN

While Andrew Shuster was contemplating his financial situation and the three Dutchmen were preparing to travel to Antwerp, Vialls was endeavouring to discover a profitable way of disposing of the gold. Several thousand miles away, an old adversary of the UK security services was beginning to stir. Over twenty years had elapsed since Colonel Yakut, a Russian Inuit or Eskimo, had in 1990 led a group of Okhotriki, Russian ex - Spetnaz, Special Forces, to kill men in central London. The London killings were in revenge for the brutal execution of twenty of Yakut's men in the early eighties, while serving in Afghanistan. After completing their mission in London, Yakut and some of the men involved, escaped to Southampton and negotiated passage on a ship after paying a significant amount of money.

When the ship left, Yakut and the men had no idea where they were going, except that they would eventually land in Canada. In fact, they spent almost a year at sea, working as deck hands, and due to wholesome food and hard work, Yakut and the men became extremely fit. The captain of the ship was more than accommodating, having been handsomely rewarded by Yakut for arranging papers for the men. The captain's authority reigned supreme over all ranks, inclusive of the ships' officers, and he frequently reprimanded officers. To emphasis a point, he would shout and point menacingly at all and sundry.

A few days after leaving Southampton, the ship was lying off the Egyptian coast, having been unaccountably delayed. The stationary ship was airless and, in the intense heat, it became uncomfortable. The clouds of flies and other insects, which invaded the ship, did not help.

Looking over the side, Abdul Azim said to Yakut, 'It was not like this when we sailed this way on leaving Aqaba a few months ago.'

'You are correct, mind you it was winter then' replied Yakut watching the ship being besieged by 'bum boats' filled to the gunwales, with everything imaginable, while the ships crew was being enticed to make purchases. The natives also appeared to be trying to sell their sisters.

After a delay of three days, and without any explanation, the ship sailed away to cheers from the crew, and entered the Suez Canal. Negotiating the Suez Canal, the ship made its way down the Red Sea towards Aden, a Port City on the Arabian peninsular. Those on board who found Egypt hot, discovered, to their horror, Aden was an open blast furnace by comparison, and, to emerge from the shade provided by awnings, was not recommended. For those looking towards the shore, the Port area and nearby mountains, seemingly danced in the shimmering heat haze and the flies were found in greater greasy profusion than in Egypt. To many of the crew, inclusive of Yakut and his men, Aden seemed like hell on earth.

On leaving Aden, the ship sailed cross the Indian Ocean, which, to the Russians, was an experience verging on paradise. Although still hot and sticky, early each morning and in the evenings, Yakut's men stood on deck to witness sunrise, and after sunset, they wondered at the clarity of the stars at night.

When the ship eventually arrived in Bombay, the men were well and truly acclimatised and ready to experience anything that India could throw at them. While looking over the side of the docked ship, Sergeant Timurbek said to Mohammad Yousef, 'It appears the ship is about to be invaded by wave after wave of turbaned and bare headed, brown- skinned natives, wearing loin cloths.'

'That's fine by me,' replied Mohammad Yousef, laughing at the sight.

During the almost two months the ship was in Bombay the captain, for financial consideration, arranged for people both male and female to come on board, who offered Canadian passports for a price. After taking photographs, asking innumerable questions and taking samples of their signatures, the mixed group left.

Returning three weeks later, a man, referred to as Mr Warrington ,said to Yakut, 'The passports are genuine and in the holder's real names. Yours and their Asian features look similar to the native Canadian Indians and Inuit's so there should not be a problem.' Accepting the five passports from Mr Warrington, Yakut smiling broadly, ceremoniously handed each of the men their passport, and while shaking each by the hand, said, 'Congratulations.'

On leaving Bombay, the ship headed for Singapore and then sailed for Canton in China, where, during the seven weeks alongside, further documentation for Yakut and his men was arranged for a price. Leaving Canton the ship sailed for Durban in South Africa. During this extended period at sea, Yakut concentrated on teaching English to the men and making sure the documentation received a worn patina and did not appear brand new. After crossing the Atlantic Ocean, Yakut and his men eventually arrived at the

Port of Montreal in Canada and what fascinated Yakut was the location of the port on the majestic St. Lawrence River, which is far from the Atlantic Ocean.

When the five nervous men, possessing supposed -genuine documents and passports, decided to go ashore, scattered amongst other seamen, they drifted into Canada without so much as a hiccup. Over the years the men conclusively proved their documentation was genuine and when the passports eventually expired they were renewed without question. The only problem they experienced was when, in the Montreal area, they had difficulty with the French language and as a result they evaporated into other areas of Canada.

One of the major aspects of life in Canada, that was somewhat similar to the existence of the men, when young, on the Steppes of Russia, was the weather. The Canadian climate was not as cold, and in winter, although the temperatures fell below freezing throughout most of the country, on the south-western coast it maintained a relatively mild climate. However, the men found the rain irksome, but nevertheless, on the whole, they enjoyed the cold winters, semi-,hot summers and found the weather was a preoccupation of most Canadians. As time passed what aided the ex Russian soldiers was the diversity of the Canadian population, and in particular, Yakut felt comfortable in an environment where immigrants from across the world struggled. Yakut also discovered significant numbers of Canada's original native Indian population inhabited urban areas. In Toronto, approximately forty five percent of the population of the city was born outside Canada, originating from such diverse regions as Asia, the Caribbean, Central and South America and Africa.

A key factor that played into Yakut's hands was the struggle new immigrants experienced and the undervaluing of their foreign skills. Money was a problem for many as they occupied low paying jobs and he recognized an opportunity to make money. Having discussed it with the men, Yakut set up as an unlicensed money lender, having pooled for investment, fifty percent of each man's money which they had lifted from drug dealers when in London.

After only three years of money-lending, during which time nobody reneged on their loans, the investments were making huge profits. In reality the investments returned an average of sixty five percent, more than sufficient to pay an annual dividend to each of the men. Within five years the men jointly owned several properties and Yakut was successfully managing their investment portfolio through a company they set up called, 'Steppes Investments', and it proved to be very profitable.

Abdul Azim, the former Spetnaz Warrant Officer, lived and worked in Hearst, Ontario, as caretaker of an apartments block owned by 'Steppes Investment.' He was accompanied, as they drove to Toronto, by Dara Manuchehar who worked with him. Travelling from Calgary by plane was Mohammad Yousef and he was now the owner of a small trucking company. Sergeant Timurbek, who was travelling from Newfoundland, had taken to the sea, when sailing to Canada and had been associated with the fishing industry for several years.

The four men from various parts of the country were in the process of travelling to the house of Yakut in the Kensington Market area of Toronto. Yakut was now sixty three years of age and principle amongst his many interests were the activities of the Western forces operating in Afghanistan. His interest was stimulated by the fact, which he kept very much to himself, that he was in fact an ex Colonel in the Russian Special Forces (Spetnaz) and a veteran of the Russian intervention in Afghanistan in the

1980's. As a result, Yakut followed everything concerning the involvement of Western forces in Afghanistan, and the problems associated with it, mentioned on the radio or shown on television or expanded upon in the press. One thing that really registered was the way Western politicians dithered over matters concerning the numbers of troops, broken-down vehicles, the lack of helicopters and the proposed surge in American troop numbers.

What really registered with Yakut was the occasion when he read that the Head of N.A.T.O. had said he would like to see the Russians getting involved as equipment trainers for the Afghan Forces. This was proposed to broaden Russian cooperation, as they had already offered transit facilities. Yakut was far from happy knowing Russia had lost some 15000, killed, while the Afghans lost around one million during their war in Afghanistan. Yakut also thought the way Western Governments announced an exit plan was sheer stupidity. In his opinion, all the Taliban needed to do, was shoot, run, hide and lie low until the planned withdrawal then reappear and the country would be theirs again. In his opinion, brought about by his experience, the chances of an all out victory, being achieved by the Western NATO forces, was almost impossible.

Yakut collected Mohammad Yousef from the airport and brought him to his residence. On entering the lounge, Mohammad Yousef saw, for the first time in three years, and spoke with Abdel Azim, Dara Manuchehar and Sergeant Timurbek. After being shown their accommodation and having eaten and consumed various liquids accompanied by chatter and hilarious laughter, the men were relaxed. Informing the group how their money and property investments were performing, which Yakut covered in detail, he received a vote of confidence.

Looking across the table at the men facing him Yakut then dropped a veritable bomb into the proceedings when he said, 'We have received information regarding the location of ex- Master Sergeant Savchenko, the one unaccounted for in London. The information was supplied by someone who you all knew as a Major, however he retired as a Colonel, and that was Igor Sidorov. The detail has been confirmed by Captain Milailov.'

With their mouths wide open and with their minds spinning, Abdul Azim was the first to react when he said, 'We last heard of Savchenko in the eighties, when the men were executed, and, personally speaking, I would like to rip his head off. He must be in his mid sixties now! So where is the reptile?'

'Originating from Romania, on leaving the Army he returned to his homeland. Romania is now part of the European Union and the latest information states he has been located running a bar in Spain,' replied Yakut. Adding, 'we are all now genuine citizens of Canada and as such we can travel almost anywhere. Mind you there are a couple of countries we should all steer clear of,' he said while laughing.

'Abdul Azim replied, saying. 'Personally speaking, since living in Canada, I have travelled to the United States and to Mexico without the slightest problem. My proposal, as we are still working and we don't know the absolute details – is that you, Colonel, go and take a look around, then we can plan. So what do you think comrades?' Talking amongst themselves for a few seconds, the agreement for Yakut to carry out the proposed reconnaissance mission to Spain, was unanimous. Having received a positive response from the men, who, a couple of day later returned to their homes and places of employment, Yakut arranged a flight from Toronto to Madrid.

Arriving in Madrid at Barajas airport after a flight from Toronto, via London Heathrow, Yakut satisfied immigration and collected his baggage. Making his way to the exit, it was Yakut's intention to get a taxi to the High Tech Hotel. As the name indicates it's a modern hotel conveniently situated about five minutes from the Airport. On arrival Yakut paid the taxi driver, and entering the Hotel he made his way to reception, where, after booking in, he enquired about the car he had arranged from Canada, to drive from Madrid to the town of Alicante. While Yakut was unpacking, the telephone in his room rang and a very English voice said, 'Excuse me, sir, could you come to reception to deal with the documentation and other requirements associated with hiring a car in Spain?'

At the reception desk Yakut met a young Englishman, who, immediately after shaking hands, started asking questions, such as, 'Are you aware foreign visitors require a valid driving licence, and being from outside the EU an International Driving Licence is acceptable?' Yakut produced his International Licence which was accepted. Then the Englishman said, 'Are you aware of the requirements concerning third-party insurance and that the documents should be carried at all times?'

Having satisfied all the requirements, Yakut was escorted outside to the car park where the Englishman handed him the keys to a rather swish Mercedes Benz. After checking the fuel and inspecting the car for scratches and any damage, Yakut locked it, and after shaking hands with the Englishman, returned to his room. Ensconced there, he set about planning the journey to Alicante, aided by maps. Satisfied he would be able to find his way to the motorway, Yakut settled in for the remainder of the day, and after a good nights sleep and a hearty breakfast, Yakut was ready to make his way to the motorways that radiate outward from Madrid.

Having reached the NIII that weaves its way to Valencia, Yakut discovered the use of Spanish motorways involved paying a toll, calculated against the type of vehicle and the distance to be travelled. With the air conditioning on, as the journey progressed through the mostly spectacular scenery shimmering in the heat haze, traffic jams occurred. The time spent going slow or at a standstill on the N111 added significantly to the journey time and Yakut thought he might try to return to Madrid by another route. The only consolation was he was at least driving on the same side as he did in Canada, and the speed limited was 120KPH.

On reaching Valencia, not really understanding the Spanish language road signs, indicating towns and villages and places of interest, Yakut found his way onto the A7 road to Alicante. On this leg of the journey, Yakut enjoyed the views of the Mediterranean Sea and, on reaching Alicante, Yakut starting looking for a suitable hotel and settled on the 'La City of Alicante,' situated in front of the railway station. After booking in and parking the Mercedes, Yakut decided to familiarise himself with the city, and during the process, discovered Alicante to be full of attractions. While strolling along streets lined with palm trees, and hoping to locate a bar called 'Creative,' he noted shops that sold just about everything imaginable, with everything enhanced by sunshine. Returning to the hotel and having eaten a meal, he decided to get a good night sleep before continuing the search for Savchenko, and the 'Creative' bar he was supposed to own.

Refreshed and with a good breakfast inside him, Yakut began touring the area in the Mercedes, and while looking for the 'Creative' bar, in the centre of the city, he saw the huge Castle of Santa Barbara and then St Ferdinand Castle on Tossal hill. Later, deciding the bar could be nearer the beach, he found the San Juan Beach about fives miles from the city centre. Searching the area, he decided to park the car and walk along the beach. The beach was crowded with people of all ages, sunbathing, swimming and playing games and while walking, Yakut was sweating profusely. Added to which he heard a great deal of English, some German and what he took to be Spanish being spoken. There was also a plethora of good quality shops, bars, cafes and restaurants near the beach, but no 'Creative Bar.'

Engrossed in his search, he stopped to buy an ice cream, and while enjoying the flavour, Yakut decided to find a place to cool off and eat lunch. Entering a restaurant and settling at a table, he heard a waiter speaking English to a customer. When the waiter, who appeared capable of speaking several languages, came to his table, Yakut said to him, 'Do you know where the 'Creative Bar' is?' Without hesitating the waiter replied, 'There are two bars, sir, bearing the name. One is near the Mount Tossal Theme Park and the other is not far from here within the Marina area.'

'Thank you,' replied Yakut. After cooling off and eating an enjoyable lunch, he returned to the Mercedes and drove to the Marina, where he parked and locked the car. Wandering around the area, he discovered it was not solely devoted to boats and sailing, as the area also contained excellent shops, restaurants and food outlets. On turning a corner, there, in front of him, was a bar bearing the 'Creative,' name and it was obviously a very busy establishment, by the numbers of people coming and going.

With perspiration running down his face, Yakut sought refuge from the sun, in the shadows provided by a doorway. While in the shadows thinking, Yakut decided he would not be recognised, as to the best of his knowledge, he had never met Master Sergeant Savchenko. Deciding to visit the bar, Yakut left the shade of the doorway and, after crossing the sun- saturated road ,he entered the crowded bar. Once inside he was greatly relieved to find it was air conditioned and it appeared mostly English was being spoken. Squeezing through the people surrounding the bar, Yakut managed to catch a barman's eye and ordered a Carlsberg larger. Gratefully taking a drink, he suddenly heard Russian being spoken, and, focusing on the language, he saw an elderly man behind the bar on the telephone, who was saying. 'He has sold the properties and is leaving the area, so the party is a means of saying "Thank you and success with your next venture.' Then, due to the loud music being played, he could not hear anymore, but Yakut managed to maintain visual contact. When the music suddenly decreased, he heard the man saying in Russian, 'Why don't you meet me at the ferry for Tabarca in an hour from now?'

When the man left the bar, Yakut followed on foot to the terminal and found out Tabarca was an island located approximately eleven miles off the coast. While reading about the island on a poster, Yakut noticed the second man arrive, who began talking in Russian. Moving closer, Yakut could hear their conversation, which involved the party that both men would be attending, and then he heard the first man say, 'Igor Savchenko, who has a drink problem, will hopefully meet us when the ferry arrives.'

Uncertain about what to do, having parked the Mercedes, on hearing the name Savchenko, Yakut decided to follow. The trip on the ferry was uneventful and lasted just on an hour, during which time Yakut kept an eye and ear on the two men. When the ferry docked and the passengers began leaving, Yakut moved closer and followed the men ashore where he watched them meet and shake hands with a man he assumed was Savchenko. Following the group as they walked from the docks, Yakut expected them to drive off in a car; instead, after a short walk, the men entered a property. Looking around, Yakut decided that, having identified the property, he would return to the mainland and thereafter keep watch on the ferry terminal.

After an uneventful return ferry trip, Yakut collected the car and returned to his hotel. In the morning, having parked near the terminal, he checked out the arrival times of the ferries from Tabarca. Convinced nobody, who had attended a farewell party, would arrive early, Yakut left the car in the parking place and became a relaxed tourist and enjoyed himself. Making his way back to the terminal for the second arrival, he was slightly disappointed not to see anyone he was interested in. On the next visit, Yakut saw a dark green Maserati Gran Turismo being parked, and then he watched the driver push the ignition keys into the left hand exhaust pipe. A couple of minutes later a car arrived, into which the Maserati driver got, before being driven away. Not long afterwards a ferry arrived and amongst the passengers leaving the terminal, Yakut identified Savchenko and the first man he'd followed from the bar. Savchenko and the man passed within a few feet and made for the car park. To Yakut's utter amazement, Savchenko made for the Maserati. On reaching the Maserati, Savchenko wobbled slightly and had to steady himself as he bent down to retrieve the keys from the exhaust. Unlocking the Maserati he got into the car and within seconds had the engine running. Opening the driver's door, Savchenko then got out and, after shaking hands with the other man, he watched him walk away. Watching from inside the Mercedes, Yakut saw Savchenko slip behind the wheel of the Maserati and then, almost immediately, he drove away, followed by Yakut at a discreet distance. Unaware of where they might be going, Yakut was thankful he'd had the foresight to refuel the Mercedes when arriving from Madrid.

For the first thirty minutes or thereabouts Savchenko drove at a reasonable speed, primarily due to traffic density in the Alicante urban environment. On reaching the A7, the road that leads to Valencia, the traffic was less dense and the Maserati speeded up. In the Mercedes, Yakut had no difficulty keeping the Maserati under observation and on two occasions it appeared Savchenko tried to overtake vehicles, only to be foiled by others pulling out. A little later, as the traffic was slowing down and beginning to back-up, Yakut saw Savchenko swigging something from a bottle, which he assumed was probably alcohol. As the traffic began to clear, it was obvious, when they passed an accident involving a couple of cars, what had caused the back–up, and with the road somewhat clearer, the Maserati accelerated away.

A little later, from the Mercedes, Yakut could see the Maserati approaching a bridge over the road, with a lorry a few vehicles ahead of it. Then in an instantaneous flash of reflected light, Yakut saw something silver and shinning, blown off the back of the lorry, which hit the Maserati. From fifty yards away, Yakut heard the screaming of tyres and saw a cloud of bluish smoke, as the Maserati skidded and spun around, followed by a series of distinctive thumps, as it hit other cars. In seemingly slow motion, the Maserati then rolled over in a shower of sparks accompanied by the sounds of crunching steel. Flipping back onto its wheels, it stopped. Pulling up behind the wreck, which had finished up at the edge of the road, accompanied by other damaged vehicles, Yakut got out of the Mercedes and with several other people he walked over to the wreck.

Looking at the crushed wrecked car and with more people approaching, speaking Spanish, Yakut saw that the shining object he'd seen was, in fact, a thick sheet of corrugated iron. Obviously, by the way it was wedged inside the car, the sheet had shattered the Maserati windscreen and, in the process, virtually sliced Savchenko's head off, spreading his blood everywhere over the crushed interior. To Yakut, and one of the other people present, who appeared to be a doctor, who was checking Savchenko's pulse, he was undoubtedly dead, and the assumed doctor indicated this, saying in English while pointing at Savchenko.

'The man is dead.'

Unable to speak Spanish and with the sound of the authorities` sirens in the air, indicating their imminent arrival, Yakut, who knew Savchenko was dead, decided to leave the scene. Making his way back to the hotel, he picked up his possessions and, settling the account, he decided to return to Madrid, to hand back the Mercedes. Upon returning to Canada, he would report the success of the mission and the demise of Savchenko in a car accident.

FOURTEEN

While Yakut had been involved with Savchenko in Spain, the Dutchmen were getting organised and the process of cutting the diamonds had began. Five diamonds were being dealt with in Antwerp, while another five were being worked on in Amsterdam and at this juncture it was very much an assessment of the skills available and the quality of the jewel diamonds produced.

Diamond cutting requires specialized knowledge, tools, equipment, and techniques, due to their hardness. Several methods are adopted by experts to cut and shape diamonds to a manageable size, for instance a diamond can be cleaved at its weakest point – which is known as the tetrahedral plane. With a diamond held securely, a cutter can carve a groove along the plane and with a fine steel edge in the groove, it is struck hard and the shock splits the diamond.

When cleaving is impossible, a phosphor - bronze saw, rotating at some 15,000 rpm can be used, and the operator must decide which part of the diamond becomes the flat top or area of greatest surface. Lasers are sometimes used, however this method can take hours to achieve the desired result. Bruiting is another method which involves cutting a diamond by hand to obtain its shape. When cut by hand, the expert relies on the hardness of diamonds, which means crushed abrasive diamonds are used to cut and polish other cut diamonds. To create the sparkle, a diamond is placed into a holder and then it's held against a rapidly rotating abrasive diamond dust polishing wheel.

The price of diamonds is related to their shape, size, colour and clarity and the quality of the cut. Prices vary greatly based on those factors. The results achieved so far with what, in the profession were being regarded as some of the biggest and finest diamonds ever worked on were breath taking.

Ep Vanderven, accompanied by Tom Rosecrans, had been following the cutting process, and when the first diamonds were ready they surreptitiously approached two well known traders with the intention of obtaining a rough guide to the valuation of the first finished diamonds, and to test their recommendation for further cutting establishments.

The first of the two traders to arrive in the office in Amsterdam was a balding, rather rotund, middle aged Englishman called David Benton, a partner in a London auction company. After shaking hands with Vanderven, Benton was invited to lift the green baize cover off the office desk and when he did, he began to shake and almost collapsed on seeing the size of the five diamonds. Vanderven invited Benton to examine the stones, pointing at them and saying, 'Please take your time and be as thorough as you feel necessary to cover every conceivable aspect you can think of.'

After spending several minutes thoroughly examining each of the five diamonds, aided by a magnifying glass, a perspiring and nervous David Benton turned to face Vanderveen and said excitedly, 'Those diamonds are, beyond any shadow of doubt, the biggest, best quality, extra clear gems I have ever seen or inspected, and each weighs over sixty carats.'

'What about an approximate value?' asked Vanderven.

'Even in the present world recession that has resulted in a significant drop in demand, those diamonds will surpass the price paid in Hong Kong for a pink diamond, which was a cushion cut 5 carat diamond that sold for $10.7 million. That was highest price ever paid for a pink diamond at auction, at $2.1 million per carat. Your gems are perfection and around twelve times bigger.'

No sooner had David Benton finished speaking, than Tom Rosecrans walked into the office accompanied by a tall well built South African trader known as, 'The Ziegler,' and nobody, but nobody, knew his first name or had seen his passport. Renowned in the diamond industry for his exceptional knowledge and connections, 'The Ziegler,' began checking the five diamonds and after examining each through a magnifying glass and reading the recorded weight of each, he said in a broad South African accent, 'Christ man, they are beyond fantastic and around twice the size of the 35.56 carat Wittelsbach blue that fetched $24.3 million in London. Those prices confirm that, even in an unsettled economic environment, top quality diamonds maintain their value and realise fantastic prices. Please believe me when I say that, in every conceivable way, those diamonds are of the very finest cut and of exceptional clarity and quality.'

Vanderven responded by saying, 'What about the various shapes being carved, as can be seen from the different shapes on the table?'

'Tom Rosecrans replied, 'There are several basic shapes, determined by the original shape of the rough diamond and it's down to the cutter's knowledge as to what shape emerges.' While pointing at the diamonds on the table Rosecrans continued, 'On the table, for instance, there are three rounds, an oval and a pear shaped diamond. However there are also other shapes available such as the Cushion, the Marquise, the Heart, and Emerald, to name a few, and of course, there are also modern day variants.'

Having listened to Rosecrans appraisal, 'The Ziegler,' responded, saying, 'The classic shaped diamond is round, however regardless of shape or size they are all cut to sparkle and the reflective brilliance is what catches the eye. However, one should always remember, everything is dependant on the cutter's skill in shaping the stones to produce beautiful jewels.'

Ep Vanderven then said, 'so what value do you put on the five stones?

David Benton and 'The Ziegler' moved to a corner of the rather plush office and in subdued tones discussed the value for a minute or so. Then David Benton said, 'This is a ball park figure, but we estimate the five stones at around twenty five million dollars each, making the five worth around one hundred and twenty five million dollars.'

Ep Vanderven replied, 'Would you gentlemen be interested in preparing the market for their sale?'

'Christ man, personally speaking, I would be more than prepared to jump through flaming hoops for the chance,' replied 'The Zeigler,' grinning broadly.

'Me too,' answered David Benton who was perspiring profusely.

Tom Rosecrans then said, 'Gentlemen may I suggest you sit down and make yourselves very comfortable and would either of you care for coffee or tea or anything else for that matter?'

'Why?' replied 'The Ziegler'

'Because, gentlemen, those are the five smallest diamonds and we are responsible for fifty one in total. In all honesty we would like to utilize your expertise and assistance in getting further stones cut, polished and marketed.'

'Bloody Hell,' answered David Benton, in the process of struggling to his feet and wiping perspiration off his forehead, then he followed up saying, 'This is a rough estimate but based on what you have told us so far and dependant on cut, shape and size, they are probably worth something like five hundred million dollars. What would our commission be?'

Ep Vanderven answered, 'For successfully representing the owners and arranging their sale without causing complexities, you will receive ten percent. So not to create confusion, it works out at five percent each. Or we will give you one of the diamonds for you to share the proceeds of sale between you. Is that acceptable?'

With his brain spinning and perspiring profusely at the sums of money that could be coming his way as commission, David Benton replied, 'That's acceptable to me,' and then he collapsed back into the leather chair.

In contrast, 'The Ziegler,' calmly replied, 'That is perfectly acceptable.'

Vanderven then said, 'So far, ten diamonds have been dealt with in Antwerp and in Amsterdam and that leaves forty one, to be distributed and processed. Can either of you mange to accelerate the process of getting the remaining diamonds cut and polished?'

From his chair, David Benton replied, 'I could get some cut and polished in New York. What time frame are you looking at?

'About three months,' answered Vanderven.

'The Ziegler' said, 'the cutting process could be accelerated in India.'

'You have contacts there?' questioned Vanderven.

'Indeed, and they are bloody good at producing a top quality product.'

'Now, before we hand over further stones for cutting, we will want to take photos of you with these diamonds, we will also require your finger prints and passport details. This is a precaution to protect you, because, believe me, you don't want to upset the owner and his associates.'

Over the next hour several photographs were taken, with each man in possession of the five diamonds. Later, both men provided, without fuss, finger prints and lip prints on a wine glass. On the matter of passports, each had to leave the office and return a couple of hours later, having collected their passports from wherever. When handing over his passport, 'The Ziegler,' was surprisingly cooperative, and said, 'I would greatly appreciate you not divulging any of the information within my passport to third parties.'

'Agreed,' replied Vanderven.

Having made a note of the number and date of issue and taken some photocopies, Vanderven handed David Benton's passport back to him saying, 'Please report here tomorrow at ten in the morning, and at that time we will provide the appropriate amount of rough diamonds for processing in New York, and more photos will be taken.'

'What about paying for the cutting and polishing?'

'Not a problem. The firms that carry out the cutting can keep the off cuts from each stone. Some could weigh a couple of carats or more and provide more than enough finance, when cut and polished for sale,' Replied Vanderven.

'Can we have that proposal in writing and signed?'

'Of course,' replied Vanderven adding, 'You will be provided with all the relevant signed paper work on your return in the morning.'

When dealing with the, 'The Ziegler,' everything was exactly the same with the exception of finding out his real name. Which was, according to his passport, Zachary Jean Betty Ziegler, and Vanderven did not pursue the point. Having arranged for, 'The Ziegler,' to return at 11 in the morning, Vanderven had also noticed, when photocopying each mans passport, that they contained the appropriate visas for both the USA and India.

The following morning Hodding Kooyman arrived at the office with the remaining forty one rough diamonds. After removing them from his briefcase, he, along with Rosecrans and Vanderven, then split the rough stones into two halves, with the biggest stones going to, 'The Ziegler,' for processing in India. When finished Vanderven said, 'We must not forget to take further photos when each man arrives to pick up their share of the diamonds for processing.'

On arrival David Benton posed for a series of photographs with his share of the rough diamonds, and he was more than happy to oblige, as he could see a secure future in doing this properly. Satisfied with the precautions, Vanderven then said to Benton, 'under no circumstances provide more than five diamonds to the cutters at anytime, and take possession of the freshly cut diamonds before handing over the next batch. Please keep us informed at all times concerning the progress, by telephone and in writing. Understand?'

'Yes,' replied Benton.

'You will probably be asked innumerable questions pertaining to ownership and by all means feel free to mention us. Beyond that we are acting on behalf of someone and, believe me, you don't want to know who! However, screw up, and you can kiss your butt and any money goodbye. Understand?'

'Yes,' answered Benton somewhat nervously.

Having carefully wrapped up the diamonds for which he would be responsible, and after placing them in his briefcase with the relevant paperwork, Benton then shook hands with the Dutchmen and left the offices, to catch a flight that would be leaving for New York later that day. About ten minutes after Benton left, 'The Ziegler,' arrived and after an identical procedure, including wrapping the diamonds he was responsible for, he placed them in his briefcase. He also shook hands and departed to catch a flight to India.

With the balance of rough diamonds theoretically taken care of, to be cut and polished in the USA and India, the Dutchmen set about gathering the ten recently processed diamonds together. Having completed that task, Vanderven and Kooyman set off for London, where, on arrival, they contacted George Turhan-Cooper, At their insistence, as they had enjoyed their last visit so much, he arranged to meet them at the "Brace of Pheasants" in Plush, Dorset, at midday the following day. Turhan-Cooper then contacted Clavelshay by telephone, and asked him to arrange for Vialls and himself to meet him at midday the following day at the Brace. When the telephone rang at the farm, John Vialls answered, and was very surprised to hear Stanley Clavelshay say, 'John, be at the Brace just before midday tomorrow, where we will meet Turhan-Cooper who has requested the meeting.'

'Any particular reason for meeting, or is too delicate for the telephone?'

'No idea, Turhan- Cooper wants us there,' replied Clavelshay.

The following morning Vialls decided, after showering, to dress for the occasion. He chose cavalry twills, tweed jacket, checked shirt and a suitable tie, with light brown socks and highly polished brown shoes. On leaving the farm, he drove to Dorchester, where he parked and visited his bank. After leaving the bank, he drove up the delightful Piddle Valley to Plush. Arriving in the field that acted as the car park of the Brace of Pheasants, Vialls was surprised to see both Clavelshay and Turhan–Cooper stood talking in the lane. After parking his Landrover, Vialls wandered over and joined the others, who were pleasantly surprised to see him looking presentable for a change, and as they started to move off, a Rolls Royce eased into the car park. When the doors of the Rolls Royce eased open, the three men immediately recognised Vanderven and Kooyman, and after shaking hands they walked to the concrete steps and entered the Brace. Luckily they were the first to enter and immediately occupied the table recessed in the old fireplace. Clavelshay took the orders for drinks and walked over to the bar to get them. Turhan-Cooper said, 'so gentlemen, why are we here?'

Delving into the briefcase he was carrying, Vanderven produced a package and after placing his briefcase back on the floor, he emptied the ten diamonds it contained onto the table and said, 'These are the reason gentlemen.'

'Bloody hell,' gasped Turhan-Cooper, on seeing the group of diamonds that looked like glass walnuts, and then he said, 'May I pick one up?'

'Sure, after all they are yours,' replied Vanderven

Selecting the biggest gem and admiring the diamond in his hand, Turhan-Cooper said, while holding it up to the light, 'What's it worth?' 'Somewhere around fifteen to twenty million pounds,' replied Vanderven. Carrying a tray of drinks to the table Clavelshay heard a shouted, 'How much?' Arriving at the table, he was putting down the tray of drinks, when several hands grabbed at the shiny objects. Sitting down, Clavelshay indicated their various choices of drink, and while watching them enjoy their drinks, he asked, 'What was that about?'

Showing the diamond he had in his hand to Clavelshay, Turhan-Cooper said, 'How much do you think this could be worth?'

'Not the faintest, two hundred thousand pounds,' replied Clavelshay.

'A rough guide is fifteen million pounds,' responded Turhan-Cooper.

The reaction from Stanley Clavelshay was an overwhelming, stunned silence, and seizing the opportunity, as several more people had by now entered the Brace, Kooyman said, 'I think it would be more sensible to swallow the drinks and then go out to where the cars are parked, what does everyone else think?'

'Speaking for myself, I think that's a bloody good idea,' replied Vialls who then grabbed his glass and drained it while the others did the same.

Gathering up the diamonds from the table and holding his hand out for the one Turhan-Cooper was holding, Vanderven counted them and put them back into the package before returning them to his briefcase. Standing up, Vialls said, 'Let's go,' and then led the others from the bar out to the cars. Outside, where they could speak more freely without drawing attention to themselves, Kooyman produced some paper work, and placing it on the bonnet of the Rolls Royce, he indicated for Turhan-Cooper to sign for the diamonds and, when that was achieved, Vanderven handed them to him.

Now in possession of the diamonds, Turhan-Cooper took one out of the packet and handed it to Vanderven saying, 'Thank you for your help and that should take care of any past or future expenses.'

In response Vanderven said something which sounded like, 'God for Domer.'

Indicating for John Vialls to come close, Turhan-Cooper then handed one stone to him saying, 'That's for finding them and bringing them back. It should ensure your financial security for the remainder of your life.'

Vanderven then said, 'The diamonds in your possession are worth millions of pounds. The worst thing you can do is flood the market, by trying to sell them all at the same time to obtain money. Quite frankly, that would dramatically reduce their value. My suggestion is to ease them onto the market over a period of years and that way you will obtain the best prices.' Taking Turhan-Cooper to one side, Vanderven said to him, 'You have the ten smallest diamonds in your possession. Please remember there are a further forty one and they are bigger. When the remainder are being cut and polished I will personally accept the responsibility of bringing them to you, probably in batches of five or thereabout.'

'What overall value do you place on the fifty one?'

'At ten million pounds each,' replied Vanderven, 'that's over five hundred million and believe me they could be worth considerably more. They could reach, if marketed correctly, something like a seven hundred and fifty million pounds and that is being conservative. However, as previously mentioned, you should not flood the market, as to do so will destroy the price.'

Returning to the group who were chatting, accompanied by the idyllic sounds of the Dorset countryside, Turhan-Cooper said, 'If nobody minds, may I suggest, as we have received the goods and come to an amenable arrangement, that we give up on the pub and move on. Unless of course some of you want to take lunch there'

'No lunch, that's fine by me,' replied Vanderven nodding to Kooyman.

'Suits me and Vialls,' responded Clavelshay.

After some small talk and shaking hands the group returned to their vehicles and, with the exception of Vialls, they proceeded to wherever. Whereas Vialls, went back into the bar and enjoyed a half pint of larger by way of a private celebration and after finishing his drink he drove back to his farm.

FIFTEEN

Having arrived home, Vialls was absolutely positive he needed to authenticate in writing, and have verbally recorded evidence, pertaining to his ownership of the diamond in his possession. He was fully aware of where the diamonds came from and the other people involved, and thought it would be relatively straight forward. On the other hand Turhan-Cooper felt extremely uneasy about the security of the diamonds in his possession, and spent half an hour burying seven diamonds under a lavender bush in his back garden.

Sat in the lounge of his property, having kept one diamond in his back pocket, Turhan-Cooper took the diamond out and spent several minutes studying the gem and estimating its potential value. With a plan forming in his mind, Turhan-Cooper then rang Andrew Shuster and arranged to meet him the following day at College House.

Arriving in the stable yard of College House, Turhan-Cooper parked, and, after locking his car, walked around to the main door and rang the bell. Almost immediately, the huge studded door groaned and creaked open and Andrew Shuster thrust out his right hand, and while shaking hands said, 'Its good to see you in good shape George. Please come in.'

Following Andrew Shuster into the lounge, where portraits of Shuster's ancestors looked down, and before taking a seat, Turhan-Cooper said, 'I understand you are suffering financial constraints.'

'Unpaid Death Duties and the pressures are building,' replied Shuster.

'I'm actually in a position to eliminate them, with your cooperation.'

'What sort of cooperation?' asked a very interested, yet cautious, Shuster.

'Politically, your views on certain matters coincide with the views of many.'

'What are you getting at?' responded Shuster

'We have access to funds to further the cause of changing the political environment, and you always provided a warm welcoming atmosphere whenever we have arrived at your door,' replied Turhan-Cooper

'Being polite tends to add a little spice, and gets debates underway that concern the economy, foreign affairs and in particular Europe, education, manufacturing and exports and imports, as well as the deluge of immigration problems, to name but a few. Added to which, the political process is immature and politicians act as if they are untouchable. The gullible public accepts, almost without question, how the country is run,' replied Shuster.

Removing the diamond from the inside pocket of his jacket, Turhan-Cooper held it in the palm of his hand and said, 'If we obtain your absolute cooperation, in all aspects, concerning the movement, and the facilities remain freely available, I will give you this, and believe me it will more than eliminate your outstanding Death Duties".

Looking at the walnut-sized stone, Shuster thought it was a piece of sparkling crystal and he said, 'How can that help eliminate my debts?'

'How much do you think its worth?' responded Turhan-Cooper.

'Not the faintest idea.'

'Have a guess,' replied Turhan-Cooper.

'Two thousand pounds and that is way short of my financial problems?'

Turhan-Cooper said, holding the diamond up to the light and enjoying its brightness, 'Even on a bad day you should get well over ten million pounds for this, as it weights just over eighty carats. Now, that amount should more than eliminate your death duty problems. You might even have a few pennies left to buy some mushrooms.'

A somewhat shaken Shuster said, 'You are joking.'

'Far from it and I'm more than prepared to give you this diamond in return for your undivided attention and enthusiasm in supporting the movement.'

Shuster then said, 'You have my assurance. I have always supported the movement and its ideology and will continue to do so when the activities really commence. Particularly since retiring, and as you may know, in my opinion, the country finds itself in a position where public complacency has brought about selfishness, greed and politically correct Liberalism. Radical change is required, coupled to radical action and the only people with the stomach for that kind of action are becoming involved with the movement.'

'You have been talking with representatives of political parties.'

Crossing the lounge to look out of the window, Shuster said in reply, 'The aim was to debate numerous topics with party representatives. I would start each topic by outlining what their party seemed to be doing.'

'Are there any particular issues you feel strongly about?

'Turning to face Turhan-Cooper, Shuster said, 'As already mentioned, immigration, Europe, the manufacturing industry, the export of goods. As a result of my views on the aforementioned, there have been occasions when I've been asked if I would be interested in representing a party. Incidentally, it was stressed that you don't actually have to be a member of the party. This struck me as rather strange, and as a consequence, I've become even more interested in fulfilling my obligations towards the movement.'

Satisfied at the response, Turhan-Cooper walked over to Shuster and stretching out his hand with the diamond in the centre of his palm, he nodded at Shuster, which was a silent "Help yourself." Interpreting the silent signal correctly, Shuster moved forward and lifted the gem off his palm. Once in his possession, Shuster said, "Is it really worth around ten million?'

In reply Turhan-Cooper said, 'In reality it's nearer to and even beyond twenty million pounds. However, we have several stones in our possession and you should cooperate with me when you are contemplating selling the stone.'

'I need to sell it immediately,' was the response from Shuster.

'That's perfectly agreeable as far as I'm concerned; however it could take three or four months or even longer to engage the correct establishment to deal with the sale. After consulting experts in the field, I will contact you.'

'What would you like to do now George?' enquired an obviously happy Shuster.

'Nothing really, as, having obtained your guaranteed cooperation, a weight has been lifted, and you can imagine a lack of finance has also had severe constraints. However, with the money almost in our possession, we can advance a little, knowing that, in the relatively near future, massive funds will ensure dramatic changes take place.'

'Good luck to you George,' replied Shuster, and then his mobile `phone rang. After a few seconds, he looked at George Turhan-Cooper and said, 'Hector Hicks is in the drive and will be at the door in a minute or so.'

Excusing himself, Shuster left the room, and within a minute, a loud bell, indicated someone at the front door. Opening the door, Shuster was confronted by the apparition that was Professor Hector Hicks, whose long white hair and straggly beard were complimented by his wearing, what could only be described as, white Druid robes. After shaking hands with a stunned Shuster, H.H. entered the house and after Shuster closed the door, they walked into the lounge. H.H. immediately recognised Turhan-Cooper from when he had attended some of his lectures. Offering his hand H.H. said, 'It's nice to see you fighting fit again after the violence of a few months ago.'

'Thanks, its good to see you again and what brings you here?'

'The problems associated with the political situation.'

'Such as?' replied Turhan-Cooper.

H.H replied, 'Please remember the public are not stupid enough to believe it's their fault the country is in such a mess. For instance it was the government that changed the rules concerning the banking industry, and we now have a financial watchdog that is weaker than a crippled maggot. The Steel Industry was purchased by an Indian and as a result a significant amount of steel production has disappeared. Both the helicopter and tank building capability have been greatly reduced as a result of selling off assets.'

Shuster interrupted, 'So what ship building capacity do we have these days?'

H.H. replied, 'Ship building is virtually non existent.'

Turhan-Cooper responded, 'An elected body of people known as politicians has been busy absorbing money like an intravenous drip to line their own pockets. While busy ensuring they themselves have sufficient income, by increasing their pay and allowances, these same politicians have restricted public pensions and annual wage rises.

H.H. replied, 'The whole system requires modernization, and the first thing in my mind that requires attention is constituency selection. Like local councilors, Members of Parliament must have been born, brought up and live in the constituency they represent. Having parliamentarians, who know the areas they represent, will result in an excellent cross-section being obtained, with detailed knowledge of all local conditions. Parties must also stop importing potential parliamentarians from, say London, to represent somewhere in the West Country, or for that matter, why should someone from the West Country be foisted upon the people of a Northern constituency, or anywhere else for that matter?'

'I could not agree more,' replied Andrew Shuster, who stated, 'In my opinion, most of the distressing problems facing this country are down to "do-gooders" who continually pollute the political waters as a result of their lassitude. There is no such thing as absolute perfection when dealing with or relating to human beings, particularly when dealing with the intricacies associated with politics, religion, national discipline, freedom of speech, the media, et al .'

'Agreed,' replied H.H. who continued, 'In fact, I came here today to enquire about future prospects. From my perspective, I know of around four hundred people who have verbally expressed a desire for change, and in principle, appear willing to participate in marches and protests. Amongst them there are politicians and statesmen, and they are fed up with greedy, self-serving self-protecting specimens of sub humanity known as politicians. Many of those expressing a wish to take on a positive roll are ex military, and they still adhere to their codes of honour, which is somewhat alien to those lounging around in the Palace of Westminster. You know the type, who would not hesitate to tax your dead grandfather, if they thought he would pay from the grave. The type of individual who has a pompous condescending attitude that immediately causes a red mist to swirl in your brain when they start speaking on the radio or television. Bring back the Birch! That would certainly deter those who milk the system – it would prove to them they are not as tough as they think they are. Mind you I liked what I read in the papers concerning the youngsters who attacked you George. To me this country appears to be sleepwalking into anarchy as the crimes committed and the danger to police officers and the population at large is far worse than the punishments applied.'

While H.H. paused to consult some notes he pulled from within his Druids robes, George seized the opportunity to speak and said, 'A means of funding will shortly be available and on that basis alone we should be able to expand the movement and get some really positive things underway.'

Looking at George H.H. responded, 'Politics is nothing more than a game to many politicians and they never think about the political questions and situations we the people struggle to answer or come to terms with.'

SIXTEEN

At a meeting to plan a publicity stunt Nobby Watson said, 'we can pontificate about whatever from here to eternity, but what is required is a name for the movement.' Looking around he said, 'does anyone have any suggestions? George Turhan-Copper responded by saying, 'having given considerable thought to a name I have the following suggestions. PAPE (People Against Political Exploitation,) MAPS (Movement Against Political Scheming,) PANTS (Politicians Are Not Transparent Souls,) TALES (Take Away Lying Expenses Seekers,) MALES (Move All Lying Expenses Scammers).'

Andrew Shuster said, 'what about CRAPS or Can Ruin All Political Scandals.'

Johnny Mann said, 'I rather like MAPS.'

Nobby Watson then said, 'what about WRAP (Wholesale Revulsion Against Politicians.) There were several nods of approval at Nobby's suggestion and Andrew Shuster said, 'George what do think?'

George Turhan-Cooper replied, 'I rather like it, but would it not be better as Warriors Rebel Against Politicians? Whatever, I feel we should adopt the letters and then in the future various interpretations could be used.

Andrew Shuster replied, 'WRAP it is and when are we going to pull off a major stunt to gain publicity?'

Although he was heading the present movement very few of those that knew Andy Shuster really trusted him and Nobby Watson looked at George Turhan-Cooper and moving closer to him Nobby whispered, 'tomorrow night.'

It was just before midnight on a Saturday in early August and thirty men were being infiltrated into the general area in vehicles. After being dropped off the men set about concealing themselves in the nearby woods, ditches and hedgerows. Once in position one man from each group began monitoring the surroundings areas through night vision Binoculars. Added to which without exception every man was hoping the weather would continue to be overcast.

The operation was to be carried out by men under the control of Nobby Watson, who had been assisted throughout the planning and recognisance phases by, Johnny Mann, Peter Crawley and Alan Warley. These men had visited the site and the surrounding areas on several occasions to estimate distances, heights, weights, the layout of the nearby countryside and the condition of fencing and gates. One aspect that really registered was the condition of the ground, which had been compacted by the feet of innumerable visitors and as such, the ground may not show the tracks of the vehicles that would be used. Added to which, there would be little or no unadulterated evidence available for sniffer dogs to latch onto. Mind you Nobby Watson's had every intention of counteracting the use of dogs with a concoction of dried animal blood mixed with a sprinkling of Cocaine that should numb the dog's noses.

While carrying out their survey they also discovered the source of electricity to the administrative buildings and a Transformer located and recessed behind protective doors in an underground passage. Alan Warley was charged with the task of neutralising the electrical aspect of the operation. There were also some bumps and dips to be negotiated or avoided when operating and there was a very useful tarmac strip that could be partially used. Some of the area was protected by a chain link fence, while another area bordering a narrow track had rough barbwire fencing and there were a couple of five bar gates that could be used as a means of entry.

With just under an hour to go before the raid, the plant, tractors and trailers partially loaded with bales of Hay were cautiously moving into the area. Where possible they were travelling across country and using farm tracks and by doing so they were endeavouring to avoid using the local roads.

It was now early Sunday morning and with half an hour to go, Nobby Watson began leading his group of men across country, these men were dressed from head to toe in black and were streaked with camouflage cream. At exactly the same time Johnny Mann and Peter Crawley, were leading their groups from their areas. With the three groups having crept to within spiting distance of the target they all laid down and waited. Moving close to the surrounding perimeter fence a couple of men wearing night vision goggles opened the five bar gates, then crept off to monitor traffic on the A303 and A360 roads. At that time on a Sunday morning the traffic was very intermittent and the men used their Mobile Telephones set on vibration to give the all clear.

At exactly 02.45 hrs, the lights in the Administrative Centre went out as Alan Warley gained entrance to the Transformer control panel by using bolt cutters and then he threw a switch. Without the slightest trace of any lights showing, as all forms of lighting on the tractors and plant had been doctored and with the drivers wearing night vision goggles, they eased forward. Two men then ripped the crowd control rope fencing out of the ground, which allowed the tractors and plant to ease into position.

Within seconds of the powerful forklift getting into position, the first Lintel stone was lifted and lowered onto a trailer, were it was quickly covered with bales of Hay. The driver then headed for the nearby woods where after the bales were removed he operated the hydraulics and tipped the Lintel into the undergrowth. This exercise was carried out successfully for three Lintels and the whole operation had been achieved in slightly less than six minutes. Everyone involved escaped undetected across the fields to woods or hedgerow where in most instances they waited for first light. The last to leave the area was Nobby Watson who spent a couple of minutes scattering his Cocaine and dried blood mixture in gateways and around the area and painting WRAP on a couple of stones. As soon as it was light enough the tractors and forklift equipment left the area on the roads and this time they used their lights and a little later cars began arriving to pick up the men. With virtually no traffic moving while the raid was being carried out, nothing had been seen moving around the site, which proved beyond doubt and enhanced the desire for detailed planning and recognisance phases for all future operations.

In the morning when the first employees arrived for work they immediately noticed the lack of electricity in the administrative buildings. Then a little later a member of the public informed the staff three Lintels were missing and then unmitigated mayhem broke out with the police and the media arriving in doves which resulted in massive media coverage.

The television companies were the first to show the results of the raid on the news and the painted WRAP featured and a little later the newspapers were filled with photographs and long articles appertaining to the desecration of Stonehenge. Some of the newspapers carried headlines stating, "Stonehenge Stolen," "Stonehenge Removed," "Stonehenge Desecrated." Whereas the television companies featured the three yawning gaps from where Lintels had been removed and all forms of the media concentrated on the few leaflets found. However one aspect that puzzled all sections of the media was who or what were WRAP and the lack of any evidence as to why and who had removed three Lintels from Stonehenge.

George Turhan-Cooper on the other hand was totally aware of who was responsible and how the operation had been carried out and was enjoying the concentrated media coverage. Particularly when the articles in the press highlighted the leaflets found, one of which said the following?

'WRAP says t*he political circus that has dominated the lives of the population for so long requires changing. A group of HGV Truck Drivers, Hairdressers, Petrol Pump Attendants, Florists and Bricklayers, would make a better job of running the country. Politicians are only interested in lining their own pockets and what other occupation would pay for toilet rolls at a second home?*

Another leaflet said, *'WRAP say no potential MP's should seek election without hard nosed work experience and Politicians should not be younger than forty or older than sixty five. Why don't politicians live in barrack type accommodation with an area where they can eat, drink and pontificate? That type of accommodation would save millions of pounds over the duration of a parliament and prevent expenses fiddling.'*

Yet another leaflet found said, 'WRAP says *Politicians are not Aristocrats overseeing their Serfs, MP's are the servants of the people paid by the people through taxation. Should Members of Parliament fail to understand this principle then?* Oliver Cromwell's Speech on the Dissolution of the Long

Parliament, given to the House of Commons on 20th April 1653, should be applied to today's money-grabbing, snouts in the trough, bottom feeding Members of Parliament.'

Produced on a separate leaflet the speech said, *'It is high time for me to put an end to your sitting in this place, which you have dishonoured by your contempt of all virtue, and defiled by your practice of every vice; ye are a factious crew, and enemies to all good government; ye are a pack of mercenary wretches, and would, like Esau, sell your country for a mess of pottage, and like Judas betray your God for a few pieces of money. Is there a single virtue now remaining amongst you? Is there one vice you do not possess? Ye have no more religion than my horse; gold is your God; which of you has not bartered your conscience for bribes? Is there a man amongst you that has the least care for the good of the Commonwealth? Ye sordid prostitutes, have you not defiled this sacred place, and turned the Lord's temple into a den of thieves, by your immoral principles and wicked practices? Ye are grown intolerably odious to the whole nation; you were deputed here by the people to get grievances redressed, are yourselves gone! So! Take away that shining bauble there, and lock up the doors. In the name of God, go!'*

Two days after the operation and not many miles from Stonehenge, George Turhan-Copper was speaking with Andrew Shuster in the summer lounge of College House and also present was a somewhat dishevelled Professor Hector Hicks. Who like the others was more than intrigued by what had become the intense media coverage and they were waiting for the arrival of Nobby Watson and the other group leaders involved in the raid. The atmosphere in the room was very relaxed and then HH said, 'do any of you remember the episode years ago concerning the Stone of Scone being stolen from Westminster Abbey. That raid really caused a media frenzy. It would appear we will surpass that frenzy with the Stonehenge episode.'

Andrew Shuster was about to reply when the front door bell rang and he said, 'excuse me gentlemen, I think they have arrived and I should go and let them in.' Greeting the arrivals at the front door Andy Shuster said, 'please follow me,' and with that he led the group to the lounge. As they entered George Turhan-Cooper indicated for them to sit down and said as they settled, 'Bloody well done and congratulations.'

Nobby Watson responded by saying, 'many thanks and it looks like WRAP has gained maximum publicity. However right up to the last second we really did not know whether it would be possible. We knew the Lintels weighed a considerable amount and we did not know if we could successfully lift and lower them onto a trailer and there was a huge sigh of relief when it occurred.'

'You have pulled off a major publicity stunt, which has the media transfixed. It's an absolute knockout and to think you initially thought of using a Helicopter. Happily you decided against the noise, in favour of hydraulic lifting equipment and tractors and trailers. Personally I thought a couple of major diversions would have been required to keep the authorities and most of the traffic on the A303 and A360 roads away. But as it turned out at that time on a Sunday morning there is almost no traffic,' replied George Turhan-Cooper.

Andrew Shuster said, 'H.H. has come up with a proposal which involves breaking the Sound Barrier directly over the Houses of Parliament during a sitting which would probably blow the windows out. The pilot would then fly out to sea and after ejecting which would result in the aircraft crashing - he would be picked up by associates. The second proposal intrigues me and is a proposal from Chris Slade. His suggestion involves training bees to attack a target and they could be trained to attack a specific Member of

Parliament. The attack could occur when they are attending a constituency surgery or holding a public meeting. Bees would be a cheaper option than arranging for or purchasing the Heavy Plant required for another Stonehenge. However, I'm of the opinion attacking bees could be responsible for producing a great deal of sympathy for the attacked MPs and the focus would be on their plight and not on achieving or focusing on our objectives.'

HH then said, 'what we have at the moment isn't working, regardless of political affiliations, you don't require a PhD in Astro Physics to work out that change is required. Various parties over decades have been provided with innumerable opportunity to achieve and failed. Who will be effective? Who knows? What is required is a leader with balls. Personally I'm of the opinion everyone should vote and if necessary voting should be made compulsory.'

Johnny Mann replied, ' they would be better employed building nuclear power stations for the domestic market or dismantling the diabolical and puritanical aspects associated with Political Correctness, Health and Safety and the Human Rights regimes.'

Turhan-Cooper responded by saying, 'funding is a problem and we really don't have sufficient funds to produce anything at the moment, however, the situation should change very soon.'

H.H. chipped in by saying, 'once funds are available, I know a couple of printers who will print whatever Leaflets or Posters are required and they are secure and trustworthy.'

The instant H.H. finished speaking a mobile telephone began to ring and a slightly embarrassed George Turhan-Copper answered his mobile and what he heard shocked him to the core. Listening for a few seconds George turned his mobile off and indicated to Andy Shuster to come over.

When Shuster arrived at his side George 'whispered can we go somewhere and speak in private?'

'Of course, just follow me,' replied Shuster and with that they both left the lounge which left H.H. saying, 'At this juncture a sizable percentage of the country will not vote when the opportunity arises.'

On leaving the lounge and as they crossed the hall Shuster said, 'shall we speak outside on the drive or in the garden?'

'Wherever suits you,' replied George.

As they left the Porch and walked about five yards from the house George suddenly stopped and while turning to face Shuster, he carried out a cursory check that nobody could hear and then he said, 'that was Tom Rosecrans on the phone, your diamond sold late last night in New York for Fifty Seven Million Dollars. When the commission and other charges for exchanging to pounds sterling are taken out, you will have well over twenty million pounds. That should resolve your financial problems and money on loan for the movement.'

A shocked Shuster was barely able to grunt and then he stuttered a very nervous, 'twenty million pounds, my goodness, I should be able to lend the movement five million and it can be paid back when other stones are sold.'

'Your generosity will be rewarded and congratulations on being in a position to alleviate your financial problems.' Replied George as they began walking back to the porch.' On reaching the Porch Andy Shuster said, 'Any idea who purchased the diamond?'

'Apparently it was a representative of a Middle Eastern Investment Bank,' replied George.

On entering the lounge again both men walked over to one of the windows to look out on the gardens. While at the same time Alan Warley who was a former Colonel in the Armoured Corps was saying, 'For instance a significant percentage of the armed forces will not vote, primarily because they are not registered.'

At the conclusion of what Alan Warley was saying George turning to face the group said, 'Gentleman in the very near future which means in about a week or thereabouts we should have sufficient funds to really develop. I'm not prepared to say how much but the telephone call was from someone who is prepared to invest in the movement and at the moment we will leave it at that. So please carry on with your discussion.'

Seizing the opportunity H.H. said, 'from my research the baulk of the population has little or no confidence in politicians or the various political parties. The political situation in the country is verging on calamitous and new inspirational ideas to solve the inherent problems that originate from the incumbent politicians are non existent. Radical ideas are required and the process of implementing these ideas on the population would be harsh. However, politicians appear afraid to implement fresh original programmes in case it offends the puritans and do gooders, the types who foolishly believe when the dust settles everyone will be living happily ever after.'

In a buoyant mood Shuster who was listening while watching birds in the feeding in the garden said, 'once the leaflets and posters are being produced, resplendent with the movements' name. Perhaps we should consider various ways of distributing the leaflets silently at night across the country.'

SEVENTEEN

Whilst Andy Shuster was worrying about when he would receive the multi-millions of pounds from the sale of the diamond, George Turhan-Cooper and others were preparing to gain more publicity. One of the first investigations he had carried out involved the printers recommended by H.H. During his visit it was agreed that when funds were available, the printers were prepared to print whatever was required.

Having received a cheque in excess of one hundred thousand pounds for the gold, a couple of weeks before Andy Shuster's diamond sold, John Vialls was planning what to do with his windfall. One morning, while pondering his family's future, Vialls was listening to a radio discussion. One subject raised by the well meaning intellectuals and professors shocked him. They were debating the wearing of traceable electronic tags by murders and sex offenders. He could not understand why, in some cases, they were allowed out from various secure establishments on day release. During his career in one country, Vialls had witnessed the beheading of criminals as half time entertainment at football matches, while in another he had seen executed people hanging from traffic lights or suspended from bridges or flyovers. There was no way he could come to terms with or accept being lenient to certain types of convicted criminals. To his mind, if they managed to survive their sentence, and had been visibly branded, they could go free. Until hearing the views of misguided do -gooders on the radio, Vialls had not contemplated joining the movement, but as a result of the tagging discussion, he decided to join, and contacted Clavelshay. During their conversation Clavelshay had said, 'We need to develop a secret pamphlet -scattering delivery service across the country, one which cannot be traced. Do you have any ideas?'

'Not at this very instant, however I'll devote some thought to it.'

The day after speaking with Clavelshay, Vialls was watching his children riding their horses in the sand school at the farm. As his eldest boy prepared his horse to jump a fence, something caught Vialls eye. What he saw was a yellow balloon floating past with a length of string and a label attached. Later, Vialls decided to experiment with several balloons, to test their carrying capacity. After arranging for cylinders of hydrogen, oxygen and helium to be delivered to the farm, he began experimenting with the carrying capacity of balloons filled with various gases or mixtures of gases.

After filling two balloons with each of the gases, Vialls allowed them to drift away carrying nothing at first. After that he tethered the balloons to a fencing rail using fifty-foot lengths of string. By doing so, when carrying exactly the same weight, he could gauge the balloons` lifting capacity and he discovered that a hydrogen and helium mix was best. After experimenting with various sized balloons, he finally decided to use black 36" latex balloons, as their lifting capacity was significantly greater than ordinary balloons. Unfortunately the 36" balloons were quite expensive at almost five pounds each, but when filled with helium they lifted a sizable weight.

The next problem to overcome was designing a method by which the balloons would release the leaflets from several thousand feet up. After experimenting he decided to use acid to ensure release occurred after a couple of hours of floating over a city or wherever. By securing string with an accurately measured weight attached to a fence rail, he discovered that putting a couple of drops of sulphuric acid onto a small elastoplast that he wrapped around the string it eventually dissolved. Which meant when aloft, and after a couple of hours, the string would part and the leaflets would then be released from several thousand feet up to float down over a specified area.

Satisfied with the success of the experiments, Vialls contacted Clavelshay and invited him to visit the farm and gave him instructions on how to get there. On his arrival at the five bar gate at the entrance to the drive, Clavelshay got out of his car and opened the gate and while doing so he looked up at the impressive house. Getting back into his car he drove through, then getting out he closed the gate and drove up the drive, passing the barns and the sand school. Reaching an area of tarmac at the side of the house, he stopped, and as he was getting out Vialls appeared and greeted him, 'So at long last you have managed a visit.'

Looking around Clavelshay said, 'And it's very impressive.'

'I do my best,' replied Vialls.

'Of that, I'm positive! Now, what have you got to show me?'

Indicating with a wave of his hand that Clavelshay should follow him, Vialls led the way to the sand school and took his visitor to where there were some large black balloons tethered. Vialls said, 'I set these experiments up a couple of hours ago so you should witness the breaking of the string in a few minutes.'

Clavelshay replied, 'So the idea is to attach pamphlets to the string and in theory they should be released.' Just as he finished speaking there was the clatter of a small tin box, containing stones, hitting the sand. This caused Vialls to say, 'If that happened a couple of thousand feet up the leaflets would be well and truly scattered?'

'How many leaflets at a time could be carried?'

'In all honesty I don't know, as I have not used them, I've been working with small stones that weigh in at two pounds, but I should imagine at least a couple of hundred leaflets depending on their weight.'

'Nevertheless this method could be used and although each balloon is rather expensive and flight direction is dependant on wind direction, it could be used to compliment other ways that have been suggested, such as scattering leaflets from lorries and cars at night, along with other suggestions about using gliders, hot air balloons, light aircraft and trains.'

'One security aspect that must be carried out if this method is to be used, is the wearing of thin surgical type rubber gloves to prevent finger prints and DNA samples.' Vialls added, 'Now, would you like to join us for lunch?'

'I would love to, and many thanks for the invitation.'

Reaching the rear of the house, they entered a utility room that contained a sink and boiler and about twenty demijohns of, what looked like, home brewed wine on shelves. Perusing them, Clavelshay noticed elderberry, barley, gooseberry and raspberry wine, and looking at him, Vialls said, 'Would you like to sample some?'

'No thanks, but I will admit to being fascinated by the selection.'

'Amongst the many activities involved in running the farm, I really enjoy making my own wine from the cereals, fruits and berries found or produced on the farm,' responded Vialls as they left the utility room and crossed a hall into the kitchen. On hearing the kitchen door, open Maureen Vialls turned away from the food she was preparing and said in a delightfully soft American accent, 'And who do we have here?' 'This is the one and only Stanley Clavelshay, whom you have spoken to on the telephone on many occasions.' replied Vialls. Offering her hand Maureen said, as they shook hands, 'It's nice to meet you at long last, particularly after hearing some of the rather strange stories about you.'

'Perhaps you could enlighten me?' replied Clavelshay, laughing.

The children are at school, so if you go into the dining room I will bring the food in very soon,' replied Maureen, turning away to get on with what she had been preparing. As they entered the dining room Clavelshay noticed the table was already set for three people and decided not to say anything. Walking over to the window to join Vialls, they both looked out over the garden and the rolling countryside that was interspersed with woods and hedgerows. While Vialls was pointing out the boundaries of the property, they heard Maureen enter and turning away from the window, they made for the chairs and settled at the table.

During the magnificent lunch of roast chicken, new potatoes, cauliflower, peas and carrots the topic of conversation, led by Maureen, got around to the media, 'One thing about the media, that surely must change, is the number of journalists they employ, who seem to be able to earn their wages writing rubbish. Some of these items are then mooted on daytime television and, since a significant number of people appear to believe everything they hear, it then becomes the perceived truth.'

In response Clavelshay said, 'As a nation we must look forward and not back, but some youngsters seem either reluctant or unaware that they need to work to achieve their dreams. It also appears that some have not accepted that we can't all live in luxury, or be a celebrity.' Vialls joined in by saying. 'The population appears to be unaware the real power lies in the hands of the people themselves, and the welfare state is partially to blame for the unmitigated mess society is in. Too many people lack the will to get out of bed, preferring to accept benefits rather than going to work.'

Silence rained supreme for a few minutes as they enjoyed their main course, and on completion, Maureen cleared the table of dirty crockery and carried it back to the kitchen, returning almost immediately with a dessert of lemon tart and double cream which Clavelshay really enjoyed. Clearing his plate he said, 'Maureen that was delicious and fit for a King.' This prompted Vialls to say, 'Certain people even want to get rid of the Queen, saying she is not worth the money. However if politicians were as devoted to the country as the Queen, there would be no problems. What do you think would happen if the Queen was thrown out?' Clavelshay said, 'In all probability some European Union Countries might celebrate the demise of the Queen. They have no loyalty to a reigning monarch.'

While he was helping Maureen to carry the remaining crockery and utensils back to the kitchen, Clavelshay's mobile `phone rang. Having placed the items he was carrying onto the work surface, Clavelshay removed his mobile from an inside pocket. On answering, he was surprised to hear George Turhan-Cooper's voice.. Listening, for what seemed an eternity, watched by both Maureen and John Vialls, and trying to remember everything he was being told, the call eventually came to an end. Turning to face the others, he said, 'There has been some catastrophic news and, no disrespect to you Maureen, but I think John and I need to speak in confidence.'

'No problem, I can leave, or you two can wander around the farm.'

'My preference would be to take a stroll,' answered Clavelshay.

On leaving the kitchen and wandering towards the sand school, Clavelshay said, 'That was George Turhan-Copper. I'm afraid there is some very bad news. 'Turning things over in his mind as they walked in silence, Clavelshay and Vialls, passed the sand school en route to a small stream that ran through the property. Eventually, on arrival at the small bridge that crossed the stream and allowed access to other fields, Clavelshay said, 'Andrew Shuster and his wife were killed in a car crash late last night, and Turhan-Cooper has been dealing with identifying the bodies.'

'Bloody hell, that is a bit of a shock! Where did the crash happen?'

'Apparently near to junction 18 of the M4, and, from what Turhan-Cooper said, it involved a drunken driver losing control of his vehicle while travelling at speed on the opposite carriageway. It bounced over the central reservation, hit the road in a cloud of sparks that became flames and smashed into Andrew Shuster's car, killing the occupants and setting a couple of other cars on fire. Turhan-Cooper was requested to carry out an identification of Andy and his wife which was somewhat gory.'

'What about family?' Asked Vialls? While silently thinking, 'I never really liked the man as he was too much of a situation exploiter.'

'There was a son,' replied Clavelshay, 'but he too was killed in a car crash returning from University several years ago. According to Turhan-Cooper there is no direct heir or for that matter even a sideways distant relative to inherit the estate. He is of the opinion it will all be settled and sold subject to probate rules and regulations and of course, after the tax authorities have grabbed their share.'

'What about the diamond money?'

'Turhan-Cooper is dealing with that at the moment and is talking with the Dutch contingency, as apparently, according to T.C., they kept everything in their names. So T.C. is hoping the huge cheque has not been officially assigned to Shuster and can be reassigned to himself.' Continuing to walk across the fields Vialls pointed out a couple of men in the next field using metal detectors. He understood that area of the farm to contain evidence of an ancient settlement, probably from as early as the Bronze Age. As they approached the men using the detectors, they stopped searching and walked over to Vialls, who shook hands with them and asked, 'Anything of interest today?'

Delving into a bag over his shoulder, the older of the two searchers withdrew some items, one of which was an old horse brass and a coin dated 1775 with a small hole through the middle. Examining it, Vialls said, 'It looks like someone punched a hole through it and then used it as a washer for a fencing nail or something similar.' The man held out his open palm and in the middle of his hand was a small very dirty coin. Handing it to Vialls he said, 'It looks like early Roman and once it's been cleaned up we should be able to trace its origin.' 'So nothing has turned up that is really valuable, which we could count as treasure trove?' 'Not as yet,' the laughing reply and then Clavelshay's mobile telephone rang again.

Moving away a few yards, Clavelshay heard Turhan-Cooper saying, 'Can we meet at the Brace of Pheasant at midday tomorrow as there are several points that I want to discuss with you, and can you contact Vialls as I would like him to be present too?' Clavelshay said, 'I'm actually with

Vialls at the moment and will let him know.' 'Many thanks,' then silence. Seeing that Clavelshay had finished speaking on his mobile, Vialls moved towards him and Clavelshay said, 'T.C. wants you and I at the Brace of Pheasants at midday tomorrow for a discussion, and before you ask, he did not say what it was about, but we can imagine.' Leaving the detectors to continue their hobby, the two men began walking back to the house and as they reached the bridge over the stream, Clavelshay saw a fox, then two deer, and was informed by Vialls they were roe deer. Fascinated by one particular bird singing its heart out, he heard, for the first time in his life, the sound of a woodpecker, shortly after which, he spotted three pheasants. When they reached the sand school Vialls said, 'I suppose you will be heading for home now and preparing for the meeting at the Brace tomorrow.'

They arrived at the side of the house, Clavelshay shook hands with Vialls and peeled off, and as he opened the door of his car, he noticed Maureen as she joined her husband. He started up and prepared to drive home; as he did so, he acknowledged the waves of both Maureen and John Vialls. Moving down the drive, Clavelshay happily carried out the gate procedure at the entrance, after what, to him, had been an exhilarating experience of listening to and seeing nature at its best. Having spent much of his life wandering the world at the behest of the British government, since retiring and becoming teetotal, Clavelshay was learning so much about nature and the environment and really enjoying it .Driving home with the car radio on, he was listening to members of the public being asked to imagine assisting the government in sorting out the economy. The response was a list of somewhat wild ideas that had Clavelshay laughing aloud. For example, selling all the Queen's swans was mentioned and getting lawyers to work for nothing was another. Someone had actually suggested getting prisoners to generate cheap electrical power by being forced onto large treadmills in the prisons. Reaching his house an hour or so later Clavelshay wondered what the heck the followings day's meeting could be about, and prepared himself to be shocked.

The following morning Clavelshay left home with plenty of time to spare, and when he arrived in Plush, he parked in the field that was acting as the car park for the Brace of Pheasants. Locking his car, he wandered along to the entrance, and being the first to arrive, bought himself a half pint of lemonade shandy and moved to the table in the alcove. A few minutes later Vialls arrived and was greeted by the barmaid as one of the regulars, and after obtaining a pint of bitter strolled over to the alcove and slid along the bench to sit next to Clavelshay. After about ten minutes of small talk and some laughter, they were both surprised when Clavelshay's mobile rang. Answering it, Clavelshay nodded a few times, and then the call finished. Turning to face Vialls, he said, 'T.C will be late and he will be accompanied by Tom Rosecrans. No mention must be made of the movement or if necessary it can be referred to as the gallery.'

'I don't have a problem with that,' replied Vialls.

After just over an hour of small talk and subdued laughter, they both noticed Turhan-Cooper accompanied by Tom Rosecrans enter the bar. After ordering a couple of drinks they came over to the alcove table and after sitting opposite Vialls and Clavelshay, T.C. said, 'Sorry for being late as I picked up Tom from Bristol airport before driving here. For information concerning the Shusters, to date, the funeral arrangements are set for Saturday 29th at 1100 hrs at Saint Paul's Church in South Aweil; the Church is off Silk Street. Incidentally, I have agreed with the undertakers that I will settle the funeral account, and the double internment will be carried out at the Moonsend Cemetery. The funeral director emphasized the church is very small and it won't take many people; he also stressed parking will be difficult. However, there will only be a couple of people present, as a blanket has been thrown over anything to do with the Shusters. I'm assuming those present will be me, you, Stanley and you John, if that's agreeable.' 'Fine by me,' replied Vialls, followed by Clavelshay. Should further information become available I will pass it on to Stanley.'

After a few seconds silence, during which time T.C. took a couple of swigs of his drink, he said, 'Tom has sorted out the Shuster financial hiccups. The money, from the sale of his diamond sale in New York, was paid into his account and was about to be transferred when news of Andy's death reached Tom. So, as a consequence, there is a distinct possibility of me becoming a multi millionaire. However, in reality, the money is surplus to requirement as it was assigned to Shuster to resolve his financial problems and to help fund his gallery. In fact, gentlemen, the real reasons you were invited here is to witness Tom signing the cheques.'

Handing Tom Rosecrans a small piece of paper with something written on it, both Clavelshay and Vialls watched Rosecrans write and sign three cheques, then hand them to Turhan-Cooper. Nodding his thanks, T.C. said, 'I'm prepared to distribute this money, which was originally Shuster's, as follows, and as a consequence of what I'm about to do, please don't become filled with an inflated sense of your own importance. As far as I'm concerned, the amounts are your entitlement – and a small a percentage of the overall total.' He offered a cheque across the table to Clavelshay, who did not look at it, but neatly folded it and placed it into his wallet. On the other hand, on accepting the cheque offered across the table to him, Vialls read it and almost exploded with excitement when he read it out.

'It says "Pay John Vialls one million pounds!' 'Yes, and you deserve it for recovering the diamonds.' Rosecrans laughed, 'It won't bounce.' Shuffling along the bench, which made Clavelshay get to his feet, Vialls just managed to suppress a wild scream as he said, 'Excuse me for a couple of minutes.' He strode across the bar and out of the Brace and once outside, he went over to the signpost. While stood there he found he was shaking like a leaf, and having the greatest difficulty suppressing an overwhelming desire to shout out loud. Inside the Brace, Clavelshay removed his wallet from his pocket, and, carefully unfolding the cheque, found that it, too, was for a million pounds. Easing out of his seat, Clavelshay joined Vialls at the signpost, where he said to him, 'John, I prepared myself for a shock, but not in a million years would I have contemplated anything like this.' Vialls said, 'You are fixated by that word "million,' and then he burst out laughing and offered his hand to Clavelshay, adding as they shook hands, 'Bloody hell Stanley, what a pleasant shock!' Turning back towards the Brace and on a sign from Clavelshay, they both strode off and made their way back to the bar.

As they sat down at the table, Rosecrans said, 'You may have noticed the cheques are drawn against an account in a Dutch Bank, so they will take a few days to clear and as I said before, gentlemen, they will not bounce.' T.C. asked, 'Are we going to partake of a celebratory lunch or do you guys wish to end this meeting and deal with certain financial affairs?' Clavelshay replied, 'A celebratory lunch would certainly be in order and it would be my pleasure to buy four bottles of Champagne, one for each of us, to be consumed at our leisure when driving is not involved.' 'I'm more than happy to partake of lunch,' replied Vialls.'

After ordering a selection of dishes from the fine menu plus four bottles of Champagne, the four enjoyed lunch, and over an hour was happily spent indulging in good food, small talk and a little laughter. Satisfied with the success of their unexpectedly rewarding meeting, and after settling the bill, T.C. said, as they left the Brace and were making their way to their cars, 'I'll see you two on Saturday at the Shusters' funeral. Should there be any hiccups in arrangements before then, I will inform Stanley.' After shaking hands and wishing each other well, they got into their cars and left Plush and the Brace of Pheasants and made their way to their various locations. Vialls went straight home and after talking with Maureen, left almost immediately for Bristol Airport, where he bought a ticket and flew to Luxemburg. There, he successfully paid his cheque into an offshore account he had been using for many years. Whereas, Clavelshay paid his cheque into an account he had in the Channel Islands. After successfully completing their financial expeditions both men were back home the following day, leaving more than sufficient time to prepare for the Shusters' Funeral.

The most efficient leaders trust their subordinates and inspire confidence throughout the ranks. Unfortunately in the experience of Vialls, the same could not have been said of Andrew Shuster, who had fallen a long way short of being a natural leader. In fact, Vialls was convinced Shuster had been involved in various types of meddling that solely benefited his own interests. Whatever, that was all in the past. He was dead and gone. Arriving in South Aweil, Vialls managed to park his car and make his way to Saint Paul's Church where he met up with Turhan-Cooper and Clavelshay.

The three men, who had made an effort to be suitably dressed for the occasion, were standing in front of the church door. When the two hearses arrived they watched the two coffins being removed and then expertly carried into the church. Even Turhan-Cooper, who was a rock solid atheist, entered the church and listened with the few people present to the vicar's tributes. When the Church ceremony ended, all present watched as the coffins were ceremoniously taken out to the hearses.

T.C. and Vialls took advantage of a lift in Clavelshay's car, as he had managed to park only a few yards from the church, and they followed the hearses to Moonsend Cemetery, where, finding themselves the only people present, they walked over to the huge grave and watched as the two coffins were lowered into the grave to rest side by side. After the vicar had delivered the, ashes to ashes and dust to dust' sequence of the ceremony, each of them threw a few handfuls of soil into the grave. As the gravediggers began shovelling the excavated soil back into the grave, the three men eased away and returning to Clavelshay's car left Moonsend Cemetery.

EIGHTEEN

Having paid for and attended the funeral of the Shusters over a month previously the financial situation concerning Turhan-Cooper was now well and truly resolved. As a result of the death of the Shusters the tax authorities wanted their share of the estate and it was rumoured it would be put up for sale to recoup the outstanding inheritance tax. On hearing the rumour and as yet not having seen anything in writing concerning the sale, Turhan-Cooper was nevertheless, following every conceivable aspect concerning the College House Estate. While waiting for definitive information concerning the estate, Turhan-Cooper discovered the Shusters were almost five hundred thousand pounds in dept and that was primarily due to unpaid inheritance tax. No wonder the tax authorities were so keen to recover the money that was owed to them. Whatever was going on behind the scenes concerning the estate T.C. was determined to purchase it as the facilities available were absolutely essential for what he had in mind.

During the period of waiting T.C. had several discussions with H.H. to formulate a future plan of action and several matters that were raised by H.H. rang bells loud and clear.

For instance H.H. raised the point that within a short period of time the world's population will reach nine billion and there would be a massive problem associated with feeding that number of people. He also mentioned the Russian ban on exporting wheat as they had significant problems and their reluctance to export would cause problems elsewhere. H.H. was suggesting one of the most important things to get over to the pubic was produce as much of your own food as possible in other words the second world war slogan of, 'Dig For Victory,' should be applied, as he felt self sufficiency should be the norm. Installing such things as renewable energy installations for electrical generation or solar panels for hot water, small wind generators should be encouraged. Also H.H. did not waste anytime in reminding anyone that we live on a small island and the world is a mere speck of dust floating and turning within the vastness of the Universe.

When in discussions with retired Colonel Alan Warley T.C. found he was more of the opinion to save money and to get better organised. Warley thought the County Police Forces should be amalgamated into a single National Police Force. Somewhat akin to the armed forces whether they are Navy, Army or Air Force, they are national. With the correct administrative infrastructure, why can't the police and for that matter the fire brigade be national? Particularly as the island we inhabit is by comparison much smaller than many American Sates. Alan Warley was also concerned about Climate change and was convinced the power of nature would be demonstrated with ever increasing fury, as mankind in all its wisdom denied nature its rightful place concerning the future of planet Earth. In Warley's mind civilisation had developed so fast over the last hundred years and the mass construction that had taken place had interfered with nature. For instance the flood plains where houses had been built and all the tarmac and concrete used for road construction had in some areas interfered with the run off of rain water causing floods.

All of the aforementioned provided a great deal of thought for the formulation of the various leaflets and posters. Added to which several of the other people T.C. had been talking to were for instance convinced Community Service was not really working and the whole punishment system required dramatic overhauling. Others thought politicians who fiddled expenses and had not divulged every conceivable aspect concerning their personal details should be publicly flogged and others thought hanging should be brought back for certain types of murder. While others generalised by saying such things as, do we really require a General to tell us the government consists of wasters. Then others mentioned problems associated with Political Correctness which appeared to have been responsible for bringing about a lapse in standards and national discipline and when combined with endemic laziness and a general acceptance of mediocrity. It was a disaster. As another said, falling from the sky never hurt anyone; it is the sudden stop when you hit the ground that hurts and the required change will undoubtedly bring about some pain. One of the last people T.C. spoke with was John Vialls and he suggested any confirmed drug addicts should be dealt with by him, as he would cure them of their addition by using methods learnt during his career.

While waiting for the official details appertaining to the College House Estate auction T.C. formulated a very large report or reference document concerning all the aspects discussed with various people. Then all of a sudden he received the details concerning the auction of the College House Estate and on the given day he produced his body at the premises where the auction was to take place. Entering the auction company's premises early T.C obtained a seat directly in front of the lectern from where the auctioneer would look down on him and other people. When the lot associated with the sale of College House came to the fore T.C. listened to the explanations concerning the property and he also noticed there were several people manning telephones. While waiting for the auction to start he looked around the room and the sensation he felt in his stomach was akin to the first time he was inside an aircraft that lopped the loop and in his past he had experienced that. Then the auction started with an opening bid of two million pounds followed by a bid via telephone of two million two hundred and fifty thousand and that was followed through the telephone with a bit of two and half million pounds. Sitting tight and determined to succeed T'C heard it reach two million seven hundred and fifty thousand via the telephone and as the auctioneer said, 'for the first time,' and then followed almost immediately by, 'for the second time at two million seven hundred and fifty thousand pounds,' T.C bid three million pounds and there was an audible gasp from the people present and with the Auctioneer looking at the telephones for a response, nothing was forthcoming and the Auctioneer once again said, 'for the first, time,' looking around he said, 'for the second time and soon after he said, 'for the third and final time,' and in total silence he then brought the hammer down and then he said, 'sold to the gentleman sat in front of me.' Showing his number for the auctioneer to record T.C. then made his way to the office where he suddenly realised he would have to pay sustainably more due to the commission that would be added.

In the office when asked how he would like to pay T.C. produced his cheque book and wrote and signed a cheque for the requested amount and immediately received a receipt. He then proudly said, 'it won't bounce,' all of which was reminiscent of Tom Rosecrans a few weeks previously.

He was then asked to confirm his home address and provide the address of his Solicitors. Asked what he knew about the property, the staff was astounded when they realised he had known the Shusters and over the years he had occasionally stayed at the house. Then T.C. was astounded to learn the house was fully furnished as nothing had been removed. It was also explained that his solicitor and he should receive all the relevant documentation confirming his outright ownership and the keys of the College House Estate within twenty eight days. At the end of the administrative formalities a couple of the staff came forward and shaking his hand they wished him well.

Fourteen days had elapsed before any paperwork arrived at T.C.'s residence and then it started in earnest and it fell into two categories. The first was for his signature and return to the solicitors and the second category was for his records. Whatever on the 26th day the keys were delivered to his house and he was officially informed that he was now the outright owner of the College House Estate. Resisting the urge to rush to his newly acquired property, T.C. set about meeting with various Letting Agents to discus how to go about renting out his original property and what the financial advantage would be. After selecting what he thought were suitable agents he arranged to let his original residence for a minimum of six months. In his mind, that would provide more than sufficient time to decide whether to sell or continue to rent it out. When he finally decided to drive to his newly acquired Estate, ten days had elapsed and just before entering the drive he stopped and emptied the overflowing mail box. As he drove up the drive under the canopy of Oak trees he found it exhilarating and yet rather worrying that what stretched before him was legally his. Pulling into the stable yard as he had done on the previous occasions, he parked and getting out of the car and carrying the pile of mail he walked to the front door. Turning around T.C. looked out over the front lawns and he concluded they were definitely overgrown and in need of cutting and required sorting out. Placing the mail on the ground and with the house keys in his hand he selected a couple of the largest and trying them in the lock he opened the main door at the second attempt. Picking up the mail he entered the large porch with some of the Shusters waterproof outdoor clothing still hanging hooks and then he unlocked another door and entered the house fully. Placing the mail on a table and looking around it was glaringly obvious nobody had been inside for almost three months as there was an array of cobwebs and a significant amount of dust.

Going from room to room T.C. was somewhat horrified to find the house was exactly as the Shusters had left it and during his tour he found dirty clothing waiting to be washed and washed clothing awaiting the iron. While deciding what to do with all the personal effects of the Shusters he returned to the table and began opening the mail and he was horrified to find the Shusters were behind with Council Tax payments, Electricity and Water and appeared to own money all over the place. Not wishing to draw attention to the property he decided to settle all the outstanding debts and every payment was accompanied with an explanatory letter covering the death of the Shusters and his position as the new owner of the College House Estate.

****

While Turhan-Cooper was wrestling with the mound of administrative detail concerning his property in the West Country, in London and East Anglia men who had been adversaries during his career were stirring. These men were Hizor Tizmasi, Orol Denggizi and Ajdar Kuli and they had been part of the renegade Russian Spetnaz group led by

Colonel Yakut Yakut that killed fellow Russians under the Chiswick flyover some twenty years previously. When Yakut Yakut and others of the group left and eventually ended up in Canada these men decided to stay in the country. As the years passed having initially been very much wanted illegal immigrants, they successfully established themselves as employment organisers. In particular they dealt with the East Europeans that came into the country both legally and illegally to work predominately within agriculture in East Anglia. During the process of learning English and working extremely hard they eventually became fully legal residents themselves and actually began the process of applying for citizenship.

As the years had passed and they met significant numbers of East Europeans on a couple of occasions they came across individuals who not only came from the same county, but on a couple of occasions they actually met people who originated from the same town or village. Very seldom did they speak in their native tongue and over the years they concentrate on learning English and became extremely competent in spoken and written English.

One thing they noted as time passed was the attitude of certain sections of the British people towards work and how in many instances rather than work for a living, they would claim benefits. Originating from the former Soviet Union the men were somewhat bemused at the attitude of certain executive types, company directors, bankers, and other forms of the managerial hierarchy, from the higher echelons of the national work force. To them it appeared as if many senior managers were detached from the reality of striving to earn a living by getting up early and working like slaves. While a significant number of their employees did not qualify for a pension, had no savings and continually struggled to pay rent or a mortgage. Then having struggled all their lives, when they achieved retirement age, they continued to struggle to survive on a state pension of less than £100 a week. In some instances ordinary workers were forced to work until they keeled over. While their bosses, some of whom were guilty of wholesale greed could retire on substantial pensions, which sometimes ran into thousands of pounds a week.

While in their case they had worked very hard and having saved over the years and pooled any surplus money they eventually acquired property and enjoyed a certain amount of financial security. Then purely by coincidence one evening, they were all watching the same television programme that was investigating unsolved crimes in the country. About half way through the programme and much to their surprise there was an appraisal of the evidence concerning the attack and killing of Russian Diplomats in London. The men had been members of the group led by Colonel Yakut Yakut that carried out the attack almost twenty years earlier. The reporter was saying he had been informed by the Russian Embassy that they were of the opinion renegade Russian Special Forces had carried out the attack. The reporter then mentioned that a group of Spetnaz Special Forces deserted Afghanistan in the mid eighties and went to Iran and helped that country with its war against Iraq. It was thought the group that was headed by a Colonel Yakut Yakut then went onto Lebanon where they helped train dissidents from Western Countries and helped to train Hezbollah. Apparently they also mentioned a contact with the Israeli Army in Southern Lebanon that ended with the Israelis taking a beating after a helicopter was shot down. It was an assumption that it was the same men as the commander of the Israeli force that took a beating reported seeing some unusually dressed somewhat older men standing on the edge of a ravine giving a single finger salute, as they allowed him to escape in a helicopter. Looking at a sheet of paper the reporter then began reading out some names and the first one was Colonel Yakut Yakut, followed by Warrant Officer Abdul Azim, then Dara Manuchehar and a Sergeant Timurbek. These men according to the information the reporter was relaying were extremely dangerous and were members of a very specialized Spetnaz unit known as Okhotriki.

As soon as the programme finished the telephone rang in Hizor Tizmasi's house and answering he heard Oral Denggizi say in a Russian, 'did you see the programme on television?' 'Yes and I was about to contact you about it and what about Ajdar Kuli?' 'Denggizi replied, 'I have contacted him and he has suggested we meet at your place as soon as possible.' 'That's fine by me lets say in half and hour and inform Kuli.' 'Will do,' replied Denggizi ringing off.

Well within the half and hour mentioned on the telephone the door bell rang and both men came into the house. Taking them into the lounge the first thing Tizmasi said was, 'our names were not mentioned but we need to be cautious and above all we must contact Captain Milailov and he in turn will contact Major Sidorov and between them as they are the only people who know where he is, they will warn Colonel Yakut that his name is in the open and that people are hunting for him.'

Oral Denggizi said, 'I have an email address for Captain Milailov.'

'In this case speed is important and we need to be careful as it could be intercepted. No name, I suggest using the ten partial word codes we were taught you can say, in the opening email the Christian Eskimo and his followers have been identified. Then by using variations of the code, send several emails that will eventually present the clear overall picture. Would that be possible?'

'Yes, I'm familiar with the codes and will send off something like that,' replied Denggizi. The codes work something like this – When working in Tibet the locals always praised the – Yak. It was very amusing how they sometimes tried to – utter complex prayers. But of course as you know they have been named. So using the code what has been said so far is - Yakut named. By sending several emails over a period it would be possible to say - Yakut named on British television and needs to be warned.

'Incidentally, where does Captain Milailov live these days?'

'In the town of Pavlov which lies south of Moscow.

Feeling somewhat more secure after the meeting knowing they had not been named and identified on British television the visitors went their separate way. When he got home Oral Denggizi sent a range of emails over a couple of days that in essence said in Russian. 'Yakut named with others on British television and needs to be warned to prevent his arrest.' In fact Captain Milailov did not have a computer but always went to an Internet Café three times a week to read emails received at his email address at the café. Having deciphered the code he manage to send a detailed message spread over more than twenty innocuous emails spread over a week using a similar code to Yakut Yakut in Toronto Canada.

In Toronto Yakut Yakut who was in fact a Canadian citizen did not use his original name and he warned the others named to be extra cautious for anything that may appear different.

****

While the Russians were engaged in warning each other, Turhan-Cooper had managed to settle the outstanding bills incurred by the Shusters and as a result he was now fully registered with the utility companies as the owner of the

College House Estate. With all the administrative detail taken care of concerning the property T.C. started to contact several of the established and trustworthy seniors within the movement and invited them to College House for a house warming party. He also stressed in communications that when travelling to the party please try to share vehicles, to avoid traffic congestion with too many cars in the local lanes leading to the property.

Spaced out over almost an hour, more than twenty cars eventually arrived at College House and parked in the Stable Yard. Acting as a chaperone and car park attendant John Vialls escorted the occupants of the vehicles, to the front door where they were formally greeted by Turhan-Cooper. Who then handed them onto Nobby Watson who was recognised by some of the guests as he escorted them to the large Conservatory at the rear of the house. On entering the Conservatory the guests were provided with whatever drinks they so desired from a bar run by three young ladies. On leaving the Conservatory for the walled garden the guests were greeted by contractors using three gas powered barbeques, on which they were preparing beef burgers, chicken, pork chops and sausages and in the process creating the most delightful smells. As the guests mingled there was much laughter and hand shaking and in certain instances more than forty years had slipped by since individuals had last met, when serving in the Armed Forces.

With all the guests now present, who were obviously enjoying themselves as they wandered in the garden, with a drink in their hand or a Berger or whatever type of food on a plate. George Turhan-Cooper as the host was circulating amongst the guests shaking hands with individuals within various groups who were merrily chatting. While others with a keen interest in gardening were admiring the Hydrangea's, Camellia's, Magnolia and the abundance of other Shrubs and flowers. Holding the attention of one group that T.C. approached was Professor Hector Hicks, who he heard saying, 'many of those here are ex Special Forces and as such have passed some the toughest selection courses possible. It may come as a surprise to many of you, but when young and impressionable I actually served in the Parachute Regiment.'

'What battalion?' questioned one of the men.

'I spent almost six years in the First Battalion, serving in Cyprus and visiting Libya, Denmark, Malaya, Aden, Norway, Nigeria and few other places during the late fifties early sixties.' That statement was greeted with broad smiles, nods of approval and a round of solid hand shakes.

After taking a swig of beer H.H. continued by saying, 'As evolution has progressed complexities have occurred. What complexities? Well you remember the early grunts that were used as a method of communication, when you were first in the Military, which eventually became a language. In civilian life there is a problem that affects everyone and it concerns the grunts made by politicians as a type of language which the public have difficulty understanding and when coupled to their lack knowledge. It causes complexities! It's not correct to condemn all MP's, as a couple are excellent, however a significant number of modern politicians are out of touch with the reality of the everyday struggles the population endure to eke out a life and severe complexities have arisen. These complexities need to be simplified and the people gathered here could do it.'

When T.C. approached a group admiring the massive trunk of a very tall Scots Pine tree he heard Nobby Watson saying, 'we could of course storm parliament as we definitely have the expertise.' In response to hearing what was being said T.C. said, 'please don't get involved in anything like that, unless things get really bad and you receive permission.'

Nobby Watson replied while laughing, 'we will bear that in mind,' and then he handed T.C. a piece of A4 sized paper and T.C. noticed others in the group had what looked like copies of the same paper in their hands and then heard Nobby Watson who after the Army had been a Prison Officer say, 'I revived this as an email a few days ago and have been distributing it amongst the guests and many a true word is said in jest.'

Looking at the piece of paper T.C. read the following. *Let's put the senior citizens into jail and all the criminals into nursing homes. By doing this the senior citizens would have access to showers, hobbies and walks. They'd receive unlimited free prescriptions, dental and medical treatment, wheel chairs etc and they'd receive money instead of paying it out. They would have constant video monitoring, so they could be helped instantly, if they fell, or needed assistance because of illness. Bedding would be washed twice a week, and all clothing would be ironed and returned to them. A guard would check on them every 20 minutes and bring their meals and snacks to their cell. They would have family visits in a suite built for that purpose. They would have access to a library, weight room, spiritual counselling, pool and education. Simple clothing would be provided, such as shoes, slippers, pyjamas and legal aid would be free, on request. Private, secure rooms would be provided for all, with access to an outdoor exercise yard and gardens. Each senior citizen could have a Personal Computer a Television, radio and daily phone calls. There would be a board of directors to hear complaints, and the guards would have a code of conduct that would be strictly adhered to. While the senior citizens were living in luxury the criminals would suffer the effects of cold food, be left all alone and unsupervised for many hours and lights out would be at 8pm. It would be possible to have a shower once a week and their accommodation would be a tiny room and for the privilege of such luxury they would have pay £900.00 per month and have no hope of ever getting out. Justice for all we say.* Having read the paper T.C. looked at the group facing him and said, 'who ever wrote that, should be congratulated and as Nobby said many a true word is said in jest, although I personally think there is distinct element of possibility written there.'

Moving away from Nobby and his group T.C. was crossing the main lawn feeling very happy with the way the guests were inspecting the gardens. Arriving at another group that was gathered underneath a large Cherry tree, he stood listening to a man called John Brennan saying, 'it may interest you to know that having paid my dues and served in the Parachute Regiment for twenty two years and being from a family that can trace its ancestry back to the 1500's. By birth and family tradition I'm a true Brit and in my mind a strong government is required to get the country back on course and providing economic immigrants with benefits is not the way forward. Having a house in Spain provides an insight into immigrants arriving in Spain and believe me they are only entitled to benefits if they work legally and pay into the Spanish system. There is no way immigrants entering Spain can plug into the system without contributions. Whereas in the United kingdom, benefits are thrown around like confetti, at a wedding.' Before T.C could say a word Peter Crawly was saying, 'In my opinion individual immigrants or group of immigrants who become British Citizens and live under the protection of British Law. Who then get actively involved with and choose to fight for an organisation we are in armed conflict with, should be tried for Treason and be executed. This nation's quality of life is being eroded by groups who are determined to abolish democracy and reduced the nation to medieval standards. Those types also want to subjugate women and kill those who fail to share their beliefs. Harsh measures are required to counteract the creeping Cancer that is slowly eating its way into our way of life.' Another man called David Spinks replied by saying, 'It appears as if the United Kingdom has lost its way and politics has become a joke. So much of a joke that in some areas, individuals always vote for the same party no matter how inept or corrupt it may have been while in office. As far as I'm concerned the individual candidates for each constituency seeking election to parliament must have been born, been brought up in and live in that constituency. By adopting that method we would elect MP's who know areas really well.'

Before anyone answered T.C. moved away to the Coquet lawn that was hidden behind a beautifully maintained Yew hedge, were a group of women guests were trying their hand at Croquet. While watching the game T.C. heard one of the younger women called Janet Parker saying, 'I'm somewhat frustrated by the individuals who belief that if we stay as we are politically, everything will solved. Well in my humble opinion the present style of government is responsible for causing multiple problems. This little island nation has achieved great things in the past and since time in memoriam it has been populated by miscellaneous groups of people who primarily originate from our old empire. Incidentally, there are significantly fewer racial problems here, than in other countries. However this country has been guided down an exceedingly slippery slope by successive governments. Present day Politicians are neither Left, Right nor Centre, and it appears their personal ambitions amount to nothing more than gaining parliamentary protection for their money grabbing antics.'

Stella Locery who T.C knew quite well from various meetings they had attended replied by saying, 'the decline experienced is a significant predicament, for the population who have been let down by an old fashioned political system.

The most worrying aspect is the number of politicians who have never struggled to earn a living in the mines, steel works or in a quarry or been in a road maintenance gang for a single day. Agreed some have been involved in other white collar occupations. However their white collar illusions of superiority are exposed when they are caught milking the system and then what happens to their ambitions?'

While walking back to the barbeque Turhan-Cooper was chuckling to himself at the reactions he had heard while wandering around the garden. While enjoying a burger he was convinced by the general attitude of the guests that the time was right to get whole heartedly involved. His next thought involved thinking about who he could whole heartedly trust concerning the underground facilities available at College House. He decided that Nobby Watson, Stanley Clavelshay, Hector Hicks, Alan Warley, Peter Crawley, Stella Locery, Janet Parker, John Vialls and Chris Slade would form the inner circle and they would be the first people to be individually shown the facilities available.

When the house warming party came to an end and the guests left T.C regarded it as a great success and over the following days he received around fifty letters of thanks that contained many compliments. On receipt of the letters T.C. then wrote to the individuals forming the inner circle and invited them to visit and it was then that he had every intention of making them familiar with all the facilities available.

NINETEEN

Turhan-Cooper dispatched letters to the members of the inner circle inviting them to attend a briefing at College House and received a positive response by telephone from each member. As a result each was given a different day and time for the briefing, and on arrival each was shown the facilities available beneath College House and in the grounds and the entire inner circle was surprised and greatly impressed with the available facilities.

When asked what they thought about setting priorities, during their briefings, Stanley Clavelshay came up with the best suggestion. His suggestion involved contacting every Member of Parliament through their constituency office with an identical letter. Deciding not to immediately use the services of the printers recommended by Hector Hicks, T.C. set about producing the required letters and lists on his personal computer. On completion of the task and as ever acutely aware of security he deleted all traces of the documents and then he removed the hardrive from his P.C and destroyed it. His method of destruction involved smashing the drive to pieces with a hammer and chisel and then placing the pieces into his multi-fuel stove, where they distorted in the heat and some parts actually melted.

Turhan-Cooper then concentrated on emphasising that all the letters should be sent at exactly the same time from a variety of locations spread around the country and far removed from College House. Copies of the letters and a list of every Member of Parliament that had been sent a letter were then forwarded to the editors of most the National Broadsheet and Tabloid Newspapers and some Local papers. The following is the content of the letter sent to each Member of Parliament and to the media.

Dear Member of Parliament,

WRAP would like to take this opportunity to remind you that you were elected to represent this constituency wholeheartedly. As far as can be ascertained you have fallen a long way short of that responsibility and that is primarily due to your woeful lack of leadership skills. When coupled to the overall view of politicians held by the public at large you are beyond a disgrace. The people of this country when lead by tough experienced leaders have beaten everything thrown in their direction for centuries. Unfortunately, at the moment the political parties appear to be filled with guilt-ridden, liberal-thinking, pseudo intellectuals; who could not lead a horse to water let alone a Bayonet or Cavalry charge. To the general public, politicians appear as a collection of selfish individuals, within a governmental system that is self-protecting and self-regulating, which is only advantageous to the somewhat characterless incumbent politicians.

WRAP says the only thing politicians have been extremely successful at is using their suspect abilities to waste billions of pounds and set up strange Quango's. Having failed to demonstrate clear leadership and communication skills that would benefit the whole nation it is time for a change. The people in your constituency are not responsible for your soft delicate conscience and an intellect that cannot accept the tougher side of life and your inability to resolve problems. Rest assured, the bulk of the population many of whom have superior intellects can cope; even when you politicians have not the faintest idea about how to achieve national improvement. As previously mentioned it is now time for change and unlike you WRAP are not puppets that are being manipulated. WRAP expects you to use your questionable, initiative, determination and leadership skills to quickly bring about recognisable change that will benefit the general public.

WRAP will of course be monitoring every action while at the same time using our collective skills to bring about change. The type of change the public desire with or without your help. So take control of your muddled thinking and stop spouting nonsense and focus on the things that really matter. Dramatic change is required in the present day political system and either you or your associates achieve it, or we at WRAP will go flat out to achieve it.

Regards,

WRAP.

Accompanying the politician's letters to the press was the following.

To whom it may concern,

The attached letter has been sent by WRAP to every politician, inclusive of the Prime Minster and all Cabinet Minsters and we at WRAP have mixed thoughts about its reception. WRAP thinks many politicians will try and ignore it or be prevented from seeing it by their agents and assistants. WRAP is also aware many politicians are manipulated by their parties who in turn are to a certain extent manipulated by the media and those who donated huge sums of money. WRAP would be extremely grateful for any publicity.

Regards.

WRAP.

One thousand letters were prepared to cover all the current incumbent Members of Parliament and a significant number of the press both National and Local. Every envelope was addressed by Turhan-Cooper while wearing surgical gloves and he used many different coloured ink pens for the task. When the job was completed he placed a self adhesive stamp on each envelop, the stamps were purchased at many different Post Offices and if tested would not aid DNA. After sending the packets of letters off to the inner circle members, from various places in the South and West of England he then burnt the pens. In a letter to each inner circle member within each packet T.C. warned them about security and to wear surgeon's gloves when handling the mail. On receipt of the packets containing the letters the members then spent several days driving around posting letters in various parts of the country.

During the time when the first reactions began emerging, from the local press in different parts of the country, Vialls was again experimenting with the balloons. As it would be difficult to supply everyone with gas cylinders, he found by inflating the balloons with a bicycle pump or by mouth the lifting capacity remained almost identical. His next problem would be to distribute as many of the balloons as possible with instructions concerning the acid method of release. A major concern was the type of acid, however he discovered by using battery acid from a car battery worked well although it took longer to work.

As a direct result the national press picking up on the story, they began asking questions about whom or what WRAP stood for? Some thought it stood for Why Run Away Play, Women Rally All People, When Radio Attracted People. Whatever the media suddenly began taking a tremendous interest in what had occurred. The first conclusion they reached, concerned the obvious difficulty politicians had in coming up with vibrant new ideas and plans that would effectively benefit everyone. While a couple of broadsheet columnists thought the political situation with its long list of failures had become a desperate issue, which meant any new ideas that could improve the situation would have to be extremely radical. Further articles in the press stated it was somewhat obvious that the present parliamentarians don't have the ability to provide real solutions, primarily because the politicians appeared frightened, of upsetting the public. Or was the collective thinking process of the politicians so suspect that if it did not benefit them personally and it upset the public, the parliamentarians worried about the public taking to the streets in protest. The media reminded everyone that such a situation had occurred previously, when the people marched in huge numbers to protest against the imposition of the Pole Tax.

While the press was gaining momentum in their efforts concerning the publication of letters despatched to the politicians, they had all sorts of investigative journalists and others seeking the origins of WRAP. On the other hand George Turhan-Cooper was now dealing with the printers and arranged for half a million leaflets to be produced. He had ordered and collected a hundred of the large black balloons which he passed to Vialls for distribution. Satisfied with the despatching of the balloons and with the instructions that explained their inflation and the instructions on how to tie the leaflets correctly so they released when the acid did its job T.C. concentrated on security.

The leaflet produced for distribution to the public read as follows: WRAP says *Political complacency is responsible for the rapid decline of this country and its culture. Primarily brought about by the ever increasing numbers of MP's who leave school, attend University and then enter Parliament. As a result they have little if any back breaking experience of struggling along the streets of real life, that are clogged with pain and misery. Politicians must be strong, very experienced and filled with National Pride and be more than prepared to stride across the world to enhance the future prospects of this country. The British Lion should be roaring a full throated challenge, not whimpering and wiping its eyes and nose in shame.*

WRAP says *you don't need to be an intelligent individual to work out it's time for a change. The Civil Service is packed with educated individuals who endeavour to guide and keep the MP's informed. Unfortunately it appears the Civil Service is being ignored and the Politicians have failed miserably to expand and implementy opportunities that have been presented, that would have enhanced the quality of life of the British population. This is primarily due to the concerted efforts of the MP's who selfishly try to increase their personal power, wealth, influence and status while ignoring or causing major problems .*

WRAP intends to shake the establishment to its foundations with positive action and bring about change. Politicians alone did not create the current mess, as corporate greed within Banking and associated industries have also contributed to the unmitigated financial havoc, which resulted in tax payers bailing out the Banks. To become involved with WRAP we recommend you write to your local MP and enclose this leaflet. Change is approaching! WRAP will soon start organising protest marches and of course more information and suggestions will be following soon.

WRAP.

John Vialls was assured no details of who printed the leaflets would appear on the leaflets and he waited for the information from Turhan-Cooper from where to collect the leaflets. In the meantime Vialls decided not to shave and commenced growing a beard and as an extra precaution he also had some very large and picturesque transfers of the female form pasted on his forearms to act as tattoos, which would divert people's eyes. He also fixed false number plates on the Horse Box he would be using.

When the day arrived to collect the leaflets from the printers Vialls was very scruffily dressed and departing at 7am he drove the hundred plus miles to Driftton. Pulling into the printers yard Vialls parked and lowered the tailboard to allow easy access and while pulling on some surgical gloves he made his way to the office where on entry he was asked how they could help and he responded by handing over a yellow disc which indicated the WRAP leaflets. Within a minute a fork lift was lifting the boxes of leaflets into the Horsebox and during the process Vialls checked that the leaflets did not indicate who the printers were. Within twenty minutes the loading was completed and satisfied all was secure Vialls returned to the farm where he began planning the delivery of boxes of leaflets to inner circle members.

Nobby Watson was the first to be issued with leaflets and balloons and he collected them when he met Vialls in the car park at Maiden Castle, in Dorset where sixty thousand leaflets, were loaded into his Range Rover. When the transferring of the boxes was completed they covered at some depth almost every square inch of the vehicle. This process was repeated over a period of two weeks in several places around the country.

When it was confirmed all the leaflets had been received Turhan-Cooper gave the order for them to be distributed. Many methods were used ranging from two private aircraft flying at night scattering almost two hundred thousand leaflets over northern towns. A selection of the black balloons scattered thousands of leaflets in the London area and the same applied for Portsmouth and Southampton. A couple of the balloons intended for Portsmouth or Southampton or the Isle of Wight ended up in France and a week or so later the French press began asking questions. While other leaflets were scattered from cars travelling through towns and villages at night and in the Bristol area leaflets were scattered from a couple of Hot Air Balloons floating peacefully over the West Country. The distribution of leaflets was completed in five days and immediately reactions began to rock the media into establishing who or what WRAP really was. As a consequence the media immediately connected WRAP with the removal of the stones at Stonehenge as a method of gaining publicity.

The media coverage became hectic and within a month many more thousands of leaflets were distributed around the country and questions were being asked in the House of Commons. The parliamentary questions were brought about because leaflets were being read by millions of people around the world as a result of being published on various internet sites. The questions being asked in the Commons concerned finding out whom or what is WRAP and what were its intentions. The Member of Parliament who asked the questions received the following letter addressed to them in the House of Commons.

Dear Sir / Madam,

The intentions of WRAP are to instigate a Coup unless of course you the incumbent Members of Parliament can *sort out the mess you have created.*

WRAP

In fact whenever a question was asked concerning the movement the person or organization that asked the question received the same note. Whenever a note was received it was handed to the Police to carry out various types of forensic tests and to date nothing had been discovered that would be of assistance.

Then something happened which eventually shook the whole political establishment to the core and it was due to a couple of ex Special Forces men who were operating under the control of Nobby Watson. These men had taken it upon themselves to closely monitor several MP's to establish their habits, routines and mannerisms. Having spent several months covering every conceivable aspect, they then asked Nobby if they could set up a snatch squad. After the proposal was brought to Nobby Watson's attention, he broached the subject with George Turhan-Cooper and much to his surprise TC gave permission to make plans to carry out a snatch.

Nobby Watson with the others then spent several more weeks visiting the constituencies of Colmbrag, Pipestag, Ivorygreen, Emmsime and West Tersity and although widely dispersed they checked and re-checked every conceivable aspect concerning the proposed targets. While checking they discovered it was possible to set a clock by the accuracy of the targets habits and routines. The most worrying aspect to the highly trained men, who were carrying out the observations, was the targets over confidence. In short the targets did not have the faintest idea about personal security or the slightest idea they were being monitored. During their surveillance the men established home addresses, telephone numbers both static and mobile even those that were ex directory. Their railway journeys, vehicle makes and numbers and the routes they habitually took were all recorded. Plus they and their homes and the immediate areas surrounding the homes had all been photographed.

On the chosen evening for the snatches the groups of men who were to carry out the tasks were fully equipped and had every possible aspect covered. The five selected targets were because of their habits easy to follow and because of the routines they unknowingly adhered too, they arrived at their respective railways stations at precisely the times forecast. Once onboard the trains each target settled into their first class compartment and seemingly relaxed. The individual snatch member on each train used their mobile telephones when they reached specific points on the journeys. Of course they did not speak but after dialling the number they tapped the telephone with a coin twice to indicate all was running to schedule.

At each of the railway stations the targets would arrive at other snatch team members were waiting in cars or using a motorcycle, that would be used to follow the targets taxies and the bus one of them caught. How would they identify the target? When the target left the train and entered the station forecourt and made for the well illuminated exit, the man directly behind the target wearing a brilliant red cap and pointing was the indicator. When the targets left by taxi and by bus for their homes shrouded by the night, they were followed. As the journeys progressed the mobile telephones were again used with three taps to indicate all was progressing according to plan.

The MP for Colmbrag who caught the bus adhered to his established routine and popped into a public house for a quick tipple. On leaving the pub and after walking less than one hundred yards, in partial lighting a technique for disarming a sentry was used. The only modification was instead of crushing the targets testicles with a full blooded kick as he toppled forward, they used another technique. Within seconds he was handcuffed, gagged and sacked up and he and his briefcase were inside a car and being driven away. While in the back of the vehicle the MP suffered the effects of crashing face first against the pavement when his ankles were ripped away, It only takes one man to implement the technique and it was used without a single scream, shout or any effort to resist against all the targets.

The MP's for West Tersity and Ivorygreen were overpowered after they paid for their taxis and were in the process of opening the gates at the start of drives of their homes. The MP for Pipestag was snatched just short of his front door by men coming out of the shadows and the MP for Emmsime was overpowered in the stairwell of a block of flats. To snatch the five targets a total of twenty five men were used, one man on each train, whose job was to identify the target, who then joined the men with the cars and motorcycle on arrival at the targets rail destination. Four car drivers and one motorcyclist and the five unarmed combat experts who overpowered the targets, the reaming men then helped with picking up and thrusting the battered targets into vehicles.

When the last vehicle arrived at the old agricultural workshop facilities in the grounds of College House, it was three o'clock in the morning. The MP's had suffered almost continuous verbal abuse while restrained on the journey and when they arrived they were dragged out of the vehicles. When dragged and prodded into the pitch black outbuilding, when the sacks were ripped off their heads, the MP's were confused by the total darkness. Taken one at a time into another room that was well lit, each MP was searched and anything found inclusive of watches and mobile phones were removed, then each was forced to strip off their outer clothing. After their outer clothing was removed inclusive of shoes and socks and placed in a plastic bag they were escorted to a darkened room. When a light was switched on, the MP's suffered severe shock on recognising the blood stained partially battered faces of the almost naked fellow politicians. Entering the room Nobby Watson dressed totally in black, looked at the MP's and said through his balaclava, 'good morning gentlemen tomorrow you will be tried for incompetence and sentenced.'

As Nobby Watson turned away five men dressed from head to toe in black, brought in five folding chairs and reams of rope. Unfolding the chairs they then forced each MP onto a chair and physically restrained them with rope. With the MP's secured the men left the room and then they returned and threw buckets of cold water over them. After pulling the sacks back over their heads, one of the men then turned on several hours of repetitive Chinese music.

When George Turhan-Cooper paid a visit at 0600 hrs the only sound he could hear after the Chinese music was turned off, was grunting, coughing and sobbing. Three MP's were sobbing because having wriggled and struggled against the restraints, the chairs had toppled over and they had hit the concrete floor, where they were left in pain, wet, cold and uncomfortable. It was all just too much for T.C. and turning to one of the guards he said, 'they are remarkably quiet for people who are normally so vociferous.'

As a result of what he had seen, on returning to the house T.C. contacted Vialls for suggestions that would frighten the life out of the MP's. Over the telephone Vialls suggested with his interest in Herpetology or the scientific study of reptiles and amphibians, the MP's should be pitted. Once Vialls was informed they were about to be pitted he said he would visit a friend and obtain some snakes to use in the pits.

A couple of hours later while still restrained and attached to the chairs the MP's where carried out of the building and lowered into two pits containing a couple of inches of cow and pigs dung. After being left for an hour or so to contemplate their situation while inhaling the smell, the sacks were suddenly removed which allowed them to study their predicament. A little time later the gags were removed and that was mainly so the men in black could study the MP's reactions when they were able to speak.

Nobby Watson returned to the building that had once been an agricultural workshop containing a series of inspection pits which were being utilised to contain the MP's. On arrival Nobby looked into the pits and was seen and although he could not be identified as he was dressed from head to toe in black, he heard the MP for Pipestag shouting.

'I need to use a toilet.'

Nobby took a deep breath while thinking the media will be looking for all sorts of angles and then he said, 'welcome to the real world, no chance of using a toilet here, so you can mess yourselves, as you have messed the public about.' Then Nobby heard the MP for West Tersity shouting, 'my suit was ruined and I'm also hungry and thirsty,'

'Tough luck,' replied Nobby, 'you are overweight and it will do you good.'

The MP for Ivorygreen shouted, 'why are we here and who are you?'

Nobby replied, 'you can shout as loud and as long as you like. You have been snatched to stand trial for the broad spectrum political and financial mismanagement that has caused the population stress and misery.'

'What about our Briefcases, Mobile phones and other person effects?' questioned the MP for Emmsime.

'Some very interesting reading in the Briefcases and the contents of your wallets was even better. Particularly as you and your fellow Parliamentarians think you are a new fully protected untouchable Aristocracy. But we the Serfs have proved differently. Believe me you are going to suffer. Who are we? That would be telling! Some of you are bloodied, you are restrained, unshaved, dishevelled and your expensive underwear will be soiled. Oh yes and you stink beyond imagination and you will spend hours shivering and moaning. Rest assured we are experts, trained at great expense to resolve problems. To date you are by far the biggest problems we have ever dealt with.' Turning away Nobby Watson said to one of the guards, 'cover them up,' Nobby then watched as several dozen short planks were slotted into place over the pits and then he watched sheets of canvas with large holes in to allow air to seep through being spread over the planks. When the canvas was in place two vehicles were then driven in and parked over the pits.

As Nobby moved to speak with one of the attendant guards he heard the sounds of coughing and retching coming from the pits and then he whispered, 'uncover them in six hours.'

TWENTY

Early the following morning Vialls shaved and removed the transfers of naked women from his forearms as he had no intention of returning to the printers. A couple of hours later, he removed the false number plates and put the original plates back on the horsebox. After which he drove the farm Landrover to a Herpetologist friend. Where he spent several enjoyable hours looking at and handling various reptiles and as a result, he purchased two North American Mud Snakes (*Farancia abacura*) each being about six feet in length. These snakes are black and orange with smooth shiny skin and Vialls selected them because they are aquatic and accustomed to living in swamps and marshes. After placing the snakes into a large transparent plastic tank he'd brought with him, Vialls then returned home.

In the evening Vialls turned on the Television and was immediately engrossed by the news concerning five missing Members of Parliament who were named as James Mandrake-Porter, Scot Calipure, Peter Lambridge, David Pitcairn, and George Petherton, representing the constituencies of Colmbrag, Pipestag, Ivorygreen, Emmsime and West Tersity. Three of the missing MP's were apparently millionaires and either Lawyers or Solicitors. One of them was a Chartered Accountant involved with Merchant Banking and another had been involved in the Adverting Industry. There was a great deal, of media speculation and assumption associated with the news. However, one item of the news focused his attention and that concerned the police making a request for anyone who may have witnessed anything to come forward, as they were offering a substantial reward. Early the following morning after a good night's sleep, Vialls not being a person who regularly bought newspapers, drove to Yeovil, where he purchased a selection. On returning to the farm he focused his attention on reading virtually every article relating to the missing MP's.

Although engrossed in the various articles Vialls was acutely aware of the difficulty associated with believing everything reported, as news hounds and others sometimes massage facts to suit the situation. In particular he recalled the story concerning a woman rescued during the Iraq war. The news mentioned a brave woman defending herself until she ran out of ammunition and when captured, she was beaten and raped. The press said, when the rescue mission was underway they came under intense fire and after retaliating they carried out a frantic search, eventually locating the woman after which they carried her to safety. The truth was much different to the articles generated by the press. As Vialls was aware, the woman did not fire a weapon, she was not beaten or raped and she actually received care and attention from Iraqi Doctors and Nurses. The rescue force landed unchallenged and did not fire a shot and in fact Iraqi Hospital Staff showed the soldiers where she was and even helped to move her to a waiting helicopter. Added to which in the past Vialls wondered on whose side the BBC really was on - particularly as they are funded by the public. Although WRAP, was frequently mentioned, on completion of his analyses Vialls was convinced nobody had any idea who carried out the snatch. Particularly as the politicians had been snatched from all over the country and nobody had a clue about where the missing politicians could be located, inclusive of trying to establish contact by their mobile phones, which were obviously switched off.

During the hours the Politicians were confined under the planks, canvas and vehicles, the sounds of pleading, grunts, groans and moans emanating from the pits were continuous. When Nobby Watson arrived at the end of the six hour period and the Politicians were being uncovered, the first thing he registered was the overwhelming smell of vomit. On the strength of that he decided it was time to up the pressure and then Peter Lambridge the MP for Ivorygreen looked directly at Nobby and mumbled, 'why are you doing this to us?'

'Because you are Politicians and if you think this is tough, think again.'

Peter Lambridge replied, 'we are up to our ankles in animal excrement.'

'That makes a change, as you are normally full of money grabbing crap.'

Satisfied with the situation, Nobby turned away and left the building to drive to College House. In the lounge Turhan-Cooper was watching the news and as a result of what he was hearing and seeing he was determined to visit the printers to ensure they maintained their silence. While making his mind up to pay them a substantial reward for maintaining complete silence, he heard the front door bell ringing. Opening the substantial door he waved Nobby Watson in and indicated for him to enter the lounge, where Nobby updated him on the progress so far. When Nobby left, T.C. then contacted Vialls and after talking with Vialls he decided to visit the printers.

During the time Vialls was preparing to visit the agricultural workshop, Turhan-Copper had made arrangements to meet the owner of the printers. While discussing the situation without mentioning the leaflets or WRAP on the telephone, he found out it was the owner and two other men after normal working hours, who produced the leaflets. Satisfied silence would be maintained, when he arrived at the printers, he handed the owner a cheque for one hundred thousand pounds to ensure silence. The shocked yet delighted owner said he would pay the two men twenty five thousand pounds each to maintain silence.

Arriving at the agricultural workshops carrying two canvas bags Vialls was greeted by Nobby Watson and after putting the bags down; he was given a black Balaclava by Nobby to hide his identity. As he was putting on the Balaclava Nobby said, 'what is your intention?'

While picking up the bags Vialls replied, 'to frighten the life out of them.'

'Sounds good to me,' replied Nobby slinging a camera over his shoulder.

As they approached the area containing the pits Vialls detached an appalling stench and then he heard strange noises. What he heard was in fact a couple of the Politicians retching, coughing, and moaning while another appeared to be sobbing. Creeping to within a couple of feet of the first pit on all fours to avoid detection, Vialls then untied one of the bags and eased the snake over the side into a pit. The reaction of the Politicians as the snake slid over the edge was explosive, as they screamed and struggled against their restraints and threshed their feet and ankles in the dung, while pleading for help. Stepping forward Nobby began taking photos of the struggling Politicians and then Scot Calipure the MP for Pipestag screamed, 'why are you taking photos?'

'To send pictures of you weak kneed pathetic Politicians to the press.'

Standing up so he would be seen, Vialls watched a snake with its tongue flicking, slithering onto the lap of Peter Lambridge the MP for Ivorygreen and then the snake started to slither up his body. When the snake reached his right shoulder the overweight Politician was terrified and as the snake began to slither around his neck and up his left cheek, he was sweating profusely and shaking like a leaf. When the snake hissed in his ear Peter Lambridge fainted and as his body slouched forward, the snake fell off and slithered towards James Mandrake-Porter.

Satisfied with the effect, Vialls released the second snake into the other pit and the reactions of David Pitcairn could only be described as cool, while George Petherton's reactions were explosive by comparison, with Petherton's maniacal screams and shouts for help filling the building. Looking up at Vialls as the snake slithered onto his lap and started up his chest, George Petherton hysterically screamed, 'save me save me.'

Looking down at him Vialls replied almost shouting, 'no chance.'

As the snakes slithered around the pits passing over the laps, chests and heads of the Politicians the screams reached a crescendo. Looking into the pits Vialls could see the snakes had achieved the desired affect. The wide eyed look of terror on the faces of the Politicians and the perspiration bubbling on their foreheads indicated success. During the process Nobby Watson who had openly laughed at the spectacle, had taken photos that would be loaded onto a computer before being reproduced and sent to whomever T.C. thought appropriate.

Satisfied with the result achieved Vialls recovered the snakes, by leaning over the edge of the pits and lifting them off the bodies of couple of the Politicians. Equally satisfied with the photo shoot Nobby instructed a couple of the guards to throw buckets of water over the Politicians, which they carried out with a certain amount of pleasure. The effects of the water were later enhanced by the cold wind wafting around the agricultural buildings, causing further discomfort and uncontrollable shivering. Added to which the whole operation would amount to nothing if they did not start the next phase soon.

Having not eaten or drunk anything for over twenty four hours, the Politicians were dragged and carried one at a time from the pits into a warm room. Where the restraints were removed and the chairs were taken away. Each MP was then ordered to strip. Each flatly refused and tried to buck the system while subjecting the men in black to a barrage of verbal protests concerning, Grievous Bodily Harm, Torture, Human Rights and Political Correctness. Ignoring the threats the men in black overpowered each Politician and quickly stripped them and while laughing at their blotted bodies they forced each into a room containing buckets of warm water, soap and towels. While being forced into the room Peter Lambridge shouted, 'you people are primeval.' While the Politicians attempted to clean the filth off their bodies, their soiled underwear was partially cleaned by the men in black. After trying to wash themselves from a bucket, each MP was allowed to put on their wet, stained and dung splattered underwear and given back their socks. After which each was offered food and water, before each was separately locked into a secure room.

Several hours later, the Politicians outer clothing was returned and after dressing the MP's were brought one at a time from the secure room and once again restrained. This time masking tape was used to cover the MP's eyes and than a blindfold was used followed by a black bag being pulled over each MP's head. When this was completed each Politician was carried out to a specific vehicle and forced onto the rear seat, where they were covered by blankets. After which each MP was taken for a lengthy drive which was intended to disorientate them before being brought back to College House. On their return each was guided out of the vehicle he'd been in and eased onto a stretcher by four men where they were once again restrained. The men in black then carried each stretcher into the house and down the flights of steps to the underground briefing room. When the restraints were removed from the stretchers each Politician was guided to a front row seat where they were left, watched over by men in black until all five were present.

Although still restrained when the black bags, blindfolds and the masking tape was removed there was an air of total bewilderment when they saw fellow Politicians sat alongside them in the brightly illuminated room. While nervously and suspiciously looking around, they all saw the stage, lectern and about twenty men in black lurking in the room. Not having the slightest idea where they were, or why they were in the brightly illuminated room, they were amazed when a large Teddy Bear walked across the stage to the lectern accompanied by a large Penguin. In fact Turhan-Cooper was the Teddy Bear and Professor Hector Hicks was the Penguin.

Turhan-Cooper was the first to speak and the well modulated voice emanating from the Teddy Bear said, 'good evening gentlemen and apart from looking scruffy, no doubt you are wondering why you have been treated in such a way and wondering why you have been brought here? You will undoubtedly be interested to learn every man in this room has undergone similar if not even tougher treatment. The conclusion we have reached from the information obtained so far confirms you are overweight, weak kneed pathetic specimens of trough snuffling money grabbing political nonsense. In a nutshell there is not a leader amongst you.' Turning away from the lectern the Teddy Bear, indicated for the Penguin to take its place at the lectern.

Arriving at the lectern the first words from the beak of the Penguin were.

'You can release their arms.'

From the lectern H.H. watched men in black releasing the arms of the politicians who were then allowed a couple of minutes to stretch and move their arms vigorously. Satisfied at the result H.H. then said while pointing his right flipper, 'you may participate by asking questions.' The first question was not a surprise when Scot Calipure said, 'why were we kidnapped?'

Hector Hicks replied, 'recently you received letters from an organisation know as WRAP. Perhaps you also recall the press coverage concerning the recent episode at Stonehenge. You are being addressed by members of WRAP and before you ask, we will not divulge who WRAP is.'

'So why were we kidnapped? questioned Scot Calipure.

'To protest against the quality of Members of Parliament, as there appears to be nobody in government with proven leadership qualities. Once upon a time politicians dealt with problems and resolved them. Now politicians appear determined only to look after themselves by lining their pockets. The public is hacked off by you and the way the country is being manipulated by a group of inexperienced do gooders. Incidentally, we have proved beyond any doubt that you are all extremely unfit and beyond pathetic.'

'We were tortured,' shouted George Petherton.

'How many people have you seen beheaded? How many women have you seen stoned to death for virtually nothing?

How many people have you seen hanging from traffic lights or from motorway bridges? My guess is never or none as you have absolutely no worldly experience. A slap on the face is regarded as torture by you specimens. Believe me if we wished to torture you we have the expertise. At worst you have been slightly inconvenienced and that is nothing to what is likely to happen should we decide you deserve special treatment.'

The most vociferous was Peter Lambridge who almost screamed, 'I'm a Lawyer and when I find out who is responsible for what has occurred action will be taken.'

In response the Penguin replied, 'so you are a Lawyer and then David Pitcairn who was sitting next to Lambridge was heard by the Penguin saying, 'for Gods sake shut up.'

From the lectern H.H. said, 'Lawyers are fleas on the back of humanity who enjoy sucking every ounce of blood that can be obtained. Particularly since instigating the compensation culture, which is so prevalent now. You are nothing but a narrow minded, ill informed, inexperienced, uneducated individual!'

'I'll have you know I went to Oxford University.

'Precisely my point, Mr Lambridge, you are uneducated and arrogant, with little if any real work experience except, School, University and Parliament.

'So what about your standard of education?' responded Lambridge

'H.H, replied, 'I attended a superior University, compared to where was it? Oh yes, Oxford, that urban establishment.'

'Where is superior to Oxford?' shouted Lambridge

'We require MP's who are not the horses pulling the party cart, MP's who are familiar with hard physical work and don't try and swing the lead while claiming various expenses. You are there to serve the people not rip them off.'

'Where is superior to Oxford? Shouted Lambridge once again.

'When will you liberal thinking bunch of greedy millionaires be prepared to provide the working class with a fair deal. If you stop shouting at me I may divulge where. But first of all you types had better realise winning as a nation is extremely important. The present philosophy of just taking part is not important. In international affairs there's no such thing as a friendly competition. For your information, it's a winner takes all and a no holds barred environment. You liberal thinking do gooders are determined to ban all forms of competition. When will you realise there are winners and losers across the board in every aspect of life? At the moment to emphasis the situation you are big time losers. So realise whether it concerned taking the old eleven plus to go to grammar school or passing the Common Entrance to attend a Public School. Or passing the required A Level grades to enter Cambridge or even Oxford. The whole of life is competitive. Can you remember the school sports? Were you determined to win? As opposed to taking part, which is very much the modern attitude. You people need to wake and get realistic. Stop trying to protect everyone. You should know a minority will always be academically superior. While the majority of the public are skilled in practical hands on subjects. Even you Mr Lambridge will obtain the services of a tradesman for various tasks which are beyond you. Oh yes, I almost forgot to mention, I graduated from Kings College, Cambridge.'

James Mandrake-Porter then said, 'politically we are heading in the right direction by embracing multi culturalism.'

'Really, inclusive of allowing Sharia law in this country.'

'The government stands for traditional British values.'

'Just like we used to have, I don't think so,' replied H.H adding, 'the German's have said Multi Culturalism does not work as immigrants endeavor set up a separate culture within the host nation. While there are idealistic idiots in Parliament there is little chance of restoring British Culture as the predominant culture on this Island. What chance do we the British people have in the watered down multi culturalism prevalent at the moment? How are we protected? What about Democratic principals?

David Pitcairn then said, 'What exactly do you people want?'

'We will let you know in due coarse. However we need to get several points over and the first one is the electoral procedure. Not one of you has been elected by a clear overall majority in your constituency. Yes, you were elected on a first past the post majority. However if all the votes cast against you for other parties and the people who although registered to vote, did not vote were added up? The result indicates not one of you is a true representative of your constituency. Further more not one of you was born and brought up in the constituency you represent, you are imports. The system requires updating.'

'But that is the present system,' responded a calm David Pitcairn.

'Asylum seekers claim benefits and in some instances they immediately begin to undermine the country. For instance Islam is seeking more religious rights at the expense of our Christian rights. This is a Christian country and our rights were achieved over centuries as a result of war, hardship, death and sacrifice. We have fought two world wars in the name of democracy. Our rights have been hard won. But now our rights are being stretched by anyone with the ability to beg for benefits when they arrive here. You are the people who are supposed to represent the population in Parliament and you appear blinded by your own greed. You most certainly don't appear to care about the how consequences affect the public. There are a couple of million unemployed and yet foreigners are allowed to arrive and many immediately claim benefits.'

'But that is the system in force,' responded James Mandrake-Porter.

H.H. replied, 'It is glaringly apparent politicians who are supposed to represent the people are extremely soft and not very experienced. I will agree it's not solely your fault, as it concerns the policies of several previous governments.'

Scot Calipure responded to H.H. by saying, 'we are aware of the foreign workers entering the country. We also know many of them claim benefits for children still in their home country. Added to which many obtain unemployment and other supplementary benefits.'

'Well bloody well get something done about it,' shouted the Teddy Bear while walking to the centre of the stage. While stood staring down at the MP's. Turhan-Cooper said, 'governments over generations have spent irrationally and some of the money spent on overseas development has been wasted. We just don't understand why we give ridiculous amounts of money to other countries when we can't fully afford to look after our own people and country. Particularly when the next government to be elected, then has to sort the mess out, the previous government caused due to financial mismanagement. Then the previous government then concentrates on lambasting the incumbent government for endeavouring to sort out the budget deficit caused by them. No logic to it and the financial balance is wrong and as a consequence thousand of jobs are lost. Once again the public suffers due to the gross mismanagement and lack of understanding of the elected politicians.'

David Pitcairn a Chartered Accountant involved within the world of merchant banking said, 'the current financial situation has been partially brought about due to disorganized procurement programmes coupled to the Banking Industry. When the government is involved contracts are negotiated, that sometimes; benefit people with a more than a vested interest. Some former politicians are employed by some of these investment companies and as a result they have settled into a routine for earning copious amounts of money. Sometimes warnings have been issued, which have been ignored until its too late and then the government bales out the Banking Industry. Banks have spent far too much money on inferior goods when alternatives were readily available.'

H.H. responded by saying, 'the financial situation has become critical and somewhat farcical. With the current state of affairs it is once again the serfs who are going to suffer while Bankers make large profits and get massive bonuses. Why? Maybe in years to come the economy could become like that of Germany in the nineteen thirties and we might require a wheel barrow to collect our pay.'

Walking to the centre of the stage another man appeared who was dressed from head to toe in black including a balaclava and this man was in fact Nobby Watson. Looking down on the politicians he said, 'enough of this nonsense, so there are financial problems. So why do we spend millions of pounds each year keeping convicted killers alive and well? Believe me the majority of people in this country are in favour of capital punishment. Five pounds for a rope that can be used several times is infinitely cheaper than keeping convicted killers alive.'

Peter Lambridge responded by saying, 'in the past errors have occurred that involved executing an innocent individual.'

'So what?' replied Nobby adding, 'the police work hard to catch criminals and then unfortunately the courts, probation services and others fall over themselves to obtain a minimum sentence. Some people who are fined are on the dole and only pay a few pence a week. All sentences should be severe and time in prison should immediately register. It should severe enough to convince criminals not to commit further crimes that would send them back to prison.'

'What do you know about prison? Asked George Petherton.

'I've spent twenty years in prison and speak from first hand experience and believe me, time in prison is nowhere near tough enough.'

'You have spent twenty years in prison.'

'Yes,' replied Nobby not intending to say he was a retired Prison Officer.

Noting a potential situation arising Turhan-Cooper said, 'tell me why when dealing with the financial situation affecting the government which is passed onto the public. Why don't wage constraints start with MP's? If the workers are going to loose money so can the Members of Parliament. Wage cuts and job losses must be seen to start at the top i.e. in Parliament.'

'Why should we suffer?' shouted Peter Lambridge.

'Because you must lead by setting a positive example.'

'That is nonsensical,' responded George Petherton.

'Mr Petherton it is precisely because of that type of attitude why you were selected for the re-education programme being carried out here. Believe me if you persist in your nonsensical way, you will suffer.'

Peter Lambridge then said, 'As a Member of Parliament I'm a member of a national management team and as such we are guided to do the very best for the country. We try to listen to the people but in all honesty it's a waste of time they are mostly out of touch. Can you imagine trying to deal with elements of the population that get as drunk as possible using their benefits? What about the young men fathering as many children as possible without fear of having to pay a penny for their keep? What about those who go on holiday to Spain or wherever and act the drunken hooligan just to maintain British values. Or when drunk in this country they urinate on War Memorials and if apprehended they scream they are being molested. Indicating to me anyway large sections of the population are generally a total waste of time.'

Looking towards Lambridge the teddy Bear said, 'now we understand why you are a millionaire Lawyer.' Turning to face Nobby Watson, the Teddy Bear pointed its right paw at the Lambridge and Nobby understood this as a signal to remove him from the meeting. Looking up at Nobby several men in black received a signal from Nobby and pounced and within seconds Lambridge was bound, gagged and bagged up and restrained on a stretcher. As they started to leave the briefing room everyone heard the Teddy Bear say, 'tree him.'

Which prompted Mandrake-Porter to shout, 'All 'MP's work very hard at trying to maintain a healthy country and protecting the people while endeavouring to concentrate on matters that are really important.'

'What about the fiddles carried out by MP's?' asked the Teddy Bear.

'So what is so wrong with MP's protecting themselves and their future?

The Penguin responded by saying, 'So what ever happened to leading by setting a good example or is it just a question off MP's screwing the taxpayer for as much as possible. Or could your motivation be even simpler inasmuch as MP's take all they can grab and give nothing back?'

Moving to the lectern the Teddy Bear said, 'We have one more subject to raise which involves the European Union. Could you explain why we spend millions of pounds a day on maintaining out link with what in many instances can only be termed as ancient almost traditional enemies? The British people were tricked by parliamentarians into joining the European Union and you don't have to be the brightest star in the sky to see what is happening. Initially we joined a trading association and now its turning quite rapidly into a United States of Europe and very soon the there will be a President of Europe who has the power to act just like the President of the USA. A single overload that will have total control over Europe, which means the Queen or future King and Parliament and the British style of Democracy will controlled by a foreigner and become obsolete.'

David Pitcairn said, 'that is a situation that really worries me.'

George Petherton responded by saying, 'Europe is the most dynamic thing that could possibly happen to this staid old fashioned country. Think of the great possibilities that will arrive on our door step and what great advantages this country will gain.'

The Penguin looked down on Petherton and said, 'you are a total fool and symptomatic of the inherent politics of the country. The best way of describing your views is. You have not the faintest idea. Competitive advantage must be gained and it's the trade of this country and its people that matters. Not your utter bunkum. You are an unmitigated fool.'

Moving to the centre of the stage the Teddy Bear said, 'we are about to release you. We wish to stress this. We are providing you lesser specimens with an opportunity to sort out the mess inflicting this country. We will be following your every action very closely and believe this. Should you not knock yourselves out to get the message over too improve the situation relevant to the Island we live and work on there will be a Coup. The sign that will signify a Coup is underway will be the breaking of the sound barrier over Parliament. That should blow a few windows out and clear the cobwebs away. 'Pointing at the MP's the Teddy Bear continued by saying, 'Restrict them totally and you know what I mean and then deposit them.' As he began to move away across the stage the Teddy Bear watched the men in black begin restraining the MP's.

TWENTY ONE

The men in black quickly restrained the MP's and lifted the four stretchers up the stairs and carried them outside. Then after easing the stretcher restraints the MP's who were still restrained were placed on the rear seats of the vehicles and covered in blankets. On completion of that their personal belongs such as watches, wallet, mobile phones and briefcases were placed in the vehicle.

After about two hours of driving in various directions the vehicles stopped and the men in black pulled the politicians out and tied them to solid objects such as roadside trees. Their personal affects were secured in the briefcases which were handcuffed to the MP's ankles. The fifth man Peter Lambridge who had been treed, which meant being tied to a tree and soaked frequently with water was dealt with somewhat differently a couple of days later.

The first of the four politicians to be discovered was James Mandrake-Porter and he was found by a farmer driving a tractor in country lane between Droxford and Soberton in Hampshire. Seeing a figure wearing a black bag over its head tied to a tree the farmer a keen wildlife photographer who had a camera with him, immediately took some pictures from the cab of the tractor. Climbing down from the cab he said, 'are you still alive?'

A muffled voice replied, 'yes'

Removing the bag followed by the blindfold and the masking tape the farmer then set about untying the ropes and released a grateful Mandrake-Porter. The only minor problem was the briefcase that had been handcuffed to his right ankle without a means of releasing the handcuffs. While sitting on the right rear mudguard of the tractor Mandrake-Porter was taken through some narrow lanes to the farm. On arrival the farmer helped Mandrake-Porter into the house, where almost immediacy he was given a cup of tea by the farmer's wife who said, 'my goodness your face is battered.'

Greatly appreciating the cup of tea he replied, 'I was tripped up hitting the pavement with my face when kidnapped, 'my name is James Mandrake-Porter and I'm the Member of Parliament for Colmbrag.'

The farmers' wife suddenly exclaimed, 'Oh my God, you are one of those missing MP's who have filled the papers, radio and television news. 'So while you are at my mercy. Why did over a hundred politicians quit and not seek re-election at the last election? Was it due to being accused of fiddling expenses? From my observations parliament has now become an expensive farce. The benches appear to be filled by over six hundred overpaid underachieving freaks.'

Acutely embarrassed by the tirade and feeling exposed, it suddenly dawned on Mandrake-Porter that many of the public really detested MP's. Not wishing to upset the farmer's wife, Mandrake-Porter decided to swallow his pride and remained silent. Deciding to retrieve his mobile phone from the briefcase handcuffed to his right ankle, he had to struggle to open the briefcase. With the phone in his hand he quickly discovered the Battery and Sim card had been removed. Laughing at the problem he then said, 'could I use your telephone?'

'Of course,' replied the farmer's wife, 'I'll fetch it for you.'

On receiving the telephone Mandrake-Porter telephoned his wife who immediately broke down on recognising her husband's voice. 'How are you? Are you now free as they said you had probably been kidnapped?

'Yes I have been freed virtually unharmed and in all honesty I have learnt a great deal.' After providing the farms telephone number and address to his wife, who then provided the details to the police. Mandrake-Porter as a result was picked up by a police car about half and hour later. When in the care of the police he was asked innumerable question none of which he could answer. Thankfully the farmer was able to prove a point concerning being blindfolded by providing a couple of the photo's after printing them from his computer.

A Vicar, walking the family dog noticed it barking a great deal and as he approached some sort of apparition located by a jump on Chepstow racecourse the dog urinated on it. It was Scot Calipure who was found tied to a fence on the racecourse. As the Vicar nervously approached he was saying a prayer loud enough for Calipure to hear and when the Vicar said, 'are you still alive?'

He heard a muffled, 'yes.'

After securing the dog to a post by its lead, the Vicar set about releasing whomever. After removing the black bag, blindfold and masking tape and establishing it was a middle aged man, he then said 'who are you?'

'My name is Scot Calipure the Member of Parliament for Pipestag'

Recognising the MP's name from the saturated media coverage of recent days, the Vicar then called his wife on his mobile telephone to prepare her for the arrival of a visitor. Due to the large briefcase handcuffed to Calipure's right ankle the Vicar partially carried him the hundred yards or so to where his car was parked. Having assisted Calipure into the car, the Vicar then collected the dog, a Rhodesian Ridgeback called Dexter. After driving to their house the Vicar went to their garage and brought in a pair of bolt cutters and released the briefcase. After being introduced to the Vicars wife Calipure then found out his Blackberry did not work and he was permitted to telephone his wife who also informed the Police with the details provided.

In the meantime he took a bath and felt much better after disposing of his filthy underwear. Barely fifteen minutes later while having a discussion with the Vicar and his wife, he discovered how massive the media coverage had been concerning the missing MP's. As the minutes passed the Vicar was intrigued to speak with an incumbent MP and he broached the subject of education as he was a school Governor. While talking about the curriculum he said, 'education and in particular history has been watered down and swept aside and I think I'm correct in saying it's no longer a core subject.'

In response Scot Calipure said, 'I have not the faintest idea.'

Continuing the Vicar said, 'How are children supposed to learn about our history and identity? What about learning about the Black Death, which effectively swept away the feudal system? What about the execution of King Charles I which created a Republic overseen by Oliver Cromwell? What about the Industrial Revolution with the construction of canals and railways which greatly advanced industry in this country. I could go on and on concerning immigrants and invaders, from the Saxons to the Normans who conquered us. We fought two world wars and won and now we are being controlled by former enemies, who now run the European Union.'

Feeling uneasy Scot Calipure said, 'we are doing our very best.'

That is nonsensical Mr Calipure as well you know and I think I speak for a large percentage of the public when I say, 'Why are Old Etonian multi-millionaires, involved with running the country. Plus why is money collected from our Taxes being sent to China and India as aid, when both countries are significantly more prosperous than this country.'

'Because they stood for election and were voted into Parliament and we have aid agreements with the nations going back years.'

'Mr Calipure its unmitigated madness as this country should come first.'

'So what are your views concerning drugs.'

'Tell me your views first? Insisted the Vicar, really enjoying himself.'

'The arguments for and against are simple. Is cannabis any more harmful than nicotine or more dangerous than alcohol? If the Government were to legalise the use of Cannabis they would quite probably instigate some rules and regulations appertaining to purity. People use the drug as a form of 'escapism,' akin to cigarettes and alcohol. Not having indulged myself, I'm aware of people who partake regularly and to the best of my knowledge, they are as rational as can be and everyday functioning members of society.'

In response the Vicar said, 'I'm actually aware of several alcoholics who are far removed from being even one percent rational. Hopefully the use of Cannabis will not be legalised by any government as it bad enough it being downgraded. Apparently they said the same thing when prohibition ended in the USA. Many Cannabis users feel bad about their habit - knowing they are breaking the law. Would Government action bring the price down below that of the criminal market therefore making it less profitable for the criminals?'

Only a few minutes later a Police car arrived at the Vicars house and Calipure was taken away for questioning and he could offer nothing to assist the police in the enquiries after explaining his situation. He was very surprised when the police informed him they had absolutely no information about who had snatched them and where they had been held. They new about WRAP but had no idea who or what it was.

The next one to be discovered was found by a soldier who while on leave was taking some exercise in Essex. While jogging near the ruins of Hadleigh Castle not far from Leigh-on-Sea, he decided to look at the ruins. As he went round a corner he saw what to him looked like a prisoner ready for interrogation. Pulling off the black bag and removing the blindfold and masking tape he saw a well restrained middle age man. Not wishing to get involved he decided to leave and as he jogged away he heard the man shouting.

'I'm David Pitcairn the Member of Parliament for Emmsime.'

On hearing the shouts he decided to return, as he was more than aware of the missing MP's from recent media coverage. Picking up the still restrained supposed MP, the soldier who was as strong as a bull hefted the MP over his right shoulder and strode off. On reaching a nearby road the soldier went back a few yards into some trees and eased the MP off his shoulder and propped him against a tree trunk. Looking down at the restrained man the soldier said, 'are you really one of the missing Members of Parliament?'

'Yes, and I would greatly appreciate being released.'

Ignoring the man while using his mobile telephone to call a friend with a Van and after giving the location he said, 'Not so fast mister, my friends and I have some questions we would like to ask you as an MP. A few minutes later a blue Ford Transit arrived and within seconds the MP was picked up and thrust into the rear and driven away. A few minutes later it stopped and picked up two men and a little later it picked up another man and then about a quarter of an hour later the van stopped and parked.

Once the van was parked all those onboard gathered in the rear and looking down at the restricted MP one off then said, ' we have all just returned from six months of operations in Helmand Province Afghanistan and as we have control of you we want to ask some questions.'

'Looking up at the soldiers as he was stretched out on the Van floor David Pitcairn said, 'So how can I be of assistance?'

'When in Afghanistan we suffered regular casualties and IED's were found and detonated almost every day. The operational challenge was clear enough and we survived due our strength, versatility, discipline and organisation. Here at home the situation on the streets would be laughable if it was not so dangerous. Areas of London not very far from here are virtual no go areas. In some areas of the UK there is more trouble on the streets than in Afghanistan. We fought the Taliban and as sure as ice melts in the sun, we would not go anywhere near those areas. So what are you politicians doing about the crime and hostility present on the streets of this country?'

Pitcairn replied, 'it's a financial challenge,'

'Financial challenge my backside, what bloody nonsense you speak.'

Another of the soldiers said, 'It appears as if you are totally out of touch with reality, it's a lack of appropriate punishments. You people are far too soft in your thoughts and actions. You would find public flogging would work. You should invest in suitable equipment to flog offenders.'

'That would infringe their human rights,' replied Pitcairn.

'What utter crap! Let's get rid of this oddity before doing something we would eventually regret.'

'Yes, let's take him to the local Police Station and leave him there.

Driving the few miles to Basildon the Soldiers dropped Pitcairn near the Police Station after freeing him. Struggling inside with the briefcase dragging on the ground, when he reached the reception area Pitcairn proved who he was. When asked how he arrived he stated he was found by some soldiers who dropped him outside. He was unable to answer the innumerable questions concerning what had happened to him, although he stood up for the soldiers.

George Petherton the MP for West Tersity was eventually found totally immobilised securely fastened to a bench in the grounds of Oswestry Rugby club. Several people walked past with their dogs ignoring him thinking it was a prank, although a couple of the dogs spent a penny against his legs. Eventually a young lad riding a bicycle stopped, taking a closer look he noticed the chest raising and falling and then he removed the black bag. After he removed the blindfold and pulled the masking tape off, the man on the bench said, 'will you please tell the police.'

'Yes sir,' replied the lad getting onto his bicycle.

After cycling for about five minutes the young lad saw a parked police car and drawing up alongside the car he got off his cycle and approached the driver's window. Noticing him the driver wound the window down saying, 'yes.'

'There is a man fastened to a bench at the rugby club.'

'Is he alive?'

'Yes sir, I took a black bag of his head and he said get the police.'

'How old are you?'

'I'm twelve years old sir.'

'Are you telling the truth? If we go and its a fib we will arrest you.'

'It's the truth sir.'

'OK well drive down there and we'll see you there.'

Leaving on his bike the lad beat the Police car as he took a short cut and on arrival he found a couple of people talking with the man on the bench. Within a couple of minutes the police car arrived and the officers came over to Petherton and began untying him. While doing this they asked who he was and he gave them all the relevant information. Within seconds one of the officers was on the car radio reporting to HQ they had found the Member of Parliament for West Tersity. Less than five minutes later there were another three police cars and a Police Van on site. A Chief Inspector who was sat talking with George Petherton was satisfied he really was the Member of Parliament and he was also aware of a revolting smell saying, 'have you crapped yourself?'

'Yes, twice and peed in my pants,' replied Petherton.

Wondering what to do with this VIP and acutely aware of the smell wafting from Petherton. Who had admitted crapping in his pants a couple of times The Chief Inspector decided to escort him to the Rugby Club and gave him the opportunity to take his pants off and clean himself in the Club toilets. After cleaning himself up as best he could from the facilities available he returned to the Chief Inspector who escorted him to a police car. While in the police car Petherton emphasised the part the young lad had played and requested he should be rewarded for his efforts. Taken to the area Police Headquarters the first thing Petherton really appreciated was the food and hot drinks made freely available for him.

After the food and drink he was subjected to some very detailed questioning, but like then others he was totally unable to be of any assistance.

Peter Lambridge who had been taken out of the briefing room and treed was well and truly shaken to the core by being tethered to a tree in the open for twenty four hours. During that period around twenty buckets of water were thrown over him. Hungry, thirsty, very wet and tired he was far from happy. Added to which for some unaccountable reason he was utterly convinced he had more than met his match. During the period he had been analysing his verbal behaviour to his captors and the conclusion reached indicated they did not take any notice of anything he said. Their attitude was absolutely alien to him and very annoying as he was completely convinced as a Lawyer he was always right.

Removed from the tree Lambridge was carried on a stretcher into the agricultural building and when released the black bag and blindfold were removed and he was provided with his dry outer clothing and some food and drink. Thereafter he was again blindfolded and hooded and after sitting around for a few minutes he was loaded into a secret compartment with his briefcase and personal effects onto a cattle truck. The driver who had done this before was told to drop him off anywhere that was convenient on his drive to Northern Italy.

When dropped off he was able to remove the hood and blindfold without much effort and as his briefcase was not handcuffed to his ankle he was able to pick it up and open it easily. He had no idea where he was or how long he had been in the vehicle as he had fallen asleep. Removing his watch from the briefcase he at least knew the date and the time now. But he was wondering where he was as the vehicle number plates he could see were different. In fact he had been dropped off and left near Bolzano in Northern Italy and not far from the Austrian, Swiss and Liechtenstein frontiers. After about half an hour of orientating himself he managed to hitch a lift on a lorry going to Innsbruck in Austria and the mountain scenery they passed through was spectacular. The reason for heading for Innsbruck in Austria was he knew it had an airport. Although his Blackberry had been immobilised his Wallet containing Credit Cards and his Passport were all in his Briefcase. While at Innsbruck airport Lambridge indulged in food and drink and thanked himself lucky the UK belonged to the European Union. As although unwashed, unshaved and smelling he did not have the slightest difficulty booking a flight that took him to Amsterdam and from there he flew to Heathrow.

The first thing he did on arrival and clearing immigration at Heathrow was get money from a cash machine and after obtaining change he telephoned his wife. She was so surprised to hear from him as she was convinced he was dead. As he had not been featured in the media scramble when the other MP's had been found and interviewed. She also prepared him to face a media onslaught once they found out he was alive and in one piece.

With all five Members of Parliament present in their constituencies and involved in detailed discussions with their party Agents and others, who mostly failed to fully understand what had occurred. Particularly when the MP's mentioned that they had been informed there was a strong probability of a Coup taking place unless the nation's politicians began sorting out the mess the politicians has caused. When they mentioned the signal for the start of a Coup would be an aircraft breaking the Sound Barrier over the Palace of Westminster it generated howls of laughter and comments such, 'of no chance.'

All the five had been interviewed at length by the police and with the exception of one David Pitcairn they were unable to contribute any positive information. Whereas Pitcairn who was approaching fifty, had when young and impressionable served in the Army and after Sandhurst he was Commissioned into the Parachute Regiment. A little later after wandering over the Brecon Beacons with a heavy Bergan on his back, he spent a couple of years in the Special Forces. When snatched having experienced something similar during training, he recognized the techniques being used and every other aspect of his short internment and interrogation. With the exception of the use of Snakes, to enhance the affect of fear, which he thought was an excellent addition.

When interviewed by the police Pitcairn told them about the use of snakes, however for personal reasons he said absolutely nothing about the fact he thought ex or still serving Special Forces were involved. Due to his background every experience survived was a positive and he'd learnt a great deal about the feelings and reaction of the public concerning Members of Parliament. As a result of the recent experience he was determined to become more involved and out spoken on a multitude of political matters. Added to which he was determined to find out about WRAP.

TWENTY TWO

Three months after the snatches, in the dining room of College House Turhan-Cooper was chairing a meeting of the WRAP Inner Circle. Those present and sat around the large refectory table were Hector Hicks, Nobby Watson, Johnny Mann, Alan Warley, Peter Crawley, John Ballard, Katherine Brennan, Chris Slade, Stanley Clavelshay and John Vialls. A couple of the full Inner Circle were unable to attend and those present were enjoying small talk during a coffee break. Calling them to order Turhan-Cooper said, 'the politicians are acting positively and membership of WRAP is expanding. The expansion is primarily due to the letters sent to politicians being published in the press and discussed in detail on various political programmes on Television. As a result the press frequently reports how active the five snatched MP's have become and recently praised their vocal inputs in the House of Commons. Now you were requested in one way or another to clarify certain aspects of information and of course I'm totally aware we have discussed it previously. Added to which, I will be making notes on specifics as they arise, so let's kick off with you Hector.'

H.H. responded by saying, 'all five MP's when recently interviewed stated they were determined to ensure they understood considerably more about the lower echelons of society in their constituencies.'

'What about you Alan?' asked Turhan-Cooper.

Alan Warley replied, 'politics in its present format is absolutely unsustainable and how many times has the matter of the European Union been raised when talking to people. The public are really worried about the amounts of money the UK pays to the European Union. Particularly since many remember a referendum being mentioned that remains unfulfilled. Was that because the politicians concluded the public would return a resounding NO. I have spoken with people who rather like the European Union, but in all honesty they are a miniscule minority. While a clear majority think we should leave the European Union as quick as possible. Because they think it's a waste of money and effort. Whilst many pensioners fail to understand why we have anything to do with the EU as some Member Nations are traditional enemies of this nation going back hundred's of years. Others were convinced the amounts of money paid by this country to Brussels are ridiculous and many feel the money is being squandered. Then of course other people were not particularly happy because of the Laws and the control being inflicted on the UK from the European Union.'

Looking at Nobby Watson Turhan-Cooper said, 'what's your news?'

Nobby Watson leaned forward saying, 'the EU is influencing everything and everywhere and as a result people are worried about the punishments being handed out in the courts and in particular the sentences for Murderers. When the death sentence was abolished in the mid sixties it was felt the public would only accept a Life Sentence. Since then groups influenced by the EU and others have emerged stating a life sentence is too long as Murderers could be re-educated and therefore they could be released early. While other rock solid people felt they should leave prison in a wooden box. Many older people feel the death sentence should be resurrected as it's a cheaper option than providing three meals a day and television in these economically difficult times.'

Looking at Johnny Mann, Turhan-Cooper said, 'what's you news?'

Johnny Mann replied, 'a significant problem highlighted by the general public, concerns the quality of MP's and the expenses fiddles many have been involved with. What many people require clarified is, were the fiddles due to the way politicians have formulated their methods of claiming without submitting detailed receipts. Many people are also of the opinion MP's should only be able to claim for specific items and services that are clearly listed and nothing else. Many people also felt any MP caught out for whatever should be dealt with in public as they are public servants and the punishments should be severe. By severe many thought a public flogging in Parliament Square should be carried out for only minor offences. More serious infringements should be dealt with in various ways and some of the suggestions are frightening. One suggestion concerned publically cutting off fingers or branding their faces with two inch high letters like MP on both cheeks. Or demolishing their principle house. One suggestion I thought was good concerned banning them for life from holding more than one licence. So if married, no driving, television or whatever and if you have a television licence you can't get married and this would be enforced for their entire lives. Also a licence could not obtained through their wife or family as they would also be banned for life. Most people were saying MP's are elected to serve the people and if they cannot understand that and consider themselves to be superior, then they should be dealt with extremely harshly.'

Pointing at Peter Crawley, Turhan-Cooper said, 'and you news Peter.'

Peter Crawley who had previously expressed concern about drugs and in particular the widespread use of Cannabis, said, 'primarily it's down to nothing more than an individual's will power. Some people thought young people consider it to be normal and the thing to do. When dealing with the hard nosed reality of the situation, it boils down to nothing more than an individual possessing the ability to resist. Plus a significant aspect concerns the lack of parenting skills. Some parents are prepared to explain to their children the problems they face as they grow up. Unfortunately, in this day and age thousands of parents simply do not care what their kids get up too. Serious numbers of people have become dependent on drugs and as a result many are totally unaware to what degree it affects their families. Added to which, the majority of addicts are oblivious to any of the associated problems of being an addict. It is extremely simple to say the best solution is to avoid getting involved with drinking or smoking. In my personal opinion more emphasis should be placed on discouraging people from starting. Some people have mentioned the situation that occurred in Singapore twenty odd years ago when the executions of drug addicts took place.'

Looking at Stanley Clavelshay, Turhan-Cooper said, 'what's your view concerning the matter Stanley?'

Stanley Clavelshay responded by saying, 'drugs have never been a problem in my life. However, becoming an alcoholic reliant on booze is to a certain extent somewhat worse and I speak from personal experience, having suffered drink problems for years. The truth of the matter is, it is extremely difficult for an addict to abstain from drink or drugs unless the addict is motivated to do it and given as in my case, support from my employer. Whatever in my opinion there are far more dangers associated with becoming and alcoholic than with some types of drugs. Mind you other types of drugs cause significantly more problems all round.'

Looking towards Katherine Brenan, Turhan-Cooper who whilst making notes said, 'Katherine you once told me a story about you daughter when she was about eight years old at primary school.'

Katherine Brenan responded by saying, 'when my daughter was young her class was subjected to a talk from a female Police Officer, concerning drugs. When she arrived home she mentioned it to me and she had been deeply affected when told by the officer, drugs were hidden in girl's underwear and another place protected by underwear. When I explained that it was probably true she began crying and felt sick. Incidentally there are many smokers of (tobacco) who never touch Cannabis and there are non smokers of (tobacco) who smoke Cannabis.'

Chris Slade intervened saying, 'what does not help the situation is the utter nonsense spoken by the people dependent on Cannabis. Particularly when they proclaim Cannabis helps pain relief. That is utter bunkum and little more than endeavouring to justify their use. Why would anyone believe such nonsense when superb medications are available on prescription?'

Pointing at John Ballard Turhan-Cooper said, 'what about smoking?'

Ballard responded by saying 'when I arrived at Sandhurst I had never smoked and did not drink. Later however as a Platoon Commander in my battalion, apparently I was the only one who did neither. While in Northern Ireland the solders tried all sorts of tricks to get me smoking, even the driver of an armoured vehicle once asked me to light his cigarette. Of course I lit the cigarette without inhaling. All these aspects of everyday life are down to an individual's will power and ability to refuse to partake in whatever. Even now at my age, I have never smoked, or for that matter consumed more than an occasional beer. In context if I drink a pint of beer a once a month I'm over indulging.'

Pointing at John Vialls Turhan-Cooper said, 'tell us about the problems associated with immigration John.

John Vialls responded by saying, 'what is going on in this country is mind blowing and there is a great deal more to it than filters down to the public. For instance there are around half a million illegal immigrants in the country many of whom are working on the land. We inhabit an overcrowded small island and personally I believe the figures could be significantly greater. Leaning to his right Vialls delved into his briefcase and extracted some papers which he placed on the table and then started to hand around while saying, 'as you know I'm politically right of Genghis Khan and about as religious as horse dung. This paper will go some way to explaining the do gooding attitude of the political establishment of this country. Incidentally it was lifted of the internet in response to a petition.'

As each person received the papers they read the following.

This concerns a petition to 10 Downing Street.

The Government's response to the petition.

Thank you for your e-petition which calls on the Government to stop Islamic immigration.

Sharia law is not part of the law in England and Wales and the Government does not believe that there has been an "encroachment of Islam" upon British society. We are also proud that the UK is a welcoming and tolerant society.

The Government has always said that we would run our immigration system for the benefit of the UK and that is why we introduced a flexible points system which allows the Government to control the numbers of people coming to the UK from outside Europe, and ensuring that immigrants have the skills this country needs. We have already demonstrated that flexibility by putting a stop to low skilled labour entering the UK from outside Europe. We will continue to use the Points Based System (PBS) to ensure that we are doing the right thing for British workers and for the long-term stability of the economy.

In response to the global recession and the downturn that has hit British workers; the Home Secretary announced that from 31 March we will be even more selective in the following key ways:

Strengthening the Resident Labour Market Test (RLMT) for employers with skilled jobs on offer, so employers must advertise them to resident workers through Job Centre Plus before they can bring in a worker from outside Europe. This reinforces Job Centre Plus' active role in matching job vacancies to the skills of the resident population; using the publication of the Shortage Occupation Lists every six months to trigger skills reviews of the jobs on this list, focusing on up-skilling resident workers, making the UK less dependent on migration for the future; and raising the qualifications and salary level for highly skilled migrants to enter the UK through Tier 1 of the Points Based System by requiring a Masters degree and a minimum salary of £20,000.

Over 90 per cent of people working in this country are UK citizens and we are stepping up the help we give to get people the training and support they need to get back to work. Furthermore, given the economic circumstances and the action we are taking to be more selective, we expect the number of migrants coming to the UK from outside the EU to fall during the next financial year. Already the tighter shortage occupation list has meant that there are 200,000 fewer jobs available for non-EU nationals.

The Government is also giving serious consideration to the way people can stay in the UK. The Borders, Citizenship and Immigration Act recently became law and means that newcomers will now have to speak English, pay their way and play by the rules if they want to get on. Crucially, these earned citizenship plans break the automatic link between coming to the UK to work or study and having the right to stay here.

Finally, evidence suggests that most migrants (particularly workers from Eastern Europe and those working in high skilled sectors) are self sufficient, privately housed, employed, contribute to the local economy and don't put any significant pressure on public services. However, there are clearly some demands placed on public services – particularly the number of children in schools and the need for English language provision that result from migration. These needs will be different in different areas according to the number and type of migrants, which is why we need to improve the statistical data available at a local level so that service providers can better anticipate the likely need within their area. Improvements in statistics will also ensure that local government funding reflects changes in population.

The first response came from Hector Hicks who said, 'as has been mentioned we live on a small island and yet we are plagued by illegal immigrants. So how do they get here? There is twenty one miles of sea at our nearest point. Agreed there is a tunnel running underneath. So unless they are entering by boat, swimming or coming by air, they must be coming through the tunnel.'

'Yes,' remarked Johnny Mann adding, 'many of the illegal's are claiming benefits and some are receiving huge amounts of housing benefit because they have large families.'

Hector Hicks continued by saying, 'in my humble opinion our border security is not up to standard. I really think some of the wounded incapacitated soldiers and by that even means those that have lost limbs should be assigned after training to border security. It really cannot be that difficult to seal our borders.'

Looking around the table George Turhan-Cooper said, 'the combination of activities carried out by WRAP so far, have had a positive result. We have gained tremendous publicity and membership is growing. Concerning the membership, please make sure maximum security is carried out concerning everyone who applies to join. Firstly ex service personnel must produce the relevant discharge documents. Then whether they are civilian or ex service they must be known by at least five existing members. Now I suggest we continue observing the five snatched politicians and make it clear to other politicians they will also be snatched and subjected to interrogation if the don't adhere to our suggestions.'

As soon as there was a pause Hector Hicks said, 'on the matter of membership we have one very special applicant by the name of David Pitcairn. Who before entering Parliament served in the Parachute Regiment and the Special Forces. As we know from recent observations he is as tough as they come and is a font of political information, Pitcairn could be extremely useful and I will of course place him under my protective wing being an ex Para myself.'

Looking around the table Turhan-Cooper said, 'that's about it for today and many thanks for attending. You have provided some valuable information to work with. So let's call it a day and go our separate ways. As the members got up and prepared to leave Turhan-Cooper said, 'and we won't be breaking the sound barrier over the Palace of Westminster yet.'

After everyone had left Turhan-Cooper was sat enjoying a cup of tea when the telephone rang. Picking it up he was astounded to hear the Dutch accent of Tom Rosecrans saying, 'I will be coming over to College House tomorrow as there have been some extremely good diamond sales recently and I have some money for you.'

'You are more than welcome,' replied Turhan-Cooper.

The following morning just after midday Rosecrans arrived with Ep Vanderveen and after being ushered into the lounge and making themselves comfortable Rosecrans said, 'you will undoubtedly be interested in the amount of money we are about to give you. Incidentally all the commissions have been covered and this is the net amount.'

'How much,' enquired Turhan-Cooper bursting with curiosity.

While removing a cheque from his wallet Rosecrans said as he handed it to Turhan-Cooper, 'it's for around one hundred million pounds.'

Looking at the cheque Turhan-Cooper saw it was for one hundred and thirty six million pounds and he heard Rosecrans saying

'There will be quite a bit more in around six months.'

After spending a couple of hours with Turhan-Cooper, Rosecrans and Vanderveen left the premise and returned to London before flying to New York and while they were doing that Turhan-Cooper was making his way to his overseas investment bank in Belgium. With the cheque paid in and financially secure for the rest of his life and with the prospect of considerably more money arriving in the foreseeable future T.C returned home. Over the next a couple of days T.C. spent quite a bit of time thinking about the next moves. The first thing he decided to do was purchase some printing equipment which would be installed in the utility room.

Having decided on that he then decided to contact Vialls and invite him over to the house for a discussion.

The following afternoon Vialls arrived and after being shown into the lounge and while enjoying a cup of coffee prepared and delivered by T.C. He was followed T.C.'s movements as he went to a desk and appeared to be writing something. Vialls was stunned when T.C. handed him a cheque for five million pounds while saying, 'John, thanks to you recovering the diamonds we have more than sufficient money to cover almost every contingency and when I say thanks I really mean it. So what do you think should be the next logical step for the movement to carry out?'

In reply he said, 'firstly in my opinion every MP should receive a letter saying something along the lines of. You heard what happened to five of your fellow Members of Parliament recently. Well far worse will occur to you unless you start sorting the political mess out. Secondly what we have at this juncture is not working to the benefit of everyone. Parliament and its members are supposed to be a representative cross section of the population and in my opinion it is nothing like it. There are far too many professionally qualified individuals some of whom are millionaires totally unaware of struggling to survive. Thirdly the electoral system needs to be dramatically changed to such an extent that whoever is elected from a constituency is voted in with a clear majority from the whole constituency. That means if there are seventy four thousand voters registered the majority of all the voters must have voted for the elected member. Not the system used at present.'

'Yes, I agree with all your points. I will get onto it by firstly sending a letter to all the incumbent members in the Palace of Westminster.'

Vialls then said, 'for instance we are short of qualified British Nurses and as a result we are importing from abroad.

We need to be employing and training our own people to fill whatever posts. The reason for saying that is as simple as this. By taking qualified Nurses or other skilled persons we are depriving their skills to their own nation's people. I could go on about a multitude of actual and potential problems that all require attention.'

'So what are you going to do next John?'

'I'm off to Luxemburg to pay this cheque into my offshore bank account.'

'Once again John, many thanks for recovering the diamonds and of course the money they provided, is more than enough to do just about anything we desire to sort out the political mess in the country.'

'All you have to do is prioritise the WRAP intentions and actions.'

Printed in Great Britain
by Amazon.co.uk, Ltd.,
Marston Gate.